# ORLAN



JACQUELINE HARPMAN was born i
Being half Jewish, the family mo
Nazis invaded, and returned home
French literature she started training to be a doctor, but could not complete her medical studies when she contracted tuberculosis. She turned to writing in 1954 and her first work was published in 1958. In 1980 she qualified as a psychoanalyst. She had given up writing after her fourth book was published, and resumed her career as a novelist only some twenty years later. She has now written twelve novels and won several literary prizes, most recently the Médicis for the present novel. She is married to an architect and has two children.

Reviewing her previous novel, *The Mistress of Silence*, a haunting, Kafkaesque story, Pierre Maury in *Le Soir* called it "the product of a fertile imagination that succeeds in setting before us a world totally alien from the one to which we have been accustomed".

ROS SCHWARTZ, who has translated fiction by such authors as Ousmane Sembene, Andrée Chedid and Sébastien Japrisot as well as many works of non-fiction, has been a full-time translator since 1982. She ran translation workshops at Goldsmith's College, London University, and teaches on the part-time MA course in translation studies at Middlesex University.

*Also by Jacqueline Harpman in English translation*

THE MISTRESS OF SILENCE

*Jacqueline Harpman*

# ORLANDA

*Translated from the French*
*by Ros Schwartz*

THE HARVILL PRESS
LONDON

First published in France with the title *Orlanda*
by Editions Bernard Grasset, Paris, 1996

First published in Great Britain in 1999 by
The Harvill Press
2 Aztec Row
Berners Road
London N1 0PW

www.harvill-press.com

1 3 5 7 9 8 6 4 2



This translation has been published with the
financial support of the French Ministry of
Culture and Communications



A CIP catalogue record for this book
is available from the British Library

ISBN 1 86046 488 2

Designed and typeset in Minion at
Libanus Press, Marlborough, Wiltshire

Printed and bound in Great Britain by Butler & Tanner Ltd,
at Selwood Printing, Burgess Hill

*To Dédée and Toury*
*with many thanks for the apartment*

Novel: An extended work in prose, either fictitious or partly so, dealing with character, action, thought etc., especially in the form of a story.

*Collins English Dictionary*, 1994

# THE FIRST PERIOD

# FIRST DAY
# FRIDAY

THE OPENING SCENE takes place in Paris, opposite the Gare du Nord, in the café ambitiously named *Brasserie de l'Europe*. Its chrome, plastic and imitation-leather décor is enough to induce depression in anybody so foolish as to look at it. The time is just after 1 pm. Some customers are eating eggs mayonnaise, others sandwiches. Thirty-five-year-old Aline Berger is reading, and taking regular sips from the mineral water in front of her. Her platform will not be announced until twenty minutes before departure, and Aline does not like waiting on the vast, noisy station concourse where she can never be certain of finding a seat.

Madame Berger does not look to me as though she is concentrating all that well on her book. From time to time her eyes rove around the room and then she glances at her watch. Time is dragging. She should not have left so early, but she is of an anxious disposition and is always worried about being late. Besides, her research completed, what would she have done in Paris? She spent an hour at the Orangerie, half an hour at Smith's bookshop, there was nothing else to do but dive into the Métro. She sighs. She tries to concentrate on her book, which does not really grab her. It is the tenth time at least that she is rereading the crucial passage of *Orlando* when the transformation takes place, trying to grasp the underlying meaning. She always feels as though she only understands it superficially, and cannot bring herself to entertain the thought that maybe there is nothing underneath it. She applies herself:

> *First, comes Our Lady of Purity; whose brows are bound with fillets of the whitest lamb's wool; whose hair is an avalanche of the driven snow . . . etc.*

She yawns. Behind the words whose deeper meaning evades her, weaves another train of thought like the hidden meanders of intermittent rivers – so called because they flow in the open for a while and then disappear underground, and people think that is where they end, but they reappear a few miles further on. From my privileged vantage point of the novelist – and I have never made a secret of believing that it is mine by right – that is what I am listening to, and soon I hear something that leaves me dumbfounded:

"How about changing sex? Suppose I abandoned you, O bashful creature, suppose I freed myself from this female body and went and made my home in a boy's body? Look! the one with fair hair sitting over there, opposite me. He's slightly unkempt and has a sly look, but his wide, firm mouth indicates stubborn determination. If I were inside his head, how would you look to me? I think I would soon lose interest; without my energy, my anger and vigour which so alarm you at times, because you call them violence, you would be dull, easily put to flight, and leading a stunted life as you stumbled from one failure to the next. I have always troubled you, and you cover me up as best you can, with lipstick, long hair and silk skirts that swirl at the slightest movement. People find you charming and feminine, but I inhabit your fear and I'm stifled. If I were a man, I wouldn't chase after women, I know them too well. I would blithely confront other men, I'd do what, as a girl, I've never dared do, I'd challenge them! Perhaps I have only ever loved men in a homosexual way, but, of course, I was ashamed. I didn't dare face up to my penchant and I disguised myself – disguised? – I clothed myself in this strange body in which I have never felt at home. Sometimes they desired me, but as I didn't desire myself, I had no idea. Oh! To be a boy! All I have to do is give rein to my thoughts, which you always keep so resolutely in check, and I can imagine that other firmer body with its broad, flat chest and its pectorals moving freely. My hips have become narrow and I sense, in the nether regions of my belly, the swelling that evokes the banners of victory that are waved slowly over the fields strewn with corpses when the battle is over. You are afraid, you tense up, how boring you are! I would walk with a relaxed step, I'd look men in the face, which would horrify you, they'd be a little startled but some would turn round to gaze after me and perhaps I'd choose one of them and lead him, enthralled, into undreamed of places. Men. I know them well, I know what they like. I know I'd be more skilful as a lover than as a mistress, because I would be fearless. Girls are taught modesty and restraint, but as a boy I learned nothing because nobody had an inkling of my existence. I would set out in all innocence for unknown lands. Goodness! What a journey! They make me laugh with America, Christopher Columbus, the Amazon basin and the Poles, even the moon and Mars! The unknown is actually the opposite sex. I've snuggled up to him any number of times but never crossed the threshold. The opposite sex is further away than Vega from Centaurus. I bang my head against closed skulls and I'm unable to get through. 'A penny for your thoughts,' I say. They smile and I remain outside, frustrated, solitary, immured in this woman's body which has always succumbed to petty fears, and which you dare not leave. But I don't hold it against them, for it isn't their fault, any more than mine. We are equally enslaved to this intractable identity that sets us as far apart as the galaxies and makes us rush towards each other, trying to assuage curiosity with pleasure. Never has a woman been a man, and never has a man been a woman. Each sex possesses a knowledge which it is unable to share, and the stupid operations I know they indulge in are only an illusion, a disguise which does not affect the mind, they clothe the body and kill desire. But to inhabit a complete body ! Take three steps and change worlds! *I is another? I* is a thousand others, and, since I am weary of this *I*, why shouldn't I take leave of it?"

The blond youth has just ordered another coffee. He looks a little tired, why is he drinking so much coffee when what he most needs is sleep? I can see an overnight bag at his feet, perhaps he's taking the train too? Honestly, I'm tempted! He has long fingers with rather neglected nails, but his features are clean, well chiselled, there's something determined about him. As I observe him sitting there on an uncomfortable chair, I can see there's something graceful about him, we should be able to do something with him. He is wearing an imitation-leather jacket, the kind that was in fashion a few years ago, with zips everywhere, over jeans that are faded but not torn. I don't suppose he earns very much. Even if I weren't imprisoned in the persona of the sensible woman you have decided to be for such a long time that you find it natural, I would not pay any attention to him because he is boringly ordinary. The only thing of interest about him is that he's a boy, young, robust and not too plain. Should I go for it? If I moved in, I would make him handsome, because for me, being a young man is already such a wonderful state that no worries could spoil it. Under my influence, he would blossom, I would put a sparkle in those lifeless eyes, I would spice up his attitude. He is not a girl, he can do anything, so what makes him look so washed out? Is this the way to be wasting one's treasures? Supposing I slipped inside him? Maybe all I have to do is will it, nobody knows, because nobody has ever tried such a crazy thing. You always allow common sense to pull you up short, even when you are merely fantasizing, that's what makes you so boring. Right: I'm making a change.

A change?

* * *

It can't be done, it's incredible, and I'm doing it. I leave you without a backward glance and I achieve the impossible. I don't feel anything, I only know that I'm crossing over, I'm floating in that indefinable space between the before and the after, at a point which has, naturally, neither duration nor space, it is the absolute zero of time and it stretches to infinity. I exist for an eternity in a nowhere which I can't remember even while I'm there because *while* no longer means anything. I have no other reality than this indissoluble *I* whose being I cannot fathom but its prodigious evidence lights me up. It is at the heart of the nameless, the core of certainty, the guarantee, the immaterial foundation that permits this impossible course I'm steering with such assurance, although there is neither up nor down, neither back nor front. I know where I'm going, I have already arrived although I have barely left. I have travelled across eternity, no time has gone by, nothing has been crossed. I become embodied, I succeed, the universe falls back into place around me, I have eyes, I hear, I feel, I am!

I've done it!

Aline is over there but I'm over here. The separation has taken place. I watch in astonishment *me*, who *is* reading, yes, the verb is now in the third person singular, absorbed, in front of the nearly empty half-bottle of Badoit. Regular cleansing of the kidneys is essential for good health, my father always used to say. *Me* is sitting opposite, slightly to one side, and I am inside the fair-haired youth. I have effortlessly entered his head. He hasn't noticed a thing. Can a person be so easily evicted? He couldn't have been particularly attached to himself, he's disappeared without a murmur. I have the house to myself. I'm trembling with excitement. I feel like getting up, dancing and shouting for joy. I control myself, I must stay calm. I have just accomplished the impossible and if I were to make a song and dance about it, I would soon find myself in a straitjacket with three male nurses holding me down. Let's explore our new kingdom. Neglected nails? Worse! He bites them! He must be a fool, ruining such beautiful hands! I feel my shoulder: it is firm and muscular, and my chest, mmm! how nice not to encounter the perpetual roundness of breasts. My stomach is quite flat and my thighs perfectly hard. How I love this body, it makes me all excited. It's plain that I've always liked men a lot more than I dared admit, and I quiver at the thought of having this one at my disposal, but I must get a grip on myself for I'm sitting in a public place and I'm not going to begin my new life by doing something stupid. So I place my hands back on the table, and turn my attention towards my inner sensations. At once I realize I have a slight headache. So that's why he was looking so out of sorts! I don't like this, I didn't change bodies to feel worse than before, what has he been up to? He must have had too much to drink last night, I only feel that kind of discomfort if I've drunk cheap wine, he probably doesn't tolerate alcohol all that well. Hey! Am I weak-willed? Might I be spineless? No, let's not panic, whatever this young man is like, I am not him, I am occupying him, I can do as I please with him, but I am well and truly me, and I have never been the sort of woman who drinks or eats too much. I need an aspirin. Ah! There must be a trace of him left, for I immediately discover that my host isn't a great one for medicines, he never takes them because he thinks they *pollute*! Pollute! How ludicrous, he's afraid of acetylsalicylic acid but he gets drunk! I had some in my handbag, because I always do, I'm going to go over and ask me for some.

I get up. Something so strange happens that I nearly stop in my tracks. Now I'm a whole lot taller than Aline, my legs are longer, and I nearly knocked over the table. I have just grown ten centimetres! The view is completely different, I've risen, or objects have become lower, and it's extremely disconcerting. I feel giddy for a second. Only a second, for I don't intend to let anything mar the pleasure of my transformation.

I make my way over towards me, who is absorbed in a book.

"Excuse me."

She looks up. She seems a little puzzled. My earlier thoughts must have disturbed her. If I know her, she's been trying very hard to concentrate on her book and put them out of her mind. That makes me laugh, for she has no idea how well she's succeeded!

"Yes?"

"Would you have any aspirin? I've got a headache."

She doesn't seem as taken aback as I'd expect, but is anxious to help. I recognize myself there, all right. They say that I'm an obliging, considerate person, but it's only an appearance, the truth is that she'd do anything – within reason! – to feel loved. With her, it's a reflex, against which she battles as best she can, rarely with any success.

She opens her bag and doesn't need to rummage around because she knows exactly where everything is. She cannot stand the notorious mess that women are supposed to keep in their handbags. I wonder, now that I've left her, will she still be as methodical? She takes out the blister-pack of pills:

"You'll need two, they're a fairly low dose."

I take them and thank her with a radiant smile. She is delighted, returns my smile and buries herself in her book again.

I go back to my seat, moving gingerly, for I shan't sit down in the same way as before! I raise my cup and once again, I'm caught unawares. I think it's level with my lips, which I push out to meet the rim, but I'm three centimetres off. What a hoot! I wash down my tablets with the remains of the coffee: it has no sugar, worse luck. In fact, I notice that the headache is already getting better – that's because I hold my liquor well, even though I'm a modest drinker because I don't like the taste. Clearly the young man and I don't have much in common! But while I'm thinking of it, what's his name? Or rather, what's my name? I must have a wallet somewhere? If he's right-handed, it'll be in the left pocket of his jacket. My name is Lucien Lefrène and I live at 19 rue Malibran, Brussels.

Amazing! I choose at random and chance on someone who also lives in Brussels. Of course, we're in a café opposite the Gare du Nord, with half an hour to go until the next train, which I should have taken with her, and which I shall still take. I'm delighted, I shan't lose my old habits. Have I got my ticket? It's not in my wallet, let's try the other pockets. Huh! I'm travelling second class.

She's reading. *Orlando* by Virginia Woolf, I remember it very well, because of the class she's got to teach soon. She'd have preferred the Barbey d'Aurevilly that's in her bag, he's a writer she adores and he tells the most gruesome tales – she's so genteel, it must give her a thrill – but her professional conscience won't allow her to. She doesn't seem to be missing me. Hasn't she noticed anything at all? Half of herself has skipped off and she doesn't notice? Goodness, what a sad woman I was! I did well to leave her. The fact is, and I know this, she hated me, I was forever causing her problems by wanting things that made her blush. She'll be very relieved to be rid of me and will consider it an improvement to have lost her more mischievous half. *Orlando* irritates her, but obviously that's what gave me the idea of changing, I'll never say anything horrid about Virginia Woolf again! Oh look, she's gathering her things! She's right, it's 1.20 by Lucien Lefrène's nasty cheap watch. By the time I've crossed the street, the indicator board should be showing what platform my train leaves from. In *my* right pocket, I find a little purse full of coins, this boy's clearly meticulous! I leave twenty francs on the table and follow her. I watch her walk. She has a jaunty step and she really is a bit of all right! Her pale leather boots, silk skirt and Laura Ashley jacket are all in shades of beige with subtly contrasting materials, people ought to find her attractive but I know they hardly notice her. She walks purposefully, without looking at people so she doesn't see those she knows, and some people think she's snooty. So she doesn't notice this elegant man walking towards her, a well-preserved forty-five, cashmere overcoat slightly too warm for the time of year and a little suitcase made of pure pigskin. He devours her with a rapid glance of appraisal, tries for a moment to catch her eye, then walks past, forgetting her at once. What a waste! I on the other hand stop, intrigued by his fine allure, and smile at him. He sees me, doesn't frown, but an imperceptible cloud passes over his magnificent tanned forehead and he looks away. I don't move, I let him walk past me, admiring him openly. I'm enjoying myself. Will he turn round? I'm sure he will, I know what men are like, they love being provoked. I wait. He walks ten yards, reaches the pavement, he can't resist any longer and glances back where he can see me receive this tiny, involuntary avowal; I'm still smiling at him. He looks away quickly and sets off again. I am jubilant. He has the springy step of an expensively shod man, which draws my attention to Lucien Lefrène's shoes. They are shabby and worn like a life that someone has grown weary of. This boy was not happy, but he's young and, handsome though the passer-by may have been, lodging inside a forty-year-old can't be as much fun, with rheumatism only ten years away. Then I run to catch up with my other half. She's almost at the station, I don't want to lose sight of her. Well, what an interesting experience I've just had! Why wasn't I ever able to do that when I was Aline? Sustain a gaze, hold it, arouse desire – ooh! I tremble with pleasure at the thought of it! She takes care over her appearance, but she doesn't seem to know how to make the most of her looks. Come to think of it, I didn't really get a good look at Lucien Lefrène before going to live in him, where can I find a mirror? The toilets on the train will be locked until it leaves, there must be one somewhere in the station.

But she's got more appeal than I thought! Two boys walk past her and turn round to look at her – without breaking off their conversation, it's purely out of habit. She hasn't even noticed them. Another man who has just met his wife and is taking her suitcase from her notices Aline, forgets the woman who is entitled to his full attention for a moment and gives her a lopsided kiss. My former self walks past all that without faltering, looks up at the indicator board, 13.41, platform 16, very good, off we go. I watch her climb into her favourite first-class compartment, but I don't follow her. I know where to find her.

Let us watch our strange character who is scrutinizing the many indicator boards adorning the station walls – Customs, Métro, Lost Property, Information – and finds the one he is looking for. What should I call him? He is not Lucien Lefrène – he is going to discover some rather awkward sides to this endearing young man – he is no longer Aline, who is settling into her compartment unaware of the manner in which she has just been deserted. He is doubtless right to credit Virginia Woolf with the idea: while Aline was applying herself to an English that seemed beyond her capabilities, nebulous divisions formed in her mind, cracks yawned, *Our Lady of Purity* irritated her, she was falling apart. Such uncertainty can lead to madness, the young man's ploy had saved her. As I am not a nasty person, I am delighted, although I do wonder how she is going to survive such a loss. But I still have to find a name for this character. For lack of inspiration, the simplest would be Alain, from Aline, but that would be a lazy option! And what about the ambiguity? Alain is Alain, it is unequivocally masculine, which is not true of the character whom my mind's eye is following to the toilet. I have often admired Woolf's wisdom in keeping the name Orlando after the gender change, but using the feminine pronoun, thus maintaining the confusion in the reader's mind, and I am going to emulate her. I shall call Aline's escaped half Orlanda, and I hope that Virginia's spirit will not hold it against me and come and haunt my dreams with nightmares, so I am letting her know, if she is listening, that this is the humble tribute of an admirer and not the vulgar plagiarism of somebody devoid of imagination.

Orlanda purchased a token and went through the turnstile to find himself in front of the big mirror he had been seeking and sighed delightedly on contemplating Lucien Lefrène:

"I think he already looks different," he said to himself. "He's lost that jaded look that struck me when I was still Aline, he holds himself well and his eyes are alert. His headache's gone. Ah! I always knew that the face was a reflection of the soul, I am already more handsome than he was because I feel free as I have never been before. Maybe he had a girl incarcerated in his male body who prevented him from living, as Aline did me, and I've sent all those people packing – I don't know where to, but let's hope they stay there! He holds his head higher and he's got more colour in his cheeks. What a good-looking boy I am! Except for my hair. Oh dear! I hadn't noticed, my hair is plastered with one of those horrible gels that make your hair stand on end, like a terrified character in a horror film. I understand why that charming forty-year-old did not look particularly impressed! I must have a wash, I can't stay like this."

The station toilets provided cold water and one of those tilting bottles filled with liquid soap. Vanity can make people heroic: he leaned forward, put his head under the tap and, gritting his teeth to stop himself shivering, he shampooed his hair vigorously, and then opened his travelling bag and was delighted to find a towel. He dried his hair as best he could, combed it and found he was attractive.

I hear groans of "what a dreadful Narcissus your Orlanda is! All he can do is admire himself!" but I protest: it is the corporal frame of another that he is appreciating, like a girl thrilled with a new outfit, for he was a girl fifteen minutes ago, and a girl who was aware of boys. I entreat anyone capable of being moved by the beauty of the opposite sex to imagine for a moment living in that body that thrills them, and they will understand Orlanda. And feel a thrill, perhaps.

After a last, tender smile in the mirror, Orlanda closed his bag and then remembered that he was in the toilet, a place designed not only for self-discovery. At the same time, he realized that he needed to use it in the most conventional way. Having mentioned Virginia Woolf, I am conscious that the modesty which was still de rigueur in the first half of this century would have me stop here – *Our Lady of Modesty* is glaring at me. But we are in the Nineties, the millennium is drawing to a close and my hair is turning grey. I no longer have to display the modesty of a young girl, and I shall not put on a show of good manners that would have me avert my eyes, as I was taught to do as a child. I remember watching in astonishment and delight when a little boy took out of his swimming trunks a part of his anatomy so different from mine, held it between his fingertips and indulged in an activity that I thought could only be accomplished sitting down or crouching.

"Stop looking!" said my mother, accompanying these words with a slap which actually forced me to turn my head.

"Dear me, this child's disgusting!"

And that evening she complained to my father about my unhealthy curiosity. He shrugged disconsolately.

So, Orlanda felt he needed to pee and was immediately excited about the new experience awaiting him. He reluctantly turned away from his reflection in the big mirror, entered one of the cubicles and, with a gesture that was automatic for Aline when she was wearing trousers, raised his hand to his waist to undo the hooks, then remembered his new condition and began to laugh. He unzipped his fly and, when he was about to touch the most significant element of his transformation, felt weak at the knees with emotion. As a little girl, he had been envious of boys, as girls are, but had never dreamed of possessing their appendage. A strange temerity overcame him, and this youth who had just, in the café, explored his shoulders and thighs with a thrill, found his fingers reluctant to slide inside the fabric, as if it had been a question of Aline putting her hand inside a stranger's underpants.

"I hope she's not going to bother me," he said to himself anxiously.

And grabbed the strange little piece of flesh that governs the destiny of every human being, took it out from its hiding place, then, opening his legs slightly as he had seen men doing, prepared to satisfy the call of nature.

But, O Virginia! avert your eyes from the page! Something then happened that your intuition had perhaps supposed, but over which your delicacy drew a veil. Orlanda gazed at the soft pink thing with which he was endowed lying limply in his masculine hand, which was beautiful despite the chewed nails, and thirty years of lustful desire surged through his veins. He admired its shape, its elegant length, the graceful folds which, not being Jewish, Lucien Lefrène had not had amputated, and was enthralled. He raised his left hand and gently stroked what he was holding in his right hand. At once, a powerful thrill ran through him, he felt the rush of blood in his veins and saw, miracle! his new identity swell before his eyes and attain its full size within a few seconds – he was barely more than twenty! He trembled. Aline had witnessed this mystery hundreds of times, but she had never experienced it from the inside. Orlanda was pure desire. But who desired? Aline or himself? He did not think about it. It is I, removed from the wonder that I am describing, who ask the question. Planted squarely on his strong legs, he did what he was compelled to do. The pleasure began, he watched with delight as his hand moved up and down, feeling the waves surge higher and higher, riding the crest of the swell. He thought at first he recognized pleasure as Aline knew it, then everything was different, strange contractions caught him unawares, he gasped with amazement, his heart thumped in his hand, he nearly shut his eyes with emotion, but curiosity got the better of him. He kept them open and was dazzled as he watched his pleasure spurt out, spreading outside at the same time as it spread within.

"Christ!" he said, when it was over.

He leaned against the wall to regain his breath and watched, full of gratitude, as the mystery slowly subsided.

Then, he used the conveniences in the more traditional, but just as interesting way.

What about Aline?

What had she felt at the moment of the incredible separation?

She was caught between the Ladies of Purity, Chastity and Modesty, their brows adorned with icicles or whitest lamb's wool, when she felt a strange sensation, was it dizziness or indecision? She sat holding her breath for a second, as if torn by a nameless grief, clutching her glass of mineral water which she raised to her lips, then the sensation subsided and she felt as if she were going through a wall of silence and found herself drinking a mouthful of water.

"But I'm not thirsty!" she thought.

Aline glanced about her. The fair-haired young man opposite was looking at her with a half smile. She automatically looked away, without realizing it. Nothing seemed out of the ordinary, people were talking quietly together, drinking their beer or white wine. There had not been an earthquake. One night, a few years earlier, she had woken up with a feeling of panic, the room was shuddering, the dog asleep on her feet groaned, then everything had stopped. The morning news spoke of a medium-scale quake. Nothing has happened, she told herself, but her back was covered in a cold sweat. She thought of her grandmother who, at the slightest shiver, would say, trying to sound sepulchral:

"Someone walked over my grave."

"But you're not dead, grandma, you haven't got a grave!"

"I will have one, it's the only thing a Christian can be sure of on this earth, Lord help us!"

Aline wanted to regain her composure and resume her train of thought. I was distracted, I was reading without taking it in, I was thinking about something else, I must concentrate. Then, trying to muster her thoughts, she felt something almost indefinable. It would be too easy to describe it as a void, an absence. It was more akin to the loss of balance you experience in an air pocket when the plane drops a couple of hundred feet and there is a tenth of a second when the soul has not quite caught up with the body, and you are afraid. For Heaven's sake! What could I be afraid of? She made herself carry on reading. Goodness! how boring she was finding *Orlando*! But she had to finish rereading it if she wanted to be able to talk about it intelligently, even if it was only to criticize it vehemently. You can carelessly praise a book that is generally agreed to be a masterpiece, but you can only attack it if you are specific and know it inside-out. When her students had asked her to talk to them about Virginia Woolf, Aline had agreed at once, astonished at their interest in such an unfashionable subject. It was a few days until the next English literature class, she just had time to reacquaint herself with a work which she only vaguely remembered, but which she thought must be full of interest as that was what she had been taught, and there she was yawning through *Mrs Dalloway*, foundering in *The Waves* and unable to concentrate for more than two minutes at a time on *Orlando*. How on earth is one supposed to understand the transformation into a girl? She read and reread the passage: Orlando slept for a week, people around him were concerned, the worthy Ladies uttered admirable words. What I find exhausting is that there isn't a single line that isn't exquisitely beautiful, and yet the whole thing is horribly boring, she thought vaguely. Then Orlando woke up a woman, miraculously endowed with the usual attributes of the female sex, and did not seem especially surprised. She hesitated: Perhaps my English isn't good enough and I'm missing something? *I am the guardian of the sleeping fawn*. I'd better look at the translation. What is that supposed to mean? Until now, there was nothing of the innocent fawn about Orlando, and anyway, the trumpets will put the virtues to flight, they seem to be protecting the sleeper. And why, for Heaven's sake, does the fact that he wakes up a transsexual make him proclaim the victory of Truth?

She felt profoundly uncomfortable for, clearly, she was not able to think cogently. But of course! she did not think in such terms, and continued to imagine that she was missing something, wondering whether she was still suffering from that strange feeling that the earth was moving, when she realized that the fair-haired young man was standing in front of her and was waiting, smiling, for her to become aware of his presence.

"Would you have an aspirin? I've got a headache."

She did not even find it odd that a stranger should come and ask her for aspirin. On the contrary, this little moment of proximity gave her an obscure sense of well-being. Had she taken the trouble to think about it, she would have thought that it was a pleasant distraction from her feeling of incompetence.

"You'll need two, they're a fairly low dose."

She watched him go back to his seat and swallow the aspirins with a grimace. It's because his coffee's unsweetened, she said to herself, not noticing the certainty of her guess, which will not surprise us. Then, as she was above all a disciplined woman, she buried herself once again in *Orlando* where I cannot bring myself to follow her.

And just who was Aline Berger, before she lost half of herself in this way? I allowed myself to get carried away by Orlanda, unquestioningly accepting his scorn for her, which is utterly unfair and annoys me, for I do not like to find myself being influenced for lack of reflection. In this crazy venture into which he – she – has plunged as if it were the most natural thing in the world, there is something which inevitably astonishes and amazes me. I am too ready to forget, so it seems, that before the separation, this madness was part of Aline. *This life of a sensible woman that I have chosen*:

so she did not want him, he had either had to be stifled or to leave. Am I going to find Aline very different from the one Orlanda is staring at in amazement saying: *She loses half of herself and doesn't feel a thing?* I can see at once that we will have to go a long way back. She is twelve years old, a robust, confident girl who strides around and laughs boisterously. She rushes into the house, flings her coat down on an armchair in the lounge and her satchel anywhere.

"Goodness! You're such a tomboy!" sighs Madame Berger, her mother.

These words did not cause an explosion, Aline quietly absorbed them as she continued on her way, went into her room, dropped her jumper in one spot and her shoes in another before having a shower for, in the dilapidated school where she had had gym, they were insistent on the importance of feminine hygiene, but the showers were out of order for two weeks out of every three. Perhaps in her confused mind, she thought the jets of warm water would cleanse away those terrible words. I do not know. They slipped silently through the barriers of the memory and were engulfed by the swamps, beneath the quicksand of oblivion and were lost from view. They flowed at the mercy of the currents, formed a sediment and festered, contaminating the water that would feed the roots of the future. Some time later, Aline had her first period and, as her mother had been eager to prepare her thoroughly, she had not been surprised to find blood on her pyjama trousers one morning. She took a sanitary towel from the bathroom, and even had the presence of mind to take an extra one so that she could change it at school. The following day, at dinner, she heard her mother complaining indignantly:

"And now Madeleine's using my sanitary towels! The emergency packet is almost empty. It's unbelievable, and here was I thinking she was so honest!"

Madeleine came three times a week to do the cleaning.

"No, Mummy, I took them," said Aline.

"What? You've had your first period and you didn't tell me?"

When telling her daughter about periods, Madame Berger had not specified that she should be informed of the event.

"For goodness sake! It goes without saying! What about period pains? Didn't you have any period pains?"

The absence of period pains seemed to be bordering on indecency. The fatal words that lurked in the depths awoke and produced obscure stirrings, or rather, to use a different metaphor, they advanced stealthily, knifing her. Aline did not feel attacked head on, but with her second period, she experienced a few sharp stomach cramps and Madame Berger demonstrated her approval by advising her to spend the morning in bed. It was geometry and natural sciences at school that day, her favourite lessons, and she went, ignoring her womb, but the following month, the cramps were much worse and she stayed in bed all day clutching a scalding hot-water bottle, a treatment which, according to her mother, was the best cure in the world for the pain of being a woman.

It was the thin end of the wedge. She realized that when she was wearing a sanitary towel, it was best to avoid taking large strides, for practical reasons upon which Virginia strictly forbids me to dwell. From then on, it was one discreet capitulation after another. Her thick, unruly hair was tamed by excellent hairdressers, she learned to handle objects without breaking her nails and ideas without causing ructions. She liked to please, and that is what kills the boy within the girl. On her seventeenth birthday, her father told her that she really was becoming a ravishing young woman and her mother, delighted, agreed wholeheartedly. She had not counted on her husband for such an undisguised compliment – as a rule he was so unforthcoming. Aline certainly needed it, for she was continually fighting a nebulous, inexplicable sadness. It cannot be claimed that she regretted the freedom of movement and the large strides, for she was unaware that she had given them up. Nor can it be said that she was moving cautiously in the world of ideas, fearing the dangers, skirting around the reefs, irritated at always curbing the impulse that would have taken her straight ahead, even if it meant some painful clashes. Her passion for geometry waned – her mother often used to say that women couldn't understand figures – and she became more interested in the arts. To complete her university studies, she wrote a brilliant thesis on Proust which now sat gathering dust in the libraries along with the ten thousand other theses. She joined the arts faculty and became assistant to a professor who was old enough to afford her the hope of succeeding him one day.

In a word, a life worth living provided that she never allowed large strides to carry her towards the subterranean depths, nor powerful laughter to resonate in the sealed up passages of her memory. She did not marry, although she was one of those women whom men always want to marry, that was the only point on which she went against the wishes of her mother, who did not understand at all.

"But don't you want children?"

She avoided replying and did not wish to ask herself the question.

After two or three reasonably happy relationships, she met Albert Durieux, a calm, reassuring man who suggested that they live together; this was not much of a change for he lived in the same block of flats as she did, in the apartment across the landing on the third floor. For a while, they crossed the landing to visit each other, then Albert had the partition wall that separated the two living rooms knocked through.

Sometimes, in the morning, sitting at her dressing table and carefully applying her make-up, she would stop, stare at her reflection in the mirror for a long time, and ask herself why she was not happy while Albert seemed so to enjoy living with her. She could not shake off a perpetual feeling of emptiness; she had become so used to it that she thought it was a natural state and did not dwell on it. That was why Aline did not really feel anything when Orlanda left her.

Since she has imposed herself on me, I have been completely flummoxed for I have very little to say about her. She is like her mother, who was like her mother, like whole generations of well brought-up women who have all had the good fortune not to have received too many talents from the good fairies at birth, so they had no trouble contenting themselves with their lot. At least, that's the impression they give when you look at them from the outside, and perhaps I should be grateful to fate which, generally, does not inflict those women on me. I should certainly find it vexing if I felt obliged to write about Madame Berger, Aline's mother. There is something special about Aline, that is for certain. Her work on Proust is truly outstanding. She went through the first chapter of *Remembrance of Things Past* with a toothcomb to demonstrate in precise detail that the entire work is encapsulated in it. You only have to read the section where she shows how the stupidity of the aunts foreshadows not only Mme Verdurin, but also the senile Duc de Guermantes, ensconced in an armchair at Odette's, who was to become Mme Forcheville, and who allows himself to be introduced to just about anybody. But she has confined her talents rigidly to her profession, and even there she is grudging. It was suggested that she adapt her thesis for publication for a more general readership, and she said yes, because she never dares say no, but did not do it.

"So much has been written about Proust!"

For, through having tried to become what her mother discreetly suggested she should, she does not feel that she is unique as each person is entitled to feel and that she has something to say that she alone is able to say.

I recklessly followed Orlanda to the toilet and left Aline outside her compartment. She always boarded the train as early as possible so as to choose the seat she preferred: by the window, with a table, and facing forwards because she liked seeing the countryside ahead. She folded her coat and placed it on the luggage rack, left her little suitcase on the floor and took out *Orlando* with a sigh. Everything oppressed her and she was already bored at the thought of the three hours she was to spend in the train. On arrival, Albert would be on the platform, happy to see her after these few days apart. She would have to be cheerful, she said to herself and felt tears welling up.

"Why am I so sad?"

And the answer formed in her mind, clear and inescapable, even though we know it was incomplete: because I'm always sad and I pretend to be happy. I feign a cheerfulness that I do not feel, and Orlando's constant enthusiasm makes me want to scream. I find him ludicrous, but it's out of jealousy. I'm depressed. I'm bored. I am the most boring person imaginable and I have no means of avoiding my own company. I would not put up with me for an hour if I met myself socially and I wonder how Albert can stand me, and even worse, be convinced he wants nobody else but me. She was shaken by a brief sob. I think I envy the happiness I give him, which is absolutely crazy. He is probably as lacking in imagination as I am, I can't find any other explanation for such an absurd choice. I would hate to live on my own, he distracts me from myself. The worst thing would be a perpetual dialogue with this boring soul that I'm cursed with.

She blinked determinedly to fight back her brimming tears, thinking: this is ridiculous! *Orlando* clearly isn't the right book for me, and she put it away in her briefcase. She took out Barbey d'Aurevilly, hesitated for a moment and then put it back. Heretical though it was, she needed a more potent distraction that would take her even further out of herself. She still had a choice between *Le Médecin des Pauvres* by Xavier de Montépin, that her friend Chantal who lived in Besançon had given her saying that there were some wonderful descriptions of seventeenth-century Franche-Comté, and *Darkover Landfall* which she had bought at Smith's, on the recommendation of another friend. The next millennium and an imaginary planet, that's what I need, she said to herself. Besides, she felt it would be less unfaithful to Virginia Woolf if she read something in English, even if it was by an American woman.

Orlanda leapt into the last carriage just as the imminent departure of the train was being announced. He was in such an emotional turmoil that he had left his overnight bag in the toilet and had had to run to retrieve it. Aline was not very athletic, so, tearing along, weaving in and out of the crowds and hopping nimbly over the piles of luggage were all new pleasures for Orlanda. He was very young, the body he inhabited enjoyed excellent health, and the twelve-year-old spirit that inhabited him rediscovered the joy of taking huge strides and regaining its lost vigour. When he jumped onto the train, he was not even out of breath. Grinning, he thanked heaven for his new existence, though heaven probably frowned on his antics, and smiled at a woman weighed down with luggage who had also run but was gasping for breath.

"Allow me to help you," he said, picking up a suitcase without waiting for her reply. She frowned suspiciously, he did not insist and, having put the suitcase down in the nearest compartment, continued on his way after giving a curt, mock bow. He wanted to find Aline and had to walk through some eight or ten carriages. Holding his bag high above his head, he wove swiftly between the people wandering up and down in search of their seats. He was agile and grinning – honestly, you would not recognize the young man with a headache from the café. The train gathered speed and approached the long bend that took it north. Orlanda did not lose his balance but swayed to the rhythm of the jolts. A passenger stared after him, but Orlanda did not notice him as he was looking for Aline.

She was sitting diagonally, her feet up on the seat, immersed in the science-fiction novel that Orlanda had made her buy at Smith's.

He felt a pang of jealousy and pulled a face, then consoled himself with the thought that in less than an hour her conscience would get the better of her and she would go back to Virginia Woolf. Knowing that she would not move from her compartment, he made his way back to the second-class carriages. In the first compartment he walked through, there was a group of girls on their way home from a school trip. They were jumping up and down chattering excitedly. He shot them a look of disgust and continued. A youth with a Walkman filled the air with tinny sounds, a few young men on leave from military service were snoring on the plastic seats and a mother was trying to control her three boisterous children.

"I'll pay the supplement," he decided, as he headed back to the first class.

He did not have to as he met the ticket inspector who clipped his ticket and was not concerned about what he might do afterwards. He chose a compartment that was already occupied by some business types. One had set up his lap-top on the table and was typing busily, the second was filing papers and the third was flicking through a magazine. He looked up and watched Orlanda stow his bag on the luggage rack.

"So there's nothing for me to do but be bored for three hours?"

He suddenly understood the restlessness of the unruly children. It was true that at their age I was already perfectly obedient to my mother's wishes and I would sit quietly with a magazine, champing at the bit in silence. God! Those journeys to Aunt Adèle's! She was just as bad as Proust's aunts and Ourscamp certainly matched Combray for boredom. This thought made him leap out of his seat with exasperation and he went into the corridor. There, he fumbled in his pockets and was disappointed: Lucien Lefrène did not smoke.

"Are you looking for a cigarette?"

The man with the magazine proffered a packet of Camel with a smile. Orlanda's immediate reaction was to think that he did not like Virginia cigarettes – actually, I have no idea, he said to himself, it's Aline who doesn't like Virginia cigarettes. So he took one.

"Thank you very much."

"My pleasure."

The friendly passenger lit his lighter and raised it. There are people who make you bend down to reach the flame, or who bring it so close that it is in danger of setting your hair alight and you have to move quickly out of the way, or they hold it twenty centimetres to the right and you have to twist, at the risk of ending up with a stiff neck and then say thank you. Aline, brought up to consider that it is rude to refuse a thoughtful gesture, had found a way out. She had bought a very expensive, elegant lighter, a Cartier, or a Dupont, I do not know exactly because I am less well up on such things. This would intimidate the owner of the cheap lighter who would put it away again. Anticipating the usual ordeal, Orlanda was surprised to see the flame exactly level with the tip of the cigarette. He looked up and felt a thrill. This man was not as elegant as the man at the Gare du Nord, but he had a piercing gaze and the hint of an invitation in his smile which put it on a par with the cashmere. Aline was very familiar with this sort of insistent, hard look, which she could never withstand – to look is to weigh up, make the other submit, try to take possession. Sustaining such a gaze is already to acquiesce, one second is surrender, there is no going back. Orlanda shivered. The cigarette lit, he stepped back and leaned against the window, astonished at being approached, when he was the one who had planned to provoke. Ah! What a good choice of host! he said to himself. Lucien Lefrène was really a bit of all right. He wondered what flirting was like when the person being seduced was male. *Do you live with your parents?* or *Haven't I seen you somewhere before?* seemed unlikely. He thought of *What a big bum you have!* which made him laugh, but he remembered that it was afterwards that Jupien had uttered that charming compliment, anyway, Lucien had beautifully slim thighs and a slim, muscular bottom. The man moved away a few paces without taking his eyes off Orlanda and asked him where he was going.

"Brussels."

" I'm getting off at St Quentin."

"You'll soon be there."

"Too soon," he said.

Oh! is it that direct? And even more so! thought Orlanda watching the man unbutton his jacket and put his hands in his trouser pockets, displaying his obvious excitement. He was aware that he responded with ardour, and straightened up so that his enthusiasm was clearly visible.

"Come," said the other.

Aline, being a well brought-up young lady, as we know, Orlanda wondered where he was being invited to go. He saw the man turn around and make his way hurriedly towards the end of the carriage. He walked with a firm, elegantly poised step. I hardly looked at him, he said to himself, apparently it's not him but the situation I find so exciting. Poor Aline is convinced that endless discussions and spiritual affinity are the cornerstones of desire, she read the passage about the meeting in the courtyard of the Hôtel de Guermantes very closely, but did not understand a thing. But where the hell was he going? There's no back room here. The man turned left, Orlanda caught up with him: he had opened the toilet door! Am I naive? It is of course the only place.

"Come in quick."

He slid into the narrow space, and had to step aside to make room for the man who was to be the first sexual partner in his new life and who, as soon as the door was shut, embraced him. He looked at him at last: a handsome face with strong features, dark-brown hair cropped fairly short, but above all that steely, penetrating gaze as if this man's entire soul was concentrated in his eyes. He hurled himself into the man's arms, enfolding him in a violent embrace, as powerful as the arms that held him fast and stirred up his passions. Orlanda trembled from head to foot, never had Aline been so wildly consumed with ardour. The dam collapsed and desire was unleashed, invading everything, sweeping away the last traces of Lucien Lefrène. Orlanda felt himself plunge into the fearful world of terrifying passions, where you risk your soul for a moment of pleasure, for pleasure has the awesome splendour of crime. He understood the fires of hell and the cries of the preachers who have left our century bewildered, and he knew that he was doomed. The Ladies of Purity, Chastity and Modesty withdrew with shrieks of horror, the boy's mouth received the demanding mouth of the man and he groaned at the violence of his own response. Then, he wanted to take and grabbed with both hands the hips that were seeking him. Oh! the fury of that union – blades erect, handles crossed, a pure duel, steel dipped in the milk of imminent pleasures, the panting of the combatants crushed together. Orlanda did not want to move away from the man who was trying to slide his hand against his belly. Having known nothing but the secret cavern, he tasted the prodigious novelty of the external, pole, mast, standard, he glued himself to the pole, the mast, the standard, in a second he was going to . . . I think I am in the way! It is time for me to leave, this is no place for a lady of my age, brought up in polite society with its inhibitions, I think I had better get back to Aline.

She was reading. The shipwrecked astronauts were counting their dead and gazing at an unknown sky into which they would never be able to launch themselves. Conquistadors stripped of light years, their feet would be firmly glued to the ground and their hands to the plough. Aline was about to close the book when she glimpsed the touch of madness her despondent mood needed, a strange wildness that invaded souls, shattering wisdom to pieces. Ah! How far away was Orlando, who would yield to the spirit of the century and, submitting to female modesty, would hide the ankle that perturbed the captain of the ship: a dangerous pollen was in the air, those who breathed it forgot all inhibitions, they threw their hats over the atomic engines and threw their uniforms into the nettles to give rein to the most powerful passions. What was Orlando doing, travelling through several centuries? He screwed a few farm girls, a passing queen and a young lady from the Russian aristocracy, then, having become a woman, it seems that he – she – sleeps with friendly prostitutes and marries a noble navigator: a fine match, the great liberation! and to finish, we find her in a London department store, like Mrs Dalloway herself, buying, not flowers, but sheets for a double bed! Marion Zimmer Bradley's language is certainly less exquisite, thought Aline, but I'm enjoying it, and that's just what I needed. A strange creature with very white hair came out of the forest, walked hesitantly towards an astonished but soon delighted woman, spoke to her, mind to mind, she was tender, crazy and so incredibly reassuring that Aline's eye's filled with tears anew. She imagined the sweetness of feeling totally protected, sheltered in a soul who cared for nothing but her happiness. Whoever I might be, I would be accepted and cherished, I would have to do nothing but exist to fill the loving object with pleasure, and I would forget, oh! how I would gladly forget, this whole difficult business of earning kindness. I would become innocent, bold and trusting again. She had no idea that at that very moment, Orlanda, back in the world that preceded original sin, which is to accept the power of taboos, was going from heaven to heaven, to find himself in the seventh, far above the clouds, in the blazing sunshine of a mesmerizing gaze.

They came out of the toilet when the loudspeaker announced the train's arrival at St Quentin. Orlanda emerged first and walked past the suspicious lady with heaps of luggage. He nodded to her:

"I hope you found a compartment to your liking?"

She was still staring anxiously at this extremely polite young man dressed like a thug when to her utter amazement a second person came out of the same, very confined, place. The man nodded discreetly and walked past. I hope, for the sake of our heroes, that she was such a naive soul that the scandalous implications went over her head.

Orlanda gazed after his lover of one hour who was striding along the platform. A little girl aged about ten flung herself into his arms, soon followed by another, a little younger, and the husband tenderly kissed the young blonde woman who was with them. Goodness, said Orlanda to himself, there's a man who's keen to have his cake and eat it. He's a good example, and as all that has made me sleepy, I'm going to find an empty compartment and have a snooze.

Orlanda, who naturally knew Aline inside out, had been quite right. She had gone back to Virginia Woolf and the tedium that is supposed to make you feel virtuous. As she had slept well and Orlanda's amorous exploits had not exhausted her, she read nonstop until Brussels. The eighteenth century was drawing to a close, and the clouds of the nineteenth were gathering over Saint Paul when she looked up and recognized the huge car parks full of new Volkswagens waiting to be delivered. Thank goodness! she said to herself. She closed Virginia Woolf, slipped on her jacket, picked up her little suitcase and made her way to the door. She vaguely noticed a young man who seemed to be in a deep sleep as she walked past. At least the journey won't have seemed as long to him as it did to me! And why the hell does Woolf make her hero travel through the centuries like that? That's another question for me to ponder before I ask my students. The irritating thing is that I'll have to have an answer to give them!

Orlanda, whose soul we should remember is only twelve years old, even if his body is that of a twenty-year-old, was sleeping the profound slumber of a child, and was not awoken by the loudspeaker announcing the train's arrival. He only jumped when the train stopped. He rubbed his eyes, yawned and picked up his bag. On the platform, Albert met Aline. Orlanda was absent-mindedly watching this scene which he knew only too well when, to his surprise, it dawned on him that he was thinking about Albert from Aline's point of view, in other words, as an indifferent wife whose mind was on other things. She's crazy, he thought, Albert's a real hunk! Tall, broad, athletic even, but light on his feet and his enveloping hug made you want to snuggle up to him! She may not realize she's beautiful – fair enough – but to be so blind to such an attractive man is a waste! Honestly! I was right to leave her. And to think that I don't have the slightest chance of seducing him, for he's not at all interested in boys! He sighed, alighted from the train and followed them.

Albert had put his arms around Aline's shoulders and, after asking how she was – very well, she said, for it did not occur to her for a moment to talk to him of the strange anxiety that had been plaguing her – told her the latest news. He had spent the four days working with the architects on the plans for the Bordier tower, which had been a very tiresome business.

"There's no limit to their ambitions, they're trying to compete with Foster in Hong Kong and even go one better! Régnier was thinking of dropping the whole thing, he's basically cautious, but I dug my heels in. He's terrified by the problems of internal traffic, he's so frightened that he was almost funny saying that we're being asked to build staircases and lift-shafts with a few walls around them."

Whatever Orlanda thought, Aline was aware of the strength that Albert exuded, and felt sad that she was unable to take comfort from it. She was overwhelmed. The protective arm around her, his booming voice and the way he was always on the lookout for obstacles, piloting her, avoiding a heavy luggage trolley, weaving among the stragglers – it was all useless to her because she was unable to allow herself to be protected. The danger came from within. Albert was like an army surrounding a fortress and facing the plain whereas the enemies were inside the walls, moving up from the cellars, coming down from the eaves, spreading through the corridors and slipping invisibly into the rooms where the horrified lords and ladies watch death approach. I'm in pain, she thought, and I don't know where the wound is. How could she know that half of herself was following ten yards behind and that her soul had been amputated?

"I accepted an invitation to dinner with the Lardinois this evening, as long as you're not too tired. I warned them that you would only just have got back. Régnier and his wretched Olga will be there, so will the Geilfus, Charles and Adrienne – enough people so we can cancel without spoiling their evening."

He thinks of everything. He is never caught off guard.

"I'm not tired," said Aline.

For why would she have called the feeling of despair and lassitude that plagued her tiredness? She had slept well, then worked as usual, for eight hours in the quiet of a library, nothing unusual for a person in good health. Jeannine Lardinois was a superb cook and Albert and Aline considered it a crime to miss one of her dinners.

"And I've heard from Antoine at last. He's in Guatemala. Guess what happened when his plane landed in the Dominican Republic . . ."

She was no longer listening. She felt such a sharp stabbing pain that she was frightened; while Albert steered her towards the car, Orlanda, standing at the entrance to the Métro, watched her disappear. He gave a mocking grin, he was certain that he had not seen the back of her, but he had all the time in the world.

Two minutes later:

"And why the hell have I come down into the Métro?" he wondered, annoyed. "Probably a reflex of Lucien Lefrène's, he's getting on my nerves, he is, I'll have to keep an eye on him."

Aline only travelled by car, so Orlanda knew nothing about the tram system; but he saw a map on the wall and found rue Malibran. He had to take a number 1, change at the Porte de Namur and wait for a 71. He groaned and rummaged in his pockets for a piece of paper and a pencil to make a note of all that. In Paris, Aline retained that sort of information easily, and, quite frankly, I find Orlanda rather snobbish: earlier he turned his nose up at the second-class compartment and now he's claiming to be at a loss when faced with the tram system in the city where he grew up. I am wrong, I think: he is twelve years old, and that is the age where you discover that there are things that are *cool* and others that are not – worse! I don't think you say *cool* any more but *wicked*, unless I am still behind and I do not know the current "in" word – and it has to be said that the tram is not exactly *cool*.

It was crowded. Orlanda found himself standing amid a swaying huddle of people. With each jolt, a young girl allowed herself to be thrown against him. At first, it bothered him, then he remembered that he was no longer Aline and decided that it would be fun to experience this kind of contact. She smelled of soap, which reminded him of Madame Berger, whom he did not like to think of as his mother too, because he no longer wanted to be Aline, and so he called her by her first name, Marie. Marie used to soap her daughter vigorously, and sprinkle her with Eau de Cologne and Orlanda could smell Aline's fragrance rising from the brown hair tickling his nostrils. But he found the delicate perfume of conscious femininity unbearable – it was the prison where he had been incarcerated and from which he had never dreamed he would escape. He moved as far away as he could from the girl, who did not appear unduly offended. I don't think I'm interested in girls, he said to himself. In short, I seem to have changed sex, but not sexuality.

The sharp pang Aline had felt on leaving the station took a long time to subside and she thought she would probably not go to the

Lardinois'. Albert sensed her silence and preoccupation, kept quiet and, as they had stopped at a red light, turned towards her and scrutinized her:

"You look very tired," he said.

She forced a smile.

"I really can't stand the train. Sitting still for three hours in a compartment that's freezing what with their wretched air-conditioning! I'm going to have a hot bath then lie down for half an hour and I'll be absolutely fine."

But why, if she had no wish whatsoever to go, was she forcing herself to do so? That's how I spend my life, forever creating obligations, like the twenty generations of women before me and like my mother, she thought, at the very moment when Orlanda was recoiling at the smell of soap. Hello Jeannine, hello Olga, are you over your bronchitis? There was no question of showing how fed up she was with inquiring, every time she saw her, if she was over her latest illness, or of saying to Régnier that his bashfulness irritated everybody. In what way am I different from Mrs Dalloway? She's rich and I work, as did Virginia Woolf, whose heroines never work, or so I believe, I haven't reread everything. It's such a chore! That's something else I'd never dare admit. Charles will give me an hour-long lecture on the novel-writing technique that influenced every single twentieth-century writer, telling me nothing I don't know already, without letting me get a word in. Her characters are an appalling bunch of clichés, Christ! imagine spending months in the company of Clarissa Dalloway or Betty Flanders! No wonder she went mad! Aline, my girl, you've got the wrong end of the stick. It's obvious that it was to fight against her madness that she portrayed characters who were so tightly constrained by platitudes, she must have been terrified of her own thoughts.

Albert laughed: "If you say things like that in front of Charles, he'll tear you apart, for sure."

That was when she realized that for the last five minutes she had been thinking aloud, which both relieved and reassured her – she was feeling better. Actually, talking about literature is the only thing that makes me feel free. Then she pulled a face: talking about literature? only to myself, or just to Albert, because I'd never have the guts to challenge Charles!

Sometimes Aline wondered – but so fleetingly that she did not have the time to register the thought – whether it was not because of the apartments that she and Albert lived together. The explanation goes back quite a long way. Her father had inherited an old travellers' inn, about thirty kilometres outside Brussels. When he got married and had to choose his home, he went to see it and discovered a rambling house in a moderate state of disrepair which he fell in love with on the spot, and Aline had grown up in huge rooms with low ceilings where you could run twenty metres in a straight line before coming up against a wall. There was a primary school in the neighbouring village, and a secondary school five minutes away by car. Her mother drove her there every day, but the university was in Brussels. Her father rented a little student room for her, she could not walk three paces without bumping into the bed, the table or the wash basin. The day when the tenants in rue Constantin Meunier announced their departure, Mr Berger, taking pity on her in her prison cell, decided not to rent out the apartment again. He drove her to this three-roomed flat plus kitchen and bathroom which, when empty and flooded with light, made her feel that she could once again breathe freely. She was so desperate to regain a sense of space that at first she hardly put any furniture in – a small square table and four chairs seemed too much for a roomthat measured five metres by five metres.

"But you can't live in an empty shell!" protested Madame Berger.

Aline wanted to show willing: "It needs curtains."

Madame Berger bought yards of netting and velvet, spent three days at her sewing machine, and then came and hung them.

Already showing that taste for subtle colours that Orlanda was to appreciate fifteen years later, Aline had insisted on ivory shades to tone in with the light parquet flooring. The walls were soon covered with shelves laden with books, but she continued to put her foot down when it came to furniture.

She had been there for a few years when Albert Durieux moved into the apartment across the landing. He immediately noticed this charming and discreet young woman and did the usual thing. He could not find any salt on the first evening, when it was too late to go out and buy some, and knocked on her door.

"Come in," she said, going into the kitchen.

The building dated from the 1930s, and formed an obtuse angle with avenue Molière and place Constantin Meunier. The architects' brief seems to have been to make as many apartments as possible, and there was a diagonal running through the building with two symmetrical flats on each floor, one on either side, which meant that the living rooms and kitchens were triangular, and entirely unsuitable for their purpose. Aline, who lived alone and cooked little, had not made any effort to improve the rudimentary fittings. She put the salt in a cup and held it out to her new neighbour.

"Here you are."

He did not intend to let matters rest there, and, the next day, he placed a little bunch of flowers outside Aline's door, etcetera, I shan't go into the details of an absolutely classic conquest. Aline slept in the smallest of the three rooms which looked out over the uninspiring gardens at the back. The first time they decided to spend the night together, Albert protested that a man of his size could not fit into such a tiny space and he took her to his apartment. He had made his bedroom in the front, in the symmetrical room measuring five square metres that Aline had made into her office. She willingly conceded that it was more spacious.

Salt at Aline's, bed at Albert's – that set the pattern. They met in the evening, cooked on the Molière side and slept on the Constantin

Meunier side. Aline forsook her bathroom, and Albert, who enjoyed cooking, brought his saucepans over to her flat. When they began to entertain their friends together, there was much coming and going between the two apartments, doors were left open and dishes and crockery were ferried from one to the other on a trolley.

Albert Durieux was a subtle man, he did not make the mistake of proposing marriage to Aline. He was very conscious of that private space which he should not try to enter and of which she herself, in fact, was unaware. Had this woman been asked to describe herself, she would have been quite at a loss, she felt as though she had no distinguishing characteristics. After all, everybody experiences vague bouts of sadness. Albert's enveloping strength was like a promise of security, but we already know she was unable to take comfort from it, which saddened her tremendously.

After a few months, he began to pace up and down the two apartments, going from Molière to Meunier, from classic comedy to realist sculpture. He came and went, examining, cursing and assessing, under the intrigued gaze of Aline, who did not question him, for she kept the curious and impatient Orlanda tightly chained. Then he took out a folding rule, measured up and soon started drawing mysterious sketches on scraps of paper.

"We each have sixty-five square metres, where your taste for space and my huge bulk make us feel restricted. Between us, it adds up to a hundred and thirty."

"Yes," said Aline, who could not dispute the figures.

"We could knock down the party walls, they're not load-bearing, they're only plasterboard. Imagine removing the oblique wall that separates your horrible little sitting room from mine and think what a huge room we'd have. And then, look, we'll knock down all the partitions between your bedroom, the kitchen and the bathroom, I'll put the sinks and washing machine and so on against the back wall and we'll have a huge room with a charmingly irregular shape where we can cook and eat. I'll do the same thing in my apartment, goodbye to all those sad little rooms where you're always banging into things."

They crossed back over the landing and he passionately described the irregular space he would create, full of charming, whimsical features:

"There'll be a huge bath for you to soak in and a chaise-longue for you to relax on afterwards. I'll find you one of those theatrical dressing tables you love with bulbs all around the mirror, and I'll buy myself an exercise bike. They're ridiculous things, but you do five kilometres every morning, which is necessary for a man who is desk-bound."

The huge operation reverberated in the depths. Albert knocked out the wall panels, he encased the exposed pipes and covered them with mirrors, he was poetic. As he took full charge of the whole crazy enterprise, Aline was able to let herself go and the wildest idea of all came from her:

"And you can build a covered walkway between the two balconies at the back. It will be entirely glazed, full of sunshine, with a forest of plants. We'll live in a completely closed ring, a whole world where if you walk in a straight line, you'll end up back where you started."

The notion took his breath away. As soon as he could breathe again, he swore he'd manage it, even if he had to resort to bribery to get planning permission. It was not necessary, I hasten to add, buildings inspectors are honest, but busy, and they obtained permission.

So there were weeks of rubble and months of concrete, plasterers and plumbers and decorators. They stayed with Aline's parents for nearly a year. Madame Berger could not understand why they were marrying the apartments but not their occupants.

I have told the whole story of this apartment because it illustrates the way Aline is closed in on herself, but with one door too many, through which Orlanda escaped. She does not know herself, but who does? Don't we all go through life in the same ignorance of who we are, ready to rush at any description of ourselves that would give us the illusion of having a simple identity that can be summed up in a few words?

It goes without saying that her star sign was Gemini.

She went in through the Constantin Meunier entrance and sighed with pleasure at seeing her own walls again. True, she was naturally well-organized, as Orlanda showed us on remembering his bag, but it was for the pleasure of walking around her property that she crossed the living rooms, went and deposited her briefcase in her office, then returned via the kitchen and came full circle by taking the covered walkway to reach the bathroom. There, she carefully removed her make-up before immersing herself in the bath.

*Immersing* is not an exaggeration: right at the beginning of their relationship, Aline had thrown Albert into a panic. He had been in the kitchen, which was still triangular and tiny, whisking egg whites to make "floating islands" while she had a bath, and, as she did not answer when he asked her a question, he crossed the little hall to join her. Then he caught sight of her, totally submerged, motionless, her eyes closed, her hair spread out around her, the terrifying picture of a drowned woman. He dropped the plate, which broke, rushed over and pulled the astonished Aline out of the water.

"What's the matter?" she asked innocently.

"You were drowning!"

"Not at all! I always do that. I float in the currents. It's very pleasant."

"What currents?" he asked, still too panic-stricken to understand.

"Oh, I agree, there aren't any in a bath tub, especially such a small one, but I dream I'm in a lagoon, in the tropics, being carried this way and that, I rise and fall."

It is the only idiosyncrasy that Aline allows herself. Albert found it hard to get used to. At first, he would come and sit beside her, to make sure that she emerged in time. But, having played this game since childhood, she was able to hold her breath for more than two minutes without any difficulty.

"But supposing one day you felt faint while you were doing that? You'd drown?"

"No, I'd choke and sit up."

She didn't think there was anything suicidal about it.

The tram being slower than the car, Aline was floating beneath the waves by the time Orlanda reached rue Malibran. He found himself in front of a fairly wide building, and, as there was a grocer's to the right and a newsagent's to the left, he assumed that Lucien Lefrène did not live on the ground floor. He started up the ill-lit staircase and saw, on the second floor, a business card pinned to a door. Good, he said, which is the right key? Let's hope nobody comes by while I'm trying them, poor old Lucien will look completely mad. At the third attempt, he was able to enter his host's flat. He deposited his bag on a chair and looked around him, his eyes soon wide with amazement: do people live like this? Is it possible to survive in such mess and filth? The old lino was worn down to the backing thread, the cracked porcelain sink was full of dirty dishes, there was a nasty stale smell and the bed had not been made nor the bin emptied. His home is as dirty as his nails! This boy is a disgrace! I was reckless in plumping for him without knowing anything about him, he may turn out to be a drug addict or a dealer or have syphilis. He pulled a face and felt the twenty generations of respectable women who had ruled over Aline shudder. I can't stay here before I've cleaned the place, I'll have to go to a hotel. But have I got any money? he wondered, influenced by a hereditary suspicion of men who do not have a respectable job, connections and a bank account.

"There's more to life than just sex," he sighed, "you need to eat hot dinners and sleep comfortably. Where did Lucien Lefrène keep his papers?"

The place was so small that the search did not take long. He found the bank statements in the drawer of the only table and discovered to his amazement that he had more than half a million in the bank! As Aline had just spent a week in Paris, he automatically converted it to French francs: eighty thousand French francs! At his age! So he was stingy too! If the room was filthy, it was probably because he saved money on cleaning products! And he doesn't trust his own memory, which suits me fine, he added, finding a crumpled scrap of paper on which Lucien had methodically noted down the pin numbers for his credit cards. I'm going to be able to have dinner in a decent restaurant. Goodness! It's not even seven and I'm starving, I don't suppose he had any lunch, no saving is too small for someone who is truly mean. The reassuring thing about that half million is that it can't belong to a man who buys heroin, even Aline knew that people ruin themselves buying the stuff.

Orlanda needed clean underwear for the hotel. He turned out the overnight bag on the bed. Among the dirty shirts and underpants was a tape recorder that only intrigued him for a moment. He gingerly opened the only wardrobe with a disgusted finger, saw three neatly folded shirts and, on lifting them, was utterly dumbfounded to discover a lethal-looking little black revolver. Is that what's known as a 9 mm Colt? A few days earlier, Aline had been among people who had been talking passionately about automatic weapons and had only been half listening, while Orlanda had been fascinated. He picked up the object, weighed it and put it back in its place, with a look of distaste. Why was a young man living in a hovel in possession of such an unusual object? He put off asking himself some serious questions until later, looked for the things he needed and was thrilled to come across a suede jacket. It was worn but was an improvement on the ghastly imitation-leather jacket.

How do you choose a hotel in your own city? He stood there unsure of himself for a moment – there are always the Hiltons and Holiday Inns, places which Aline considered ridiculously expensive and therefore rather vulgar – then he picked up the telephone directory, looked for a three-star in a quiet street and called a taxi.

There, in the peace and quiet of a clean room with all the usual comforts, he began by having a bath, in the manner I have already described, then he carefully examined his veins at the crook of his arm, and saw no needle marks, which reassured him completely. The impulse that made me dive in here would terrify Aline, a level-headed woman who always thinks twice before making a decision, he said to himself. I suppose it's as a result of repressing me that she's made me so feckless. I jumped into the first opening without paying too much attention to where I was going and I don't think I like the boy I've jumped into very much. Although ... Standing in front of the full-length mirror in the bedroom, he smiled: I really am attractive! Those muscular shoulders and slim hips ... and my eyes have got bigger since the Gare du Nord, because I don't look at the world through half-closed eyes. I've lived in the shadows for too long not to open them now as wide as I can. I must drink plenty of water to finish cleansing his insides after his over-indulgence, but I've already got more colour in my cheeks. On Monday, I'll go and see a doctor and have a full check-up. The liver of a boy who gets a hangover when he drinks too much might be in need of treatment. Let's go and eat, I must give this young man who skips lunch some nice red meat and vegetables if I want to enjoy all the physical pleasures his youth promises. Impulsive, certainly, but at least I didn't jump into an old man! Well, well, maybe the prim Aline had a secret penchant for young men that she would never have admitted to herself? After all, in the café, she's the one who made the choice. He burst out laughing and enjoyed his dinner immensely.

Aline, at the Lardinois', kissed Jeannine, smiled at everybody, inquired after the bronchitis, which had not been too serious, then found herself, as she cut into her slice of leg of lamb, saying to Charles that Virginia Woolf poured her madness so skilfully into her metaphors that there was nothing left for the narrative.

"Really," said Charles, "how can you think that?"

"Very easily, I find it boring. Do you remember, in *Mrs Dalloway*, the voice that rises up from the earth, actually it's not like that, it appears to be coming up from the Tube station, but it comes from the depths of time, a woman as old as the world laments lost love, her mouth is a simple hole in the earth. It's beautiful enough to make you weep, except that nobody loves anybody, everybody is afraid and everyone sticks to their guns."

"You've completely missed the point," replied Charles, beginning his lecture, and Aline bitterly regretted her lapse: I knew I should have kept quiet!

That night, she had bad dreams. She was walking down a street and noticed to her astonishment that she only had half a body, just one leg and one arm. But how can I walk? And as if that thought made her lose the peaceful equilibrium of ignorance, she began to fall and awoke screaming with fear. Obviously, as we are fully aware of the strange situation she was in, the dream is perfectly clear, her soul, reduced by half, was trying to let her know, but, as usual, she did not understand a thing. Albert took her in his arms, comforted her lovingly, and she went back to sleep. This time, she was standing in front of a mirror, but there was no reflection. Even in the depths of her dreams, she remained a woman of great literary culture, the absence of a reflection caused Count Dracula to appear, dressed in his huge cape lined with red satin, his vampire teeth protruding. She screamed again.

"If this goes on, you'll need a tranquillizer to help you get through the rest of the night."

"Give me an aspirin," she gasped.

As far as I know, aspirin only soothes headaches, not troubled states of mind, but that night, the dreams stopped. No doubt the half-Aline was lacking inspiration.

Her other half, whom we know by the name of Orlanda, but who was content to say *I*, was not sleeping either. That was because Lucien Lefrène was stirring in the depths of his soul and Orlanda, asleep, was, naturally, a usurper less vigilant over his booty than Orlanda awake. Lucien kept having a dream that confronted Orlanda with people and situations that utterly baffled him. Who was that loud, fat, whinging woman? Why that panic-stricken flight along treacherous paths and this search for dark recesses in which to hide, trembling? And who were those menacing figures who kept looming up in front of him? Orlanda awoke with a start and moaned at Lucien, the inhospitable host who inflicted his fears on his guest.

"Well, not exactly guest," he had to admit.

At one o'clock in the morning, he telephoned reception to ask for a sleeping pill. The helpful night receptionist did not have any, but recommended a nearby street corner where you could find anything: cocaine, a girl, a boy, amphetamines and probably tranquillizers. He had to get up and get dressed.

"What about aspirin? Have you got any aspirin?"

"I've got my own, because I get a headache every night."

"Give me a couple, I'll repay you tomorrow."

Thus Orlanda marked his spiritual connection with Aline, through acetylsalicylic acid. Lucien Lefrène, who did not have the same trust in Bayer, tried to continue his painful nightmares, but Orlanda, strengthened by faith, became impervious and slept soundly.

# SECOND DAY
# SATURDAY

HE AWOKE FEELING full of energy, and set about cleaning rue Malibran with the help of plenty of detergent and water and one of those disinfectants that give hospitals that grim odour of cleanliness. He was surprised not to find any clean sheets. Apparently, Lucien Lefrène was content just to have one set, which he must have washed and dried in one go at some launderette. The dubious mattress was protected by a flannel undersheet. He threw everything away and went a few doors down from number 19, to a shop that sold bed linen. He also threw out all the dirty dishes, the oilcloth covering the table, the toothbrush and two towels, and everything else that looked suspicious. He did not stop until mid-afternoon; the room had been devastated but was as clean as an operating theatre. Then, he removed the rubber gloves, threw them in the bin and washed meticulously in the tiny bathroom where naturally there was no bath tub. Finally, he put on the new clothes he had bought himself.

"Whew! It's bearable in here now. I can sit down and even contemplate sleeping here tonight, although eating here's still out of the question. There are no plates left and I don't see how I can cook on an electric cooker with only one hotplate!"

He had assembled on the table the few things he had not

discarded: Lucien Lefrène's papers, a typewriter, the tape recorder from the overnight bag and some cassettes. It did not take him five minutes to discover, to his amazement, that Lucien Lefrène was a journalist.

"So I'll never get away from the written word!"

Every week he produced articles on pop stars for a magazine that must have been very trendy because its title was hellishly esoteric, *Les Paincos* – backslang for *copains* – mates. Lucien Lefrène had been to Paris to interview a young musician who had made a *smash hit* with her latest *chart topper* – the words in italics pained the half of Aline who had not lost her love of language just because she had become a boy. Lucien Lefrène was expected to deliver his article that evening. The lady whose name must have been Adèle Dubois had chosen, as they all do, an outrageous stage name: Amouradora. Orlanda could only bear to listen to half of Lucien Lefrène's conversation with her. When he learned that Amouradora had remained a simple girl, that she very much hoped to meet a man who would make her a happy mother, but that her career etc., he stopped the tape. If he had to write, he would write, but he did not feel he could cope with transcribing what he had heard. Aline had a lively pen, which she always restrained because the academic powers that be were so easily shocked. Orlanda could not see how Amouradora could be inspiring. He thought for a second and then recalled the article on *The Alcalde in Difficulties*, an imbroglio in three acts, which Lucien, who was no longer Chardon but was now Rubempré after Mme de Bargeton had fired him, wrote in twenty minutes: "on the round table in Florine's boudoir, under the gleam of the pink candles which Matifat had lit", and automatically cast around for the bookshelves to take down a copy of Balzac's *Lost Illusions*. There were no bookshelves. Very well, he said, let's not lose heart, there must be a bookshop near here. Yes, but no Balzac, and as it was already five o'clock and time was pressing, he took a taxi to a large bookstore in the city centre and another one home again.

What worked for Rubempré will also work for me, he said, flicking through the beautiful Pléiade edition, the only attractive object in the horrid room that would now be his home. He was going to plagiarize.

"The alcalde's daughter was there, played by a real Andalusian girl, with Spanish eyes, Spanish complexion, Spanish waistline and Spanish gait: a Spanish girl from head to foot, with a dagger in her garter, love in her heart and a cross dangling from the end of a ribbon over her bosom". Further on: "Ah! this alcalde's daughter makes you drool with love and arouses wicked thoughts. You want to leap on to the stage and offer her your heart and your hearth, or maybe an income of 30,000 francs and your pen." And then: "I was able to get to Act III without making any disturbance, without the police being called in or the audience being scandalized, and from now on, I believe in the power of public and religious morality which the Chamber of Deputies worries so much about that you might suppose there is no more morality left in France." That's brilliant! Orlanda said to himself, reading every single word – I could have quoted the whole thing, I restrained myself – that's good writing! That hypocrite of a Balzac, who pretends to despise journalism, wants to show that he can do it just as well, if not better than anybody. OK, I have to replace the word "Spanish" with a contemporary word, let's say sexy, and as the Chamber of Deputies isn't concerned with morality any more, but, I suppose, insurance companies don't like people ripping out the seats in the concert halls, I'll substitute "vandalism". He began confidently: "Amouradora appears, swaying rhythmically on three-and-a-half-inch stiletto heels, seven veils revealing her beauty with such art that when you have seen it all, you want more." He filled two pages and called a taxi to take him to his newspaper.

"Are you out of your mind!" they said. "That's not suitable for our readers!"

"Then I'm not a suitable journalist for your paper."

And that was how poor Lucien lost his job.

Then he went for dinner and decided that after a day where virtue had cost three bottles of domestic cleaning fluid, he deserved to have some fun, which, as we know, meant cruising. We will not follow him. The first time, in the train, I did not know him yet, and I had no idea what would happen. Well . . . I confess I suspected as much and perhaps my curiosity made me linger, but I shan't repeat that indiscretion. The fact is that pornography has always bored me and I cannot imagine that things I would find boring to write about would make interesting reading. We must return to Aline who is preparing for a dreary Saturday.

She awoke late with no desire to get up, but her mother had taught her that you do not stay in bed when you are not ill. Albert had left a note on the kitchen table to remind her that he had a meeting with a client. He would be back around one. She reheated some left-over coffee – apart from hanging oneself and other dramatic gestures, is there anything that is a clearer symptom of depression than reheating coffee, at the risk of it boiling, when you have everything you need to make some fresh? She wandered around the flat and found herself at her desk, emptying her briefcase and watching *Orlando* slide gently over Marion Zimmer Bradley. She did not feel like working, but what else could she do? It was Saturday, a big city hummed around her, she felt alone in the middle of a desert. I feel bad, she said to herself, but did not ask herself what was hurting. There is an open wound in my soul. She thought about these words, and as she had no idea how appropriate they were, found them melodramatic, so she shrugged and sat down, but did not open *Orlando*. I'm not going to read it a fourth time, I'm sure I won't get anything out of reading it again. It's time to think. The previous evening, Charles had mentioned Vita Sackville-West at least ten times, his words were a thick forest of things that have been said before and Aline had silently fantasized about a machete.

He resolves everything with pre-digested ideas, as if his culture and his vast store of information – he knows a lot more than I do about everything – were only useful to him for showing off. He worships Virginia Woolf and probably thinks that it would be unseemly to try and understand her? Somewhere in this text is the meaning, but perhaps it is not the same meaning that Woolf intended. "*A farce? the writer having fun?*" I don't believe a word of it! Wasn't it in *Marshlands* that Gide tried to make Angèle see just how serious his jokes in fact were? She mechanically glanced up at the bookshelves under the letter G, then shrugged – my instinctive tendency to check everything is a waste of time here, I can see that it would only be a distraction from what I should be thinking about. There's no doubt that I admire the effrontery of an author who makes a character go to bed a boy and wake up a girl, after a deep sleep, but I can't continue to value my ability to think, or to teach my students how to study a text if I leave it at that. For ten years I've been teaching them that you shouldn't look for the meaning of a book anywhere but within the book itself, not in the author's life or in the writings of critics and other commentators. Vita Sackville-West can go to hell! I know that view irritates Charles and annoys smug old Duchâtel, who has never dared to think for himself, but Albert, being an engineer, finds it completely natural, for he believes that the stability of a building depends on the way it is built, and not on the personality of the architect. Poor Virginia, who was continually on the verge of suicide, begins to laugh, plays and jokes: it's time to take her seriously! We're in 1928 . . . hold on! When did her madness begin? Aline quickly flicked through a chronology: 1915, and she drowned herself in 1941. How odd, thirteen years after and thirteen years before! Then she began to laugh: Aline, my girl, I've told you not to bring real life into it! Just remember that the beginning of this book is bubbling with joy, she holds her Orlando from the start, she dances with him, she jumps, bounces, runs, climbs trees, flings herself to the ground or snatches up her pen. She enjoys herself like a kid and teases her reader, she provokes and mocks her reader, until ... until Sasha! cried Aline feverishly turning the pages, until Sasha! Before which, he plays with his Moor's head which he decapitates anew with enthusiasm, he screws an old queen without complaining, he's clumsy and a bit dumb, he's a child who's sometimes good and sometimes boisterous but always enthusiastic. He darts from one toy to another, taking nothing seriously, and then suddenly he discovers passion. Which makes him discover suffering. And then, he sleeps for a week and wakes up changed, but not yet into a woman. It is his soul that is different, he no longer laughs, there's no longer any question of rolling with girls in the hay, that's an image, I don't think Woolf is that specific, but there are still fleeting love affairs, I'll have to reread the text closely. After that, he writes. Good! But he already wrote before, the important thing is, undoubtedly, what he no longer does, which is to slice at the Moor's head and run around all over the place. I suppose that in the meantime his parents died, they're never mentioned, the years begin to pass but he doesn't grow any older.

At what time of life do the years pass without your growing older? Aline mused. She felt a thrill, as though she were on the brink of discovering something. She waited. Nothing came. And so she continued.

He invites the poet Nick Greene to visit him, is disappointed, experiences the terrifying passion of the Archduchess Harriet Griselda, and flees to be ambassador to Constantinople. And that's the bit where I get aggravated, and reread the passage ten times, and I can't find anything in the text that helps me understand what comes next. He's made a Duke, gives a sumptuous feast, seems to spend the night with a stranger, sleeps for a week, etc. all that happens swiftly, Woolf is blithely making fun of her characters.

And of me! thought Aline who was still turning over the pages when she came across a little phrase that was perfectly in keeping with the rest: "But nobody has ever known exactly what took place later that night." That is how that sly creature had me believe that the meaning of the transformation is to be found in the events that immediately precede it! Through saying that we know nothing of Orlando's life in Constantinople, she convinces us that she is concealing something in the gaps in his so-called biography, that she has devised a treasure hunt and that we have to find the clues.

And then the bells started clanging in Aline's head:

"But he never was a boy!" she exclaimed. The seven days in bed – didn't my mother din it into me often enough – were puberty! It's all allegorical, and Virginia is telling her own story. As a child, she was strong and passionate, she waged war against the Moors in the attic, she had a girlfriend whom she adored and who began to neglect her, preferring boys, so she withdrew into study and reverie – I must ask Jacqueline if that isn't what's known as the latency period – she learned to tell herself stories to keep herself amused in secret.

She was ecstatic:

Childhood is when the years pass and you don't grow any older! And then the moment for the big transformation came, and she had to change from being an asexual child into a woman, and Truth forced itself on the reluctant little girl. She would no longer climb trees, she would no longer be a warrior, she would wear skirts and become coy. Poor Woolf is trying to protect her character from the fate that she suffered. She distanced Purity, Chastity and Modesty who so cruelly governed her life, but, of course, she doesn't succeed, and later we will see Orlando blushing, concealing her ankle from the ship's captain.

She was breathless with emotion.

It's so obvious! I can't possibly be the first person to realize it. There is that passage where Orlando, now a woman, repeats: "*I am growing up*". And then there were the servants! The servants don't age any more than she does. They are there until the end! The world around us changes when we grow up, and so does the weather. The summers of childhood are hotter and brighter than those of adulthood, and the winters are colder! My childhood days certainly seem as far off to me as past centuries! This time I really ought to go and see what the commentators had to say.

How easy she finds thinking! I am amazed, I probably thought, like Orlanda, that only boys have strength. But thinking has no sex, it is neither female nor male. In fact, Aline's reserve is useful to her: she will back up her theories so solidly with the help solely of the text, that they will be utterly convincing. Alas! who will care? A received idea is not dislodged by reasoning, no matter how thorough. The idea that for Virginia Woolf *Orlando* could have been an autobiography of her inner life will seem enticing, but if it is not in the textbooks, it will be forgotten.

Aline decided it was time to make notes and that on Monday she would go to the library to consult the critics. She began to write.

I watch her. She is in her element. She is no longer the dejected woman at the station, nor the amputee walking listlessly beside Albert. Her pen races over the white page, tracing the gracious arabesques of thought. Like flights of migrant birds forming hieroglyphs in the pale dusk, the letters joyfully unfurl their intricate curves, the vowels are gracefully joined to the consonants in a lithe dance that continually stops and starts. Oh dear! I am being taken over by metaphor, Virginia is contagious, soon I shall be comparing the movement of the pen to that of the waves, to the sparkling crest of foam edging the northern beaches, to everything that undulates and sways. But I see that, curiously, my mind always suggests movements that leave no traces. Am I so influenced by Charles and his rejection of any new ideas? Let us talk of nice parallel lines, like the furrows in a ploughed field and the plants that will soon be growing there, of the yarn that the shuttle draws in and out of the weft. I don't think I am very good at images, for I have come down to the banal comparison with knitting which continuously loops the wool. Let us pull ourselves together. What I sense is the great burst of enthusiasm that sweeps Aline from short sentences to long paragraphs balanced by whos and whiches, those beautiful bar lines that create rhythm. The happy band of words falls into place quite naturally, it proceeds in orderly fashion and comes to rest on the page. Aline is inside herself and also on the page where she watches herself land, led by a confident hand, the faithful partner, the good servant of each intention. Orlanda, who during this time is scrubbing vigorously, would shake her head saying: But, my girl, if you enjoy writing so much, why on earth spend your time writing about other people's books! Write your own! Such an idea did not belong to Aline. She would reply, I think, that the conception and gestation of a work is a man's job, without realizing that she is working on a book by a woman, for her mother had so profoundly etched her convictions on her daughter that Aline obeyed them without even being aware of it.

You may point out that Orlanda is scrubbing, and that brushing and scouring are the prerogative of women, and that I am getting confused over sexual identity. But look how he is doing it. A woman maintains her home: Orlanda is eliminating, throwing away, getting rid of things. It did not even occur to him to wash the dirty sheets. Can you picture Madame Berger acting thus? He still had the mania for cleanliness that had been instilled into him, but he did not give a fig for Lucien Lefrène's belongings.

At one o'clock, Albert found Aline writing and if, the previous evening, he had been slightly concerned by her tired air, he felt reassured.

# THIRD DAY
## SUNDAY

ORLANDA'S SATURDAY NIGHT lasted until the small hours of Sunday. He returned home very tired from the interesting activities which my discretion – unfortunately! – prevented me from witnessing, and fell into such a deep sleep that he was not disturbed by his host's dreams. At eight thirty he was awoken by the telephone. He automatically got up, went over to the chest of drawers and picked it up without thinking.

"Is that you at last, Lucien?" croaked a hoarse voice that instantly grated on his nerves.

Lucien? It took him a few moments to remember his connection with that name.

"Yes," he replied, but said no more as he did not know who he was speaking to.

"When did you get back? You ain't called me for a week."

It was the voice of an elderly woman, rasping rather than hoarse.

"I've been very busy," he ventured cautiously.

In front of him there was a mirror which he had deemed in good enough condition to escape the dustbin. He gazed at his reflection, still enchanted with his new appearance: his hair was tousled, there were dark rings round his eyes and his chin was rough, but he thought he looked pretty good. Very good. He gave a smug grin. What a gorgeous young man! I was very lucky, in my haste and recklessness, goodness knows who I might have picked!

"So busy you couldn't phone your own mother!"

His mother! He jumped. So Lucien Lefrène had a mother!

"And you're never in. I've been calling you for three days, you told me you'd be back on Thursday."

"I was delayed," he said, panic-stricken at her plaintive, demanding and cantankerous tone. Madame Berger had never spoken to Aline like that.

"Anyway, you're here, that's the main thing. I'll be expecting you. I need you to do some shopping for me. Me foot's bad again and your sister ain't no use, you know 'er, I can't ask 'er for nothing."

And a sister? A sister and he knew what she was like! Orlanda sighed. A young man is drinking a coffee in Paris and he turns out to have a whole family in Brussels. The only one missing was the father, unless Orlanda was in luck and poor old Lucien was fatherless.

"Hurry up and come round. And, by the way, pick up a bottle of whisky on the way. I'll pay you back. I ain't got nothing to offer visitors."

Ah! ha! thought Orlanda.

After a further chiding, Madame Lefrène hung up. Go there? said Orlanda, but I don't know where this lady lives! There's no reason why I should care about someone with a croaky voice and sloppy speech. *Your sister ain't no use, you know 'er, I can't ask her for nothing.* Huh! Just because I've changed sex, it doesn't mean I'm going to change the way I talk. He went back to bed, determined not to worry about his filial duties until he had had enough sleep. He felt no curiosity for Lucien Lefrène, a man with a healthy bank account but poor hygiene, and wondered vaguely how he would get rid of the boy's family. A bottle of whisky! Honestly! He was dropping off to sleep when he jumped. The screeching voice reverberated, demanding the countless sacrifices and gratitude that were her due. But this time, who was dreaming, his host, alarmed by the telephone call, or him? He took two aspirin. You do not break into someone else's life without the risk of suffering some inconvenience; he told himself again that he knew very well he had not thought of everything.

The fact is, I didn't think of anything, not even of locking the door, he added an hour later as the door opened and a young girl appeared before him.

"What's all this?" he grunted, under the duvet.

*This* was wearing a mini-skirt that was so tight it made her slim hips bulge, and an imitation-leather jacket – Christ, they're everywhere! – she had naturally blonde hair but it was in need of a wash.

"Ah! So you're home! How long have you been back? You haven't called me for days."

"I was busy."

The girl flung herself on the bed, threw her arms round him, and, to Orlanda's horror, grabbed his mouth and began a kiss that left no doubt as to the intimacy of her relationship with Lucien Lefrène.

How awful! The woman is his girlfriend! He tore himself away from an embrace that was becoming dangerous.

"And I'm still very busy. I've got to go, I've overslept."

But where the hell will I go? he groaned inwardly.

"You go off for a week, you don't call me when you get back, and when I come round, you say you've got to go! Don't you love me any more?"

"I'm supposed to love you, am I?"

Honestly, Lucien was impossible!

"What on earth's the matter with you?"

On leaving Aline, Orlanda had intended not to take her weaknesses, but he had moved too fast to check every piece of luggage. At the sight of the tears that suddenly filled the girl's big brown eyes, threatening her mascara, he felt the stirring of compassion in his soul. He also recognized the irritating delicacy of feeling that had made his erstwhile gaoler unable to defend her interests. What is this emotion at the sight of a girl crying, he thought crossly, if not the residue of poor old Aline, of her endless sacrifices and her obedience to an over-apprehensive mother? There's no way I'm having any of that, he added, leaping out of bed because the young lady, doubtless anxious to verify her lover's ardour, had slipped her hand brazenly and accurately under the duvet.

Now up, he was shocked by his nakedness and hurriedly sought a clean pair of underpants in the chest of drawers. While he was pulling on his jeans, the young lady looked around the room in amazement.

"What's happened here? Have you been burgled?"

Poor burglars! thought Orlanda thinking of the rubbish he had thrown out.

"It was disgusting. I cleaned up."

"What about these sheets? You didn't have these sheets, or this duvet?"

She stretched out, slid under the pillow, said something about how nice it would be to baptize such lovely new bed linen together and Orlanda felt his hair stand on end, announced that his mother was waiting for him and he had to leave straight away.

"I'll come with you," she said.

Then she added that, honestly, she didn't know what had got into him today.

But when they were downstairs, Orlanda remembered that he did not know where this mother lived and wondered which way to turn. He stood on the pavement, while the girl headed for Place Flagey and he followed. While he hesitated and pretended to dither, she led him to a little street in the Molenbeek district. From time to time, she took his hand, or pressed herself against him, which made him very tense. She chattered a lot and he learned in passing that her name was Marie-Jeanne, and in his mind that name became associated with imitation leather jackets and unkempt hair.

We must not forget that Orlanda is twelve years old, the age at which boys find girls irritating and children are inclined to be snobbish. We will not be seeing much of Marie-Jeanne, but I must not let Orlanda's prejudices influence me and, since she is there, she is entitled, just like everyone else, to a few minutes' attention. This girl has a soul which is not adequately defined by the imitation leather and unwashed hair.

She is in love with Lucien Lefrène whom she finds wonderfully good-looking, talented and kind. At nineteen, she has already been working for three years, as a check-out girl in a supermarket. She only has two hundred thousand Belgian francs worth of savings, because of her concern for her appearance, which for a while took priority over her plans for the future. It is certain that Aline Berger has no idea of this kind of life, her family has had money for ten generations. Marie-Jeanne's grammar is dodgy and she has not opened a book since the happy day she left school, which does not mean she lacks ambition. She wants to get married, have children, a house and two cars. She thinks that all this is perfectly possible with Lucien Lefrène. She is delighted with his thrifty disposition and has given up going to the hairdresser's and stopped smoking. Her faith in the rosy future that lies ahead of them gives her strength. She still cares about her clothes, but this year she went through her wardrobe and, as everything was in good condition, she has not bought any new clothes to keep up with fashion so she has been able to save a third of her pay every month. Her mother, with whom she gets on very well, is very impressed by her strength of character.

"My mother told me that her mother only bought her a dress if the old one was beyond repair," she said, nodding pensively. "They used to unravel old jumpers and knit new ones with the wool that was still usable. You can't do that with factory-made ones," mused Marie-Jeanne, dreamily.

This mother still works as a cleaner. Marie-Jeanne is counting on the fact that when she has babies, her mother will look after them while she is out at work. Lucien takes a keen interest in the stock market, and, as soon as he is sure he has understood the way it works, he will start investing. By judiciously placing their savings, boosted by the family allowance which is quite generous after the third child, they will have a good income and their children will go to university. She sees them as doctors, engineers or lawyers. They will marry into the bourgeoisie. She will not allow herself to be intimidated by the mothers-in-law who will try to look down on her.

Yes, but, Marie-Jeanne dear, where has Lucien Lefrène gone?

"What about my bottle of whisky?"

Madame Lefrène was sitting in an antique armchair, its tapestried cover threadbare; a stool supported her left foot which was bared to let the air get to her hideously red and swollen big toe. Even Orlanda could tell it was an attack of gout at its worst. Marie-Jeanne leaned over and placed her lips on the blotchy cheek without showing any disgust.

"I think Lucien forgot it, we'll go and get it later."

"But I need a little pick-me-up!"

Orlanda stared at Lucien's mother in horror and recognized the figure that had pursued the poor boy in his dreams. She had grey hair, thinning on the top of her head to the point of baldness. Her face was puffy and her nose had the purple tinge of the hardened alcoholic. She wore a sort of bathrobe covered in stains, that gaped to reveal a night-dress too short to conceal the varicose veins in her legs. Whoever this sister is, I'm on her side, he said to himself with a shudder and wondered what he was doing there. If this woman had ever had a soul, it had been pickled in alcohol, and all that was left of her were the cunning eyes that watched the effects of her complaints on those around her. She knew that nobody was taken in by her, but carried on pretending because nobody was interested in the painful truth: nothing gave her any pleasure except drinking, and her life was hell because none of them would procure her the thing that was killing her. So she became even more scheming in her efforts to obtain the poison that nobody had the courage to deny her. When she finally got what she wanted, she seemed so happy that they felt ashamed of having made her wait. She had no wish to die, but was a total slave to the pleasure of the whisky spreading through her and did not give a damn about her liver, her heart or her brain. They'll last as long as I do, she would say, exasperating the doctors with this aberration of logic. Lucien brought the bottles, apparently out of weakness, but perhaps too out of hatred. Disgusted, Orlanda, turned on his heel and left.

"What's up with him then?" exclaimed Madame Lefrène.

"I don't know. He's acting really weird today," repeated Marie-Jeanne, puzzled.

Aline had never seen anything like it, and Orlanda only knew what Aline knew. He felt frightened and wanted to forget the dreadful sight of that half-dissipated old woman as quickly as possible. He ran for a few minutes as if he hoped that in putting the gloomy little apartment behind him he would put what he had witnessed there out of his mind, then he slowed down, shook himself, remembered that he had not had enough sleep and returned to rue Malibran. There, he took precautions, locking the door and taking the telephone off the hook.

Lucien's dreams were less perturbing than the first night. Perhaps Orlanda had done him a favour by running away?

That Sunday, Albert was going to his office to work on some drawings that had to be ready for the following day, which is not unusual in the life of an engineer, and Aline finished her notes on *Orlando.* She even painstakingly reread the chapters that precede the transformation and was delighted not to find any reference to a beard or moustache. At the most, there was mention of a light blond down on his cheeks, at the beginning. Other than that, Woolf painted them pink and chubby like the cheeks of a child. When he was in Constantinople and rose late, he emerged from his bath "*scented, curled and anointed*", but not shaven. I'm not mistaken, thought Aline. When she had finished, she reread the few commentaries she found on her bookshelves with irritation. They really are adamant, she grumbled. Edgar Allan Poe fills his stories with pale corpses and people buried alive because of his mother's dead body, that's common knowledge, and academic etiquette demands that the name Albertine be uttered with a knowing smile. Duchâtel, who had supervised her thesis, had an ironic way of pronouncing the *tine* which his colleagues thought to be in excellent taste. She filled the margins of her ten pages with quotes showing Orlando blushing, trembling and quivering with shyness before Sasha.

"The only difference between him and Clarissa Dalloway is that his reproductive organ works better," she said to Albert over breakfast.

"Will you say that to your students?"

"You don't talk about erections in a university lecture theatre."

Now she was absolutely convinced, the transformation was not the magic feat that those poor transsexuals pay so much for and which only castrates them, but which, in 1928, Virginia Woolf could not have known about.

What was a woman born in 1882 allowed to know?

These days, all knowledge is available to me, she thought.

She suddenly felt that same agonizing wrench that she had experienced on the Friday evening.

At four o'clock in the afternoon, sated with sleep, washed and dressed in fresh linen, Orlanda realized it was too late for lunch and too early for dinner and resigned himself to the joys of a fast-food restaurant where he devoured several hamburgers with distaste.

What was more, the coffee was awful. What now? he wondered, and was surprised to feel at a loss for something to do. What do you do in a city where, in short, you are all alone with no plans? Neither his host's journalistic pursuits, nor Marie-Jeanne, nor Madame Lefrène made him feel inclined to delve further into Lucien's life. He could have gone to the cinema, but who would he have discussed the film with afterwards? Was he going to be bored? The thought made him wince, and he decided to wander aimlessly through the streets and invite inspiration. It was a lovely, fresh, sunny April afternoon, and his footsteps took him in the direction of the Ixelles lakes, where he enjoyed watching the ducks which had left Aline indifferent for twenty years. Children threw them stale bread, under the loving gaze of their mothers who were glad that their offspring could enjoy themselves and get rid of the leftovers at the same time. He walked through the Cambre Abbey where he admired the splendid buildings that were finally being restored, and entered the wood. The first leaves outlined the heavy black branches with a fine green fuzz. Wasn't this the time of year when, long ago, people used to go and pick wild hyacinths in the Halle woods? He pictured the bunches of mauve bells that people used to put all around their homes, then remembered the curved branches of white hawthorn blossom whose flowers fell so quickly onto the polished floor boards. He thought about the buttercups, the daisies and the forget-me-nots. Aline had forgotten all that, but for Orlanda, the long, absorbing flower-picking expeditions felt like yesterday. He used to make tiny bouquets, arranging the colours in concentric circles and putting them carefully into Madame Berger's liqueur glasses. She admired her daughter's precision and talent – but it was me as much as her! protested Orlanda recalling the long hours spent on his knees in the grass. He always carried several baskets where he carefully arranged the little flowers. Sometimes he spent hours looking for scarlet pimpernel, which was becoming rare because of insecticides, but whose tiny petals he found particularly beautiful, and delicate little pink clusters whose name he had never known.

"Your knees are all green! And just look at your socks! Look at the state of them! I'll never be able to get them clean!"

There again, Aline gave in. Or do children always grow out of the games they once loved? Orlanda hated this idea and went down to the lake and got down on his knees in the big field to pick a bunch of daisies. Not knowing what to do with them, he gave them to a little girl who was surprised and delighted.

Then, he left the wood and set off along avenue Winston Churchill, nostalgic, like Aline, for the days when it had been called Longchamp, but you have to pay tribute to wars and victors – how many Fochs, Clemenceaux and Charles de Gaulles had replaced the sheep, pastures and lilacs of the old street names! He walked at a relaxed pace, looking at the few big old houses that had survived the property developers and saw that one of them was for sale. He crossed over, walked past a rusty gate and slipped between the laurel bushes which looked as though they had not been trimmed for ten years, to try and see inside through the dusty windows. Just then, a middle-aged man who was standing by an expensive car came over to him:

"Monsieur Leroy?" he asked – or something like that – "I was expecting you. I'm delighted you're here, as I wanted to make our appointment earlier, but you must already have left when I phoned because there was no answer."

It was too good an opportunity!

"Let's go," said Orlanda without compunction.

"I hope you won't be shocked. The house has been empty for some years, and the heirs have only just decided to put it up for sale. We haven't even had the time to give it a quick clean. But it's very sound, I checked, there's no dry rot."

And so on. The estate agent opened the door as he chatted and Orlanda made no attempt to listen to him. They crossed a spacious marble and gilt hall and walked through ornate rooms which still contained some items of old furniture that were perhaps not devoid of interest. Orlanda went over to a window and saw a sort of little interior courtyard full of plants that had gone wild. A narrow corridor led to what must have been a very beautiful library. The doors with their bevelled glass panes rattled:

"But that can all be repaired quite inexpensively," said the agent.

They went upstairs and down in such a haphazard fashion that Orlanda had the feeling of being delightfully lost. He saw narrow little rooms, vast modern-style bathrooms with swan-neck taps, and a balcony big enough for a royal family to stand and receive the acclamations of the crowd on coronation day. He was having the most wonderful time when they heard the distant chime of a bell. Puzzled, the estate agent went to investigate and Orlanda vanished as discreetly as he could while the real Leroy – or whatever – family made themselves known.

"I knew there was something about that young man in jeans . . ."

Orlanda continued on his way in excellent spirits. That's some house! he said to himself. I made Lucien Lefrène lose his job, but when I was Aline, I used to love old houses. Perhaps I could go into the renovation business. I'd buy derelict old buildings, do them up and resell them. It's as good as job as any, I wonder if the half-million would be enough? He headed towards avenue Molière studying all the façades carefully, and daydreaming.

Those who have been following him from the Ixelles lakes and who know the district give a faint smile when they see him reach place Constantin Meunier and sit down on a public bench in the middle of the square claiming, with all the hypocrisy in the world, that he does not know how he got there.

On the third floor, Aline was pacing up and down the apartment. Why did she feel so restless? Suddenly, she no longer felt like working, but that was understandable, she had just spent six hours at her desk, stopping for only twenty minutes at lunch time to finish off the remains of a stew. She opened a book, which immediately bored her, assumed she must be tired and lay down to have a nap, but she had pins and needles in her legs and jumped up again. She felt a growing exasperation, she needed to move around and went into the kitchen intending to empty the dishwasher. She was quivering with impatience, everything annoyed her, she groaned, fraught, miserable, she did not know what she wanted but she wanted it desperately. In the end she found herself slipping on her coat and rushing down the stairs without having decided to go out. Downstairs, she looked right and left, puzzled. What the hell was she doing there? She made her way over to the pitiful public garden in the centre of the square: two hedges, an emaciated tree, three daffodils which dejectedly turned their backs on a lawn suffering from partial alopecia, which would seem to prove that dog poo is not a very good fertilizer, and the bench from which Orlanda observed her arrival with satisfaction.

"Hello," he said.

As she did not know many of her neighbours, she presumed this rather nondescript young man lived nearby and therefore felt entitled to greet her. So she gave him a rather curt, discouraging nod. He got to his feet, smiling.

"Don't you recognize me?"

She was embarrassed. Orlanda knew she had an excellent memory for faces. How different we are! he thought. I would stick my nose in the air and say, with a hint of arrogance: Should I?

"We saw each other in Paris."

She could not imagine this young man hunched over manuscripts at the Bibliothèque nationale.

"You were drinking mineral water opposite the Gare du Nord, and I was finishing off a cold cup of coffee that didn't have enough sugar and you gave me an aspirin."

"So you don't live around here?" inquired Aline who had hoped for this more reassuring possibility.

Orlanda's smile turned into a little laugh.

"Oh no!"

He looked her straight in the eyes, with an insistence that should have made Aline feel ill at ease.

"Where were you going?" he added.

"I don't know," she replied.

She was furious with herself for having told the truth.

"Then I'll walk with you and we'll go there together."

Aline, completely disconcerted, allowed herself to be taken by the arm and walked three yards before turning on him.

"But I don't know you!"

"Ah! But I know you very well."

Orlanda was having fun. Aline ought to shrug her shoulders at once and say, "because of two aspirins, in Paris?" in order to get herself out of the awkward situation I'm putting her in and to embarrass me. That's what I would do in her shoes, which proves she's got it in her. But no! That's just it. I'm no longer in her and all she has left is the passiveness of the well-bred young lady, poor thing! All the same, even before, she would not have done it.

"Do you know me?"

"You're a lecturer in literature and you've written a thesis on Proust."

"Have you read it?"

"Why not?"

I must put an end to this conversation and go home, thought Aline, without moving. Why am I talking to this young man whom I don't know, even if he does claim to know me? Her restlessness, that painful feeling of emptiness, the void in her soul which she had experienced at the station and which had suddenly come back to torment her a few minutes earlier and her irritation had all vanished, but she did not realize it, and beneath the feeling of incongruity, an insidious tranquillity was stealing over her.

Orlanda did not take his eyes off her.

"Do I really look such a boor?"

She protested, unconvincingly, which amused him.

"Your manners never let you down, do they?"

And Aline realized that such an accurate appraisal of her character was making her laugh.

"Come on," he said, "let's go for a drink."

"Around here? There's nowhere."

"That's true!"

Place Constantin Meunier has avenue Molière cutting across it diagonally, with rue Rodenbach and rue de la Mutualité leading off from the other two corners. In this district, literature and the arts take precedence over civic duty, there are no streets named after great war heroes, only small apartment blocks and old, classical mansions that have been converted. The nearest shop or café is at least five hundred yards away.

"Except the ice-cream place," volunteered Aline, who did not recognize herself.

"Let's go."

She tried to regain her composure, and repeated:

"I can't! I don't know you."

"Better than you think," replied Orlanda, still laughing.

I hope I have made it clear just how reckless walking beside a young man *who had never been introduced to her* was for Aline, an extremely proper young lady who found herself discussing her work on the first chapter of *Remembrance*, and the stupidity of the aunts who were unable to thank Swann openly for sending them the case of Asti.

"You should have shown more clearly that it sets the tone for all those conversations made up of allusions between those who are in the know, which automatically exclude those who aren't, thus distinguishing the chosen from the dross, and that the Duchesse de Guermantes as well as Mme de Verdurin are included among them."

"But I didn't see that so clearly!"

"Oh yes you did," he declared firmly. "In fact, one keeps expecting you to show that the two characters are different sides of the same coin, but then you don't. Don't tell me it didn't occur to you."

"Granted, but that was nearly fifteen years ago, and people would have been shocked."

"The only difference is that the Narrator likes one of them and he finds the other ridiculous. They are fundamentally the same, but the Duchesse has the privilege of birth, and all she has to do is step into the part, while Mme Verdurin learned to entertain at the home of the caterer who supplies her table."

"I have to stop you there. I don't remember any caterer!"

"It's a way of talking. A society lady has a cook, which people envy her for: someone should do a study on food in *Remembrance*."

"Oh, there probably is one! Everything there is to be said about Proust has already been written."

"But I loved the way you showed how the passion for the mother foreshadowed the love for Gilberte, the jealousy towards Albertine and even the curious attraction for Mme de Guermantes. Jesus! That red-faced woman, with a big nose and bulging eyes!"

As she was drawn into the conversation in spite of herself, Aline wondered confusedly why this way of talking seemed so familiar.

"Bulging? I don't think so; she has a piercing look, a wandering gaze when she's bored at Mass, or tender and absent-minded, but not bulging? Aren't you talking about Mme Verdurin?"

"Goodness, I can't remember; they're so similar."

And so on. They had sat down at a table so absorbed in their conversation that they were caught unawares by the waitress handing them the menu.

"Two vanilla ices with chocolate sauce," said Orlanda.

"What?"

"That's what you were going to order, wasn't it?"

"Yes," conceded Aline meekly.

He turned to the waitress: "With a double helping of chocolate sauce."

Then he turned back to Aline:

"You see, I do know you."

She thought vaguely that he could not have found out from her thesis that she liked a double helping of chocolate sauce, but let such a disturbing thought go. And Orlanda was off again enthusiastically:

"And what about the Marquis d'Osmond? Do you remember him? He dies and the Duke doesn't want to know. He's the Duke's cousin, he'd have to turn down dinner at Mme de Saint-Euverte's."

Their conversation was so enjoyable that Aline forgot – very easily, I find – how odd it was to eat ice cream with a stranger. It is certain that at no point had Orlanda consciously planned to go to place Constantin Meunier, and that, finding himself there, he never asked himself what he was doing there. He had waited for Aline as naturally as if he had arranged to meet her, and he was not mistaken, since she had arrived five minutes later. Since the beginning of this business, his impulsiveness had been rewarded, and there did not seem to be any reason why he should deny himself. But now, heatedly discussing the Marquis d' Osmond, what was he trying to do? Goodness, no matter how much I search his soul, all I can sense is his enjoyment. Orlanda has an innocence, he relishes the moment and does not look further than the end of his nose, which, I must repeat, was a very nice nose. He has the character of a child, with the knowledge of an adult which he only uses when he needs to, and the rapt body of the recent adolescent. Aline amused him and he enjoyed intriguing her as much as he had delighted in making the man in the cashmere overcoat turn around the previous Friday. When she was embarrassed or disconcerted, it gave him immense pleasure, and it did not occur to him to spare her. He was not unkind, it was the natural cruelty of the child. Let us not forget that, from his point of view, Aline had been a prison. Now that he had escaped, he had come back to play outside the walls which had seemed insuperable, and was delightedly thumbing his nose at the gaolers who did not recognize him. This happy thief feared no police – who could guess his crime? In any case, there are no laws! The penal code does not provide for his offence, which is a double one, for he has stolen half a woman's soul and a boy's entire body. He cannot be reported: one victim is unaware of the crime and the other seems to have disappeared. Nobody is in a position to lodge a complaint. Besides, imagine the police superintendent who received such a complaint! He would immediately think the plaintiff crazy and call in the psychiatrists, for what Orlanda has done cannot happen.

I can already hear the question people might ask: "In that case, Madam, why are you claiming that he has done just that?"

How can I help it if I am witness to the impossible? Mauriac said that he had seen his Thérèse at the Crown Court, Maxime du Camp states that she gave Flaubert Madame Bovary, but Peter Cheney has never claimed that Lemmy Caution existed. Novelists are often asked if they believe that the story they are telling is plausible, probably because people confuse them with journalists, who have a duty to be reliable. I claim that Orlanda did it and I defy anybody to prove the contrary to me. You can prove that something exists, but it is quite a different matter to prove that it does not. What is more, if something has not yet been done, does that mean that it will not be? In 1910, Proust had not yet written *Remembrance of Things Past*, and clearly, it was not impossible that it should be written.

But Orlanda is immoral, that I do not deny, just as immoral as the Duc de Guermantes furiously refusing to accept that his cousin was dying. By the way, Orlanda is in the middle of saying something:

"The Duke is not immoral because he doesn't care about the death of a cousin who means nothing to him, but because he claims to despise the dinners in town when in fact he would sell his soul not to miss one."

"And Oriane is just as bad when, two minutes later, she refuses to listen when Swann announces that he only has three or four months left to live and pretends to believe he's joking."

"And the terrible *You'll bury us all!* on which that volume closes!"

"The only crime is to wear black shoes with a red dress!"

"And to think of the grandmother's death, about which he will speak so eloquently in Venice; ten lines after the last breath, he feels himself being reborn because the fog has lifted!"

"No, you've got to be fair, it must be at least twenty lines!" said Aline, and they burst out laughing.

Of course, a grumpy little voice tried to make itself heard, but Aline ordered it to be silent. Never, in the academic circles where most of her conversations took place, had she found such a stimulating person to talk to. Goodness! Can one really only enjoy talking to oneself? Ideas sparked, stimulating others, which this strange young man seized on to go one step further, then Aline caught up with him and went beyond, each one passionately developing the other's suggestions. They hated commonplaces, but they knew them all and enjoyed evoking them: the *madeleine* dipped in tea, the *paperolles*, the fumigations, Vinteuil's little phrase, everything that encapsulates images and saves you having to read.

Suddenly:

"Aren't you finishing your ice cream?"

The ice cream had melted, making yellow rivulets in the chocolate.

"It's too much," she said.

"Give it to me."

She was dumbfounded to see this stranger take her plate and delightedly scrape the bottom of the goblet with his spoon. This sort of thing is only done by people who are on intimate terms, and, of course, she had no idea of the intimacy that connected her to him.

"I'm still hungry," he said. "It must be because I'm so young."

That strange comment did not make Aline any the wiser.

"As you get older, you lose your appetite," he went on, "you eat without enthusiasm. How boring!"

That is actually true, thought Aline, for at least ten years now I've enjoyed my food, but I never eat with gusto. This thought made her forget her amazement. Besides, he was returning to Mme de Guermantes and Mme Verdurin, and she abandoned intimacy for enjoyment:

"You don't build an academic career with personal observations," she said to him. "You have to have refined thoughts within an accepted framework."

"Isn't that a subversive thing to say?"

"All the critics are adamant: the issue is whether the Duchess was based on Mme de Chevigné, Comtesse Grefulhe or the Comtesse de Castellane, and as they could not possibly be confused with Mme Arman or Mme Aubernon, there is no question of seeing Mme Verdurin as the other side of the same coin. Oriane is never described as coarse, but as haughty, because she rules over Society, which cannot be vulgar, but Mme Verdurin is coarse because she's a Verdurin. And yet, in *Time Regained*, we see Mme de Guermantes trying to persuade people to come to her *soirées* that nobody is interested in any more, like a Verdurin!"

Orlanda was amazed: she's quite delightful when she's animated like this, she's passionate, her eyes are sparkling! She always consigned me to oblivion, but when I force her to confront me, she becomes lively again, she enjoys herself, she dares. The fact is, she can't live without me.

He never asked himself whether he could live without her.

Albert was most surprised when Aline did not come home until seven o'clock. He had expected to find her at her desk, a little pale and tired after a long afternoon of work, and there she was, flushed and laughing, with the air of a schoolgirl who has been playing truant.

"Are you home already?" she asked in surprise. "Is it that late?"

"Where on earth have you been?"

She had not thought about what she would say to him, and lied instinctively:

"I went for a walk round the block, I felt restless."

"Round the block? I've been waiting for you for an hour and a half!"

"That's incredible! I had no idea of the time."

She was stunned to hear herself lie so quickly and so well, and then wondered why she did so. *I went for an ice cream with a young man I don't know and we discussed Proust which he's very knowledgeable about.* Could she say this to a man and expect him to accept it at face value? Yes, if he is trusting and you are an impulsive woman, but we have been living together for ten years and I have never done a single unpredictable thing. I am always punctual, I brush my teeth every night to please the dentist and every morning out of vanity, I pay my bills promptly, I go to the toilet a quarter of an hour after breakfast, I remember to go and have my tetanus boosters. If I talk about a twenty-year-old boy I met in the square, he'll tell me I'm ridiculously naive and that next time I'll be kidnapped, gagged and drugged, and wake up in a brothel in Rio, because in his anxiety he'll forget that they only take girls much younger than me. It's best to lie this evening and never to be so crazy as to go off for an ice cream again.

She and Albert had a quiet dinner in the big kitchen, watched an excellent film on television, and then it was time to go to bed.

Absolute madness, honestly! she thought as she stepped onto the scales, for she had forgotten, when listing her habits, the weekly weighing of a woman who watched her figure. The chocolate sauce had been a bit too runny, the ice-cream maker is sometimes careless on Sundays, that's the only indulgence where I lost my self-control. But I have to admit that I was feeling miserable and now I'm perfectly cheerful. Why the hell did that boy insist on having an ice cream with me? Not for a second did he seem to want anything other than conversation.

She was about to fall asleep when she remembered he had spoken of a mineral water and two aspirins in Paris, which roused her completely. How can having seen me in Paris lead him to the scrawny garden in place Constantin Meunier? He must have followed me, but I would have seen him in the train, she reasoned, forgetting that she had sat there with her nose in her book all the time. Besides, it's ridiculous to think he would have gone to so much trouble to wait three days before approaching me. *But I know you.* And he talks to me about my thesis as if he's read it, which I don't imagine anyone has, apart from the supervisors who had to, and even then! I'm not sure that Duchâtel ever does anything he finds tedious. For twenty years he's read nothing other than his own writings. That young man is simply a student who knows me by sight, he saw me at the Gare du Nord, he's interested in Proust and he was playing games to mystify me.

She decided that this admirable conclusion was sufficient to placate her and when Albert, who had spent a few minutes at his drawing board, joined her, she welcomed him amiably. For the next half hour, it happened that the image of the fair-haired young man sometimes floated into her mind, which, as she was being embraced by the man who was to all intents and purposes her husband, she felt was in very bad taste.

Orlanda was in excellent spirits as he left Aline and went off for dinner, for he was famished. He then went parading his delightful person in places where he could expect to be noticed. As it was a fine evening, all the tourists were out, wandering around the Grand-Place clutching their *Guide Bleu.* The tower of the Town Hall was concealed under scaffolding, so they bought postcards and explained to each other about the architectural feat hidden from view by the restoration works, so that they were either looking down, or up, but not at Orlanda's level. Anyway, they were often accompanied by wives whom Orlanda found repulsive. So he decided to forgo the splendours of the fifteenth century, and set off down the little side streets. Aline vaguely knew that you met a lot of young people wandering through the streets, but Orlanda had always paid a lot more attention to them than she had. He mingled with them and realized that it would be very easy for him to become part of the groups that formed and broke up seemingly at random. They were very friendly, offering each other cigarettes which might have been joints. He saw that both boys and girls found him attractive, but he realized that this did not interest him. The previous evening he had been to a part of the Cambre wood which even Aline knew had a particular reputation – having said that I would not follow him there, I shall not say any more – and he had had a very enjoyable time, but that experience was enough. That afternoon, he had found only a fast-food restaurant, this evening, he was in no mood for "fast sex". He decided to walk back up to the Porte Louise, he remembered that along boulevard de Waterloo there were still a few cafés frequented by the sort of company that would suit his mood. But he stopped en route; there was a big symphony concert at the Palais des Beaux-Arts, it was the interval, music-lovers were milling around on the pavement. He slipped in among them, entered the rotunda and then the foyer, and was captivated by the sight of a man standing by a pillar.

He was around forty, elegant and self-assured, like the man at the Gare du Nord and the one on the train. He held himself very erect, and had a way of standing firm on his legs which suggested perfect self-control. He was screwing a cigarette into a long, yellowed, ivory cigarette holder, and this gesture evoked one of those distant memories long buried under the dust of time but which can suddenly regain all their lustre. When Aline had been twelve or thirteen years old, the age of uncertain emotions, Maurice Alker, a friend of M. Berger's who often came to lunch on Sunday, aroused in her the embarrassment of a young person who was trying to remain unobtrusive, she felt so insignificant. How silly she was! thought Orlanda who remembered clearly a grace that was still a little gawky, the lanky tanned legs of a child who runs around outdoors, the thin chest with breasts that were just beginning to form. She kept in the background, but the perceptive gaze of the man in his forties picked up the signals of her imminent blossoming. Dozens of times she had seen him look quickly away and had never understood. And yet, how she would have loved to please him! In the evening, she thought of him before falling asleep, *if I were eighteen and he were to invite me to dinner*, and felt a delightful shiver, the memory of which now thrilled Orlanda. Would this man have eyes that crinkled into a smile, like Maurice Alker? Imitating the conqueror on the train, Orlanda stepped forward and proffered a light.

"Thank you," said the stranger, without disguising his surprise.

"Are you enjoying the concert?"

"Louis Grimbert is excellent."

" What's in the second half?"

Orlanda did not take his eyes off the man, and noticed with pleasure that he did not avoid his gaze.

"Haven't you got the programme? The Schumann concerto."

"Isn't it a bit repetitive?"

"I love every note of it."

His way of expressing himself pleased Orlanda. It was clear, individual, others might disagree, he would listen to them quietly without changing his tastes which he had had time to develop.

"You've convinced me. I'll stay."

The bell announced that the second half of the concert was about to begin. The handsome stranger gave a polite nod and turned on his heel. Orlanda waited a moment before following him into the auditorium. Aline had been to enough concerts for Orlanda to know that the ushers do not check the tickets after the interval, there were not many people and he was able to seat himself a few rows away from the interesting music lover. Then the ritual began with arrival of the conductor and the pianist, applause, the soloist sat down, stretched his fingers, concentrated, etcetera, and Orlanda, who was not there to listen, was amazed to find himself caught up at once by the vigour and powerful beauty of the music.

Let us listen too for a while. Schumann had such a brief life, we owe it to him to devote a few moments to his music. Time kills us, second after second, and we fools continue to be impatient. Ah! for tomorrow, next week, for the moment we are awaiting finally to come. But, reckless soul, it will all end! Suppose you tried instead to enjoy the present? Stop, listen. Your heart is beating, a rich blood flows through your veins, you are alive, make the most of it now, don't say that the enjoyment will come later, it is there, it is happening now and it won't last long, every note of the concerto dies away. When you come to the end of the first movement, you can play the record again, but not that of your life, which is only played once. Orlanda, who was a child, allowed the *allegro vivace* to carry him away, he was probably not afraid of being reckless and as soon as the last note had faded, he turned his attention back to the attractive stranger.

He was applauding calmly, like a man who was mindful of the requirements of courtesy, then he left the row without seeming irritated at two elderly ladies fussing with their shawls and handbags. Orlanda only caught up with him outside, when he stopped to take out a cigarette.

"Well, what did you think?"

He did not seem surprised to see the young man again and he even gave a fleeting smile: yes, his eyes crinkled like Maurice Alker's!

"The execution was too romantic," he replied. "To play a romantic work romantically is a pleonasm. I would accept that kind of interpretation for *The Art of Fugue* or *Musical Offering*, where I would appreciate the paradox, but Schumann must be treated with the utmost rigour."

Good! said Orlanda to himself, interested by this communication process, it was not the same style as the man in the train. He was not rejecting the advance, but it has to obey certain rules, which I have to fathom, otherwise he'll reject me.

"Isn't that a rather unusual point of view?" he asked in a deliberately naive voice.

"Perhaps. I have no idea. I am not a music specialist."

"Playing Bach romantically? My piano teacher used to set the metronome."

"The metronome is the rule, it's the grammar. It is only within a strict adherence to the rules that expression can develop."

Orlanda noted that he avoided the teacher and the lessons, which implied a little boy sitting on his piano stool, and only talked about the metronome. Rule number one: it's all right for us to talk, but let's get it straight, we're talking about music, as is acceptable after a concert. We are not exchanging any personal information.

However, they had started walking, and were going up rue Ravenstein side by side as if by common consent. Orlanda concentrated on making conversation. He had at his disposal Aline's tastes and ways of thinking, and used them with the greatest of ease. I am sure she too would like this man who looked like Maurice Alker, but she wouldn't dare do what I'm doing. He added with a little inner laugh that her advances might not be so welcome!

When they reached place Royale, the stranger stopped by a car:

"I'm going to have dinner, I didn't have time before the concert," he said.

There was no invitation. Once again, it was up to the young man to take the initiative.

"Oh! You neither! I'm starving. Where are you thinking of going? There's nothing around here."

"I quite like the restaurants around rue du Grand-Cerf."

"It's a very nice area. Would you have any objection if I joined you?"

"Not at all," he said, and opened the passenger door.

Good, we're getting somewhere. As long as I don't put my foot in it!

For part of the journey, the conversation kept strictly to the subject of music, which the man knew a great deal about and, no matter how much he despised his former gaoler, Orlanda could only be grateful to Aline for having taught him so much about a subject which, at twelve, was still foreign to him. As they were parking, they moved on to the comparative merits of different types of Asian cuisine and decided to go to a Chinese restaurant.

"Good evening, Monsieur Renaud," said a thoroughly European head waiter, greeting them. "Your favourite table is free."

"That reminds me!" he exclaimed as he sat down. "We haven't introduced ourselves. Renaud is not my first name. And, by the way, it isn't spelt *aud* but *ault*, like the car. My name is Paul Renault."

Orlanda winced as he uttered the name Lucien Lefrène.

The time had probably come to move on to more personal matters, for, when they had ordered, Paul Renault inquired:

"And, apart from going to concerts, what do you do?"

God! It was exhausting constantly having to find a roundabout way of explaining things!

"In theory I'm a journalist, but I've just lost – " he stopped in mid-sentence, he had been about to say *his* job – "my job," he corrected.

"But isn't that a problem?"

"Not at all. I almost did it on purpose. I was supposed to write an article on a singer. You'll understand how ridiculous she is if I tell you her stage name is Amouradora."

Paul Renault laughed silently.

"So to console myself for having to do such a painful piece, I decided to write a good article. But I wasn't used to doing so and I copied the Balzac article that launched Lucien de Rubempré's career. Nobody recognized it, that wasn't the problem, but even a poor plagiarism of Balzac was too good."

"And what are you going to do now?"

"Dream. Idle my time away. Have fun. Fritter away the money I've saved up at the expense of numerous sacrifices."

"And find yourself poor, *by the winter's first roar.*"

This allusion to the feckless Grasshopper in La Fontaine's fable pleased Orlanda. Maurice Alker would have done that too, he said to himself. He reckoned that he could, in turn, question his companion, and learned that Paul Renault ran a business consultancy. He had no idea what that might mean and was careful not to ask any questions, in case they elicited boring answers. In any case, the food was coming and, as it was only his third meal that day, he really was very hungry.

Despite everything. And supposing I'm wrong? he wondered during the lacquered duck. If in fact this man were exactly like Maurice Alker, he wouldn't be interested in boys at all. Well, I'll have dined in excellent company, and I'll have an early night! But there were lingering looks, so fleeting that he could not be sure he had intercepted them, he listened so attentively and gave tiny, barely perceptible signs. That uncertainty became a pleasure in itself and agreeably complemented the excellence of the food.

When the bill came, Orlanda took out his wallet. Paul Renault laughed softly:

"Keep your savings a little longer."

He took Orlanda's hand and guided it so gently towards his worn suede jacket pocket that there was no doubt that the gesture turned into a caress.

Then they returned to the car and left together, as though it were a foregone conclusion.

Orlanda was amazed by Paul Renault's apartment with its collection of heavy, carved oak furniture, leather armchairs that were fashionable before the war, satin light-shades with flounces and an enormous crocheted lace tablecloth on the table. Nothing has changed here for fifty years! he thought.

"What would you like to drink?"

"Water. Lots of cold water. I drank more wine than I should have with the meal."

"Just a minute, I'll get it for you," said Paul Renault leaving the room.

The young man noticed a bookcase with glass doors and Aline's reflexes took over. He went over to it: Bromfield, Pearl Buck, all twenty-seven volumes of Jules Romains' *Men of Good Will*, Duhamel's *Caged Beasts*, the Goncourt brothers and Jacques Chardonne.

"It's an old lady's library!" he exclaimed.

"You're quite right," said Paul Renault who had returned with a jug of water and some ice cubes. I haven't touched a thing since the death of my parents who had kept my grandparents' books. My books are in another room.

And, having put down the tray, he placed a strong, caressing hand on Orlanda's shoulder. The boy turned around and was immediately caught in an embrace which . . .

Oh dear! I did say that I would not follow him any more! I am afraid I got carried away by the story. But also, there is something fascinating about unrequited love and Aline's Maurice Alker made me feel nostalgic. I think he reminds me of some love affair that I did not have, because I was too young or too silly. Unfortunately, I did not have the presence of mind to turn into a boy and become adventurous. Let us withdraw. Night descends, bringing with it unmentionable pleasures, the city gradually falls silent and slumbers. I am sure there is a pretty poem to be written about the gradual drowsiness that envelops desires and souls. Darkness invades every nook and cranny and silence seeps into the shadows, a cat stalks, and beneath the closed eyelids of the sleeping, dreams and nightmares alternately unfold their marvels and terrors. Under the dark veil of sleep, terrible vows are made which are immediately forsaken for simple desires. People tranquilly eat a bowl of forbidden cherries, they sigh in the arms of a lover, the peacefulness of locked bedrooms wards off all danger, there is a moment when the last night owls and the last thieves go to bed, the cat that has killed its mouse jumps onto the window ledge and steals into the room where those it has chosen are sleeping. The rising mist is made up of a hundred thousand peaceful or terrified breaths. A child sits bolt upright in terror at a forbidden thought that has taken on the shape of a monster and the child's terror conjures up his mother, a miracle that is repeated daily. Between the day that has just ended and the one that is about to begin there is a moment of absolute suspense. I awaken and perhaps I no longer know who I am nor who is asleep beside me, so I quickly invent a name, a story in which to pour my anguish. I construct an identity, but how can I be sure that today's is truly the same as yesterday's, or that the world exists? Are we sleeping gods who do not know that we are dreaming, each of us constantly creating the world? Then the night claims me again, I tell myself that I am talking nonsense, but perhaps that is not so, nothing convinces me that that moment of uncertainty was not one of lucidity. Fear sustains the illusion, then the cat comes and purrs against my cheek, reassuring me. The first dawn bird sings, it has no doubts, it knows who it is and it must know who I am.

Goodness! Was that the poem I did not intend to write?

# FOURTH DAY
# MONDAY

ORLANDA AWOKE AT ten. Remnants of dreams were floating around inside his head and he lay there for a long time smiling vacantly and looking angelic. But Orlanda was no angel – they have no sexual organ, whereas he certainly did, and it participated so enthusiastically in his recollections that he eagerly encouraged it. He dozed a little longer, then opened his eyes wide and looked around the room: mahogany wardrobes with mirrored doors, a chest of drawers on which stood a marble slab with a porcelain bowl and jug – the grannies were still everywhere. He rose, and found a note stuck to the mirror: in the kitchen he would find everything he needed for breakfast. A bowl had been placed over several bank notes with another note: "Thank you very much." He counted them and laughed: it was the equivalent of half a week's honest work, if you remember that honest work is always poorly paid. He ate his croissants ravenously for he did not have a respectable soul and did not feel wounded by Paul Renault's misapprehension.

Aline's father had a first-class library and he had encouraged his daughter only to read good literature. At six o'clock, Paul Renault came home and was startled to find the young man still there, so absorbed in a book that he did not notice his arrival at first.

"Oh! Didn't I pay you enough?"

Orlanda tore himself away from the stormy passions of Louis Bromfield's *The Rains Came.*

"I don't need money, I told you I've got savings. But it was very kind of you. You've got an amazing library, I don't think I've ever come across such dreadful literature."

The owner of the dreadful literature frowned.

"I wasn't expecting to find you here. I must warn you that I have no liking for long-term relationships."

"Wow! Your love life must cost you a fortune!" said Orlanda thinking of the notes he had found in the kitchen. "Will you lend me Bromfield? I don't know if you can still get it in the book shops and I simply must finish it."

Paul Renault looked at the book Orlanda was holding. Even with its full leather binding, *The Rains Came* was not worth the amount he had left.

"I paid the going rate," he replied.

"Honestly, you are mistaken. But, if I can't find a job, you've provided me with a solution if I get desperate. I'm going now, all I ask is to be able to finish this appallingly bad story – it enthrals me. I'll bring it back."

The boy did not take the money. Was the novel an excuse to come back? But why would he want to come back if he was not interested in the money? Paul Renault scrutinized the laughing Orlanda and, for the first time, wondered who this young man was.

And here am I wondering who Paul Renault was: here's a character who arrives in the story without my being prepared for him at all. I was following Orlanda in his debauchery for unquestionably dubious reasons, I was not expecting him to settle down in the library and read Bromfield – Bromfield! Let all the angels in heaven disavow me if I lie: I have not the least idea what *The Rains Came* is about! And I was even less prepared for the reappearance of someone who should have been a passing character, as quickly forgotten as the man in the train, but here he is studying Orlanda and struck by his air of sincerity. He cannot know, of course, that he is dealing with a twelve-year-old soul in the body of a twenty-year-old, with the knowledge of an adult woman who teaches literature, but he has enough awareness to be disconcerted. What sort of man allows himself to be picked up as he had done the night before, and lives surrounded by his parents' carved oak furniture with complete sets of Pearl Buck and André Chamson? He had left Orlanda alone in his apartment, which is extraordinarily unwise in these times when nobody defends morality in Parliament any more. If he does it too often, he will find himself robbed of his mirrored wardrobes! Did he think our hero looked so honest that he could trust him, or did the storm catch him unawares? He claims to dislike long-term relationships: perhaps he is not bothered what sex his partner is, he wants to remain free to be able to go to concerts as he pleases? He knows very well, that when you live as a couple, there is always an evening when the other person is tired or in a bad mood, and that courtesy, if not affection, demands that you take that into consideration. He had received a very strict, slightly old-fashioned upbringing from parents who had kept furniture dating from before the war. But there had been love, otherwise he would not have allowed Hungarian oak and carved wood to rule over his home. He saw a father who was always attentive to his wife's interests. She became a devotee of *Men of Good Will*, and her husband bought her a new volume every week. Twenty-seven volumes, twenty-seven weeks, six and a half months, without fail, and when he had to go on a business trip, he had the bookshop deliver the weekly book. At the sixteenth, he got muddled up and bought the same volume twice. Madame Renault, not wishing to confront him with his mistake, reread the whole thing, every single word of it. As soon as she finished them, the books were sent to the binder to be encased in white calfskin, and it was when he was placing the sixteenth next to its twin that Mr Renault noticed that he had made a mistake.

"But why didn't you tell me?"

"I was afraid of upsetting you."

The two volumes are still there.

Paul felt overwhelmed by such consideration, and shrank from the fearful demands of conjugal life. He opted for liberty and became a libertine. At forty, he felt flattered by such a young man, but was wary of narcissism, which explains the money in the kitchen, then he tried not to think about it any more. As he was a disciplined man, he managed it. Now he was confronted with a boy who was not bothered about being mistaken for a prostitute, as though he were oblivious to the insult, but just wanted to finish his book. What was more, this boy had the straight look of innocence, nothing hinted that they had been lovers the previous night, and Paul Renault told himself that the situation was not what he thought and that his mother's book was quite safe.

"Fine, take it."

"I'll bring it back in a couple of days. If you like, I'll put it in the letter box."

Such a discreet suggestion reassured him once and for all that he had nothing to worry about.

"It's not big enough. Ring the doorbell, I'm always at home in the early evening, between six and seven o'clock."

"That's very kind of you," replied Orlanda, who left as happy as a sandboy, leaving a very baffled man behind him.

If I remember, I'll come back to him in an hour to see how he is getting on.

Orlanda thought he would go back to rue Malibran and read, but the minute he was outside, the idea of shutting himself up between those four ugly walls did not appeal to him. The weather was still fine, which is unusual in Brussels, especially in April, and he wanted to make the most of it and decided to go for a walk, wherever his footsteps took him. He walked up avenue Louis Lepoutre, crossed the square, soon reached avenue Brugmann and turned into rue Berkendael, after which he walked up rue Rodenbach at a brisk pace. He pretended to himself that he was amazed to find himself in place Constantin Meunier.

And it is true that he had not realized that, in fact, he was going home. In front of the locked door, to which he did not have the key, he felt a sort of dizziness, it was as though his whole body could feel the spacious apartment, the big strides you could take without bumping into furniture. The bicycle in the halls of childhood was much closer to Orlanda than to Aline, he was in exile, he could not go up there, nor could he go to Ohain to pick the first flowers on the lawn. For the first time, he felt the wrench of separation that was tormenting Aline. Since the brasserie at the Gare du Nord, he had been playing with somebody else's body like a person exploring a borrowed house: looking everywhere, opening drawers, experiencing the feeling of having discovered a wonderful secret in front of a pile of neatly folded scarves. In the kitchen you take a frying pan and the eggs you fry will taste different from the omelette you make at home; if it rains, the raincoat you grab on the way out makes the rain smell different. You sleep differently in a strange bed, everything is more exciting, the most ordinary gestures become new, but Orlanda, who had been continually enchanted with his new face, suddenly realized that he was not allowed to go home. On Saturday, he had rushed out to buy the Balzac without stopping to realize that he was missing his books, which is what had drawn him to Paul Renault's library. Impulse had made him leap out of Aline, for he hated prison, and now he was locked out of his own home. For a moment he knew that, furious as he had been with his gaoler, he loved the books, the huge bath tub, the glazed walkway where you could slip between fronds of bougainvillaea and the light walls of sparsely furnished rooms. This thought made him tremble with anger, he tensed and was about to turn around when the door opened to allow Aline and Albert through.

"But it's true, on Monday we were having dinner with the Geilfus!"

Albert came out first on his way to the car, and walked past the young man without noticing him, while Aline lingered for a moment in front of the mirror in the lobby. The minute she turned round, she saw Orlanda and recognized him. She started. He smiled, bowed his head and torso in a greeting that was both ceremonious and mocking. She muttered a curt "hello" and joined Albert, clattering along in her high heels, which made Orlanda laugh softly, as he was able to recognize one of Aline's little ways. She was angry, she wanted to slap him and was stamping on the pavement, but was unaware of it. She caught up with Albert, the car drove off and here I am, agonizing, not knowing which of them to follow!

Hadn't I planned to go back to Paul Renault?

Once Orlanda had left, Paul went into the kitchen and saw that the young man had washed up his bowl, plate and knife, which were drying in the rack, put the butter back in the fridge and the bread in the bread bin. A single man either lives in a mess or is meticulous: Paul Renault approved of such tidiness. Then, assuming he would forget about the boy, he started to prepare his dinner. He was a methodical, organized person: he planned to cook chicken, which he put in the oven, with a salad and vinaigrette dressing. When the bird had browned nicely, he transferred it to the microwave oven. By the time the lettuce was washed and seasoned, the chicken was cooked. He arranged his meal on a tray and carried it into the dining room. Before sitting down, he went through his records looking for the interpretation of the Schumann concerto that he preferred to Grimbert's. All this was accomplished with the utmost concentration, so he was surprised to find himself thinking about Orlanda again – let us not forget that he called him

Lucien – instead of quietly enjoying his chicken and the music as he had planned to do. Ten minutes' thought were condensed into a single sentence:

"What kind of young man picks up a man of my age at a concert and refuses payment?"

Paul Renault may well wonder, but we know the answer.

Let us wait.

A few images flit through his mind of the kind that compel me to apologize to Virginia Woolf anew, then:

"It is astonishing that a boy who can barely be twenty, and who until yesterday worked for a magazine interested in a person with an absurd pseudonym, can look at a library and immediately identify the period when it was constituted! *I don't think I've ever come across such dreadful literature*: the implication is therefore that he only reads good literature. It's true that he had spoken of plagiarizing Balzac, and of Lucien de Rubempré. I can't have opened Balzac since I left school, and I'm not sure I would remember where to find Lucien de Rubempré. Obviously, his schooldays are not as far off as mine, but did I ever get beyond *Eugénie Grandet*, which was compulsory? I preferred music to reading. This little Lucien strikes me as being a literary rather than a musical man. After all, there's probably no mystery: he likes books, but he works to earn a living. Perhaps he's still paying his way through college, and I happen to be the sort of person he's attracted to.

He thought briefly of two very young women who had shown an interest in him and told himself that he could tell, without being conceited, using only straightforward common sense, that some people did find him attractive.

"Very good, let's leave matters there, he'll bring my mother's book back and that will be the end of that."

We shall see.

Orlanda stood on the pavement and watched the car drive off in which an agitated Aline was having difficulty listening to Albert as he explained to her the latest developments in the Bordier business – we will recall that there were serious internal traffic problems to be resolved. She had been very busy all day, which had suited her for she realized that as soon as there was no specific chore for her to attend to, she once again found herself prey to that unbearable tension which, the day before, had made her rush out of the apartment. What's happening to me? she wondered, watching herself race from one job from another, and she worked even faster so as to finish without having had time to reflect on her question. At six o'clock, she had had to go home and conceal her irritability from Albert. He was also annoyed: now the Bordiers, gradually affected by Régnier's anxiety, were talking about going to Hong Kong themselves to look at Foster's tower.

"Imagine! the father and the two brothers, Régnier and me on a trip, a fifteen-to-twenty-hour flight – we'll probably have to go via Paris, or from Tokyo to Hong Kong in some old crate – and a hired car waiting for us at the airport. Five very dignified gentlemen arrive wearing suits, each carrying a little suitcase. The gang hits town! The bankers greet us solemnly, take us to see the escalators, we look at them once, and we look at them again. We have to make the journey worthwhile, it's not a question of a quick glance, and then when we've had enough of looking, it's back to the hotel. Of course the men from the bank have dinner with us, conversation, the next day we go back, they get the plans out, we unfold them, we look again, the Bordiers ask questions – you have no idea the incredible questions they think up! You want traffic flow, you got it! says the old man, and the sons agree with the boss. Can you do this? I can. Ah! you can. He can. And we're off again. We have to go back to Tokyo, wait for the plane, I don't know how many planes there are a week, and with a bit of luck I'll get to see Mount Fuji, last time there was fog and Antoine couldn't see a thing. A week, I'm sure, it'll be at least a week's work lost!"

"Can't you dissuade them?"

"You don't dissuade five-hundred-million-dollar clients who want to increase their budget!"

Aline made sympathetic noises, but she was elsewhere. She had just spent two days trying to put the ice creams out of her mind and had reached the point, to her fury, where she was wondering whether she was at the age where women are supposed to succumb to a taste for young flesh. She could only concentrate on her work. As she found purely bibliographical research extremely boring, she had set two students to work on the topic of puberty and was pleased they had not yet found anything. Her lecture had been ready since Sunday, but she continued to write and gradually found she had penned an article that was well argued, as she liked them to be. She knew the fate of this article: it would be read by a handful of people who would say: "Well! Well!" and would forget it immediately. That's where her natural modesty was a help, all her enjoyment came from thinking, she did not care about the rest. But she found it offensive that the image of the fair-haired youth with his cheeky grin kept popping up in her mind. She could not, of course, explain this strange persistence other than as an unacceptable interest on the part of a self-respecting woman. Seeing him outside her door had therefore thrown her into an aggravating state of turmoil, and she told herself she had been naive in discarding the idea that he wanted to seduce her and that she should have sent him packing more firmly. She had behaved like a kid and could not reproach a boy for having taken advantage. She did not recognize herself in the woman who allowed herself to be taken for an ice cream, and put her feelings down to a justified irritation against herself, as the car drew further from the cause of her mounting agitation and anger.

The cause stood rooted to the spot in amazement. Orlanda standing in the street had not been expecting this wrench that suddenly took his breath away. Wasn't he the happiest of fugitives? And besides, why had he come here? He no longer had any business in this apartment and if he was missing the bougainvillaea, he would grow some on the window ledges of rue Malibran! He would have stamped his foot like a twelve-year-old, but the pang was there, so violent that he felt himself turn pale and lose his balance.

So he resorted to Madame Berger's precepts:

"I must be hungry."

For *his* mother firmly believed that moods are always related to the state of one's stomach.

This is where everything changes.

Aline, sitting at the table, is tense and irritable. She cannot bring herself to listen to what is being said to her, she is so strangely haunted by the fair-haired youth that she has forgotten the young flesh theory. He is going round and round inside her head like those obsessive ideas people have when they are delirious with fever. At around fifteen, she had had bronchial pneumonia and, before the antibiotics started working, had spent a whole night repeating the names of the actors in a film she had seen the previous evening, groaning in exasperation at such a stupid mental activity but without being able to stop it. But she cannot groan while she is picking half-heartedly at Denise's Flemish-style asparagus. She has to carry on a normal conversation while Orlanda, sitting in front of a gruesome pork chop, is wondering what has happened to his appetite. Since Paris, he has operated according to a series of impulses, and now nothing is motivating him, he has no plans and no desires, and this body which is such fun to inhabit leaves him indifferent. He keeps picturing Aline, startled, then walking away, and feels drawn towards her as she forgets to answer Charles who is still talking about Vita Sackville-West. Dear Charles has reread a passage from Virginia's diary which absolutely confirms the usual theories. He takes Aline's silence for surrender and is content, but Albert is puzzled for he knows she is working tenaciously on other ideas. Orlanda pushes his plate away angrily, the meat is inedible. He asks the owner of the little restaurant where he is not having a good dinner how he can possibly turn a decent piece of pig into something so disgusting and marches out slamming the door. Aline shudders and hears herself saying to Charles, to her utter amazement, that he bores her silly. A silence falls over the table, which is quickly broken by Denise. Orlanda strides along and does not try to pretend he does not know his destination, although he wonders what on earth he is going to do there. The streets fly past him. Aline is breathless. Orlanda runs faster and faster, he crosses the avenues without looking and cars slam on their brakes to avoid knocking him down. He reaches rue de Florence, stops dead and stares at the windows on the first floor. Aline sits stock still, her fork with its piece of chocolate cake poised in mid-air. She holds her breath, suddenly she is calm; it is as though she had reached the eye of the cyclone. Orlanda sinks down in the doorway and regains his breath. He is tired from running, perhaps he dozes while Aline, relaxed, puts two lumps of sugar in the tiny cup of coffee that is bringing the evening to a close.

She was not surprised to see him downstairs, but she showed nothing, and when Albert spoke to her about her rudeness to Charles, she said sweetly that she had been very polite because in fact she had felt like throwing the asparagus at him.

"Those are the times when, for the sake of our friends, I bless your mother and the superb upbringing she inflicted on you! But what a shame we were deprived of the sight of Charles with mashed hard-boiled egg and melted butter dripping down his face."

# FIFTH DAY
# TUESDAY

THE NEXT DAY, at six, he was outside the door.

"What do you want from me?" she asked.

"Let's go and have an ice cream."

No, I am cheating, I must tell you about Orlanda's day, otherwise I would be neglecting my duty as a narrator. He was impatient to be with Aline again, and I think I share his haste. He had not been able to avoid Marie-Jeanne's visit.

He had kept the phone off the hook and the door securely locked. At seven thirty, he was rudely awoken by a frantic banging. I won't open it, he said to himself and gave in after five minutes. The sobbing girl collapsed in his arms.

"Is it true you don't love me any more?"

Orlanda may well have been lacking in scruples, but he found it awkward to have to break off someone else's relationship.

"Well, yes."

"What happened? Everything was going so well! Is there someone else?"

Demanding as my sense of duty is, there are limits to my endurance and I do not feel capable of repeating the ritual words of inevitable break-ups. Marie-Jeanne cried, raged and pleaded – she did not understand what was happening to her at all.

"We had such wonderful plans."

The situation bored Orlanda as much as it does me, he held out for fifteen minutes and then turned nasty. She asked what she had done wrong, and as he had no idea what Lucien Lefrène could have against the girl, he remained silent. She ended up with:

"Did you fall in love with Amouradora?"

This made him burst into uncontrollable laughter. When you are miserable, there can be nothing in the world more hurtful than to see a man laughing until he cries. She left, banging the door so violently that the plaster around it cracked, and Orlanda, ashamed but relieved, wiped away his tears and tried to go back to sleep. As he was not totally devoid of feelings, even though he was only half a soul, he did not succeed. So he got dressed, went out to buy bread, butter and coffee for his breakfast, which he ate as he continued to read *The Rains Came.* At some point Marie-Jeanne had probably managed to put the phone back without his noticing, because he was disturbed by its ringing and, as he was running through the tropical rain soaked and shivering, he picked it up without thinking.

"Is that you, Lucien?"

I must get used to this name, he thought.

"Yes."

"It's Annie."

I hope he didn't have another girlfriend! said Orlanda to himself, panic-stricken.

"Yes."

"You could say hello! It wouldn't cost you your dignity, would it!"

He emitted a hesitant hello.

"Stop it Lucien! I know you're annoyed with me, but we've got to talk. What's going on at the moment between you and mummy?"

Ah! so it was the sister! And she was called Annie. He remained guarded.

"What do you mean?"

"Your phone is always off the hook, she can't get hold of you, so she calls me ten times a day. My ward sister keeps telling me off. I've told mummy, but you know she doesn't care about anything."

Ward sister? What's a ward sister? It sounds like a hospital, surmised Orlanda.

"I'm not home much at the moment," he replied.

"She's furious because she has to do her shopping herself and as her gout isn't getting any better, she can't manage it."

Orlanda thought of the brief visit on Sunday morning.

"Her shopping? You mean her whisky?"

There was a silence at the other end of the phone. Then:

"That's rich, coming from you. You're the one who's been taking her a bottle of whisky every day for God knows how long!"

Every day? So this decent young man who saves his money so carefully encourages his mother's alcoholism daily? Christ! How much does a bottle of whisky cost?

"Well, I shouldn't have."

Another silence.

"What's got into you, Lucien? I saw Marie-Jeanne, she didn't go to work this morning, she was waiting for me at the canteen and she didn't stop crying. And you don't sound like yourself – it's your voice but . . . I don't know, you don't normally sound that way."

To hell with Lucien Lefrène! thought Orlanda, exasperated. Here's a twenty-year-old boy who has saved half a million wearing imitation leather and eating the cheapest brand of tinned beans off cracked plates. Unless he doesn't care about nice jackets and good food, which suggests great strength of character. He has plans for which he sacrifices everything else, yet every day he takes a bottle of whisky to a dreadful old woman who lives the other side of town? No wonder he has nightmares.

"I've decided to change my life style. Just send your mother off to be dried out, that'll cure her gout."

"But I've wanted to do that for years and you've always been against it!"

"I've changed my mind. Do what you think is right, I just want to be left in peace."

He promptly hung up and, as he was afraid Annie would call back, he took the phone off the hook at once.

I hope that's the end of his family problems, he growled returning to the tropical rains.

That was how he found himself suggesting ice cream to Aline, who was expecting it. She gave a little nod of assent and set off in the direction of the café so rapidly that Orlanda stood rooted to the spot in amazement. He caught up with her and walked beside her without saying anything.

Aline was puzzled. She had slept badly again. She had only remembered one dream, which combined the first two: she looked at herself in a mirror but only had half a body. Sometimes it was the right half that was missing, sometimes the left. She remembered that she had been very much afraid of looking down and discovering that there was nothing below her waist: I won't be able to stand up any more. But she was not thinking about it for the time being. In fact, she was not thinking about anything, and to the extent that she was aware of it, she was very glad not to, for she had spent a good part of her day wondering why she was absolutely certain she would find the young man outside her door in the evening and would accept his invitation.

"Have you given your lecture on Virginia Woolf?" he asked.

"Yes."

"Did it go well?"

She gave him a level stare. "How the hell did you know I was going to give that lecture?"

"Didn't I tell you that I know you?"

"Precisely. That's why I'm here. Proust, the vanilla ice cream with a double helping of chocolate sauce, and now Virginia Woolf: it's a bit much. Who are you and what do you want from me?"

He was amazed at her directness. Shouldn't the shy, well-brought-up Aline have stammered and blushed? I am probably the only person who can understand: they were together. Already, the previous evening, it was only when the exasperated Orlanda had left the restaurant to run to rue de Florence that Aline, suddenly beside herself, had allowed her irritation to boil over and told the pontificating Charles where to get off. We know what draws them together: Orlanda gives Aline strength. She had kept him weak and powerless in the dungeons of her soul, but the minute he emerged he encountered success after success. He is sure of himself, like a child whose confidence has not yet been undermined by anything. Lucien is a very good-looking boy now that he has clean hair and his nails, freed from the tyranny of being bitten, are growing again. He has a generous mouth and muscular shoulders, and his back has become very straight for it is no longer bowed by the burden of Madame Lefrène the mother, and slim hips, and I could go on but I shan't. Everything about him is seductive, and yet it would be wrong to imagine that it was chance that dictated the choice of Lucien Lefrène. Certainly Aline, a respectable woman, would swear on oath and in all innocence that she had not taken her eyes off her book. Let us allow her to be an unwitting liar. It only takes a glance to assess a man and, at the *Brasserie de l'Europe*, before the separation, it was still she who was in control and who spotted Lucien. Out of the corner of her eye, true, and so fleetingly that she would not have had the time to blush. The fact is that she is walking beside a young man whom she finds attractive and who has been pursuing her for several days. Only her candour, which I do not share, enables her not to be aware of it. He walks with a confident stride, he is relaxed as he could never be inside Aline, and this self-assurance strengthens him. A strange osmosis unites the two of them, Orlanda gives Aline strength, but they need to be physically close.

Nevertheless, even though he knew who he was, he did not know what he wanted from her.

"I don't know," he said.

She stopped, frowning:

"What's your name?"

He hesitated:

"Er . . . Lucien Lefrène."

"You don't sound very sure."

"Well, that's what my physical being is called."

"Really! And what is your mental being called?"

"If you're called Aline, I should perhaps say Alain. But I've never liked the name Aline, it sounds like a granny who makes jam or a spinster aunt, so I don't like Alain."

She wondered what on earth he meant, thought briefly that he was talking nonsense, and then her thought slipped, skidded, slithered and vanished into the depths.

"So," finished Orlanda, "I'd better stick with Lucien."

But, what with the first ice cream and the one they were about to have, the lie to Albert, the rebuff to Charles and the strange nightmares, that was a lot of things to consign to the depths, and Aline's soul, especially reduced by half, was not such a vast abyss that it could contain an infinite amount of heavy baggage.

"And what does Lucien Lefrène do?"

"Nothing at all any more," he replied cheerfully. "Until a few days ago, he wrote stupid articles and saved his money, but he's changed. That was someone else. I'm enjoying myself."

"Stupid articles?"

He explained about Amouradora.

"All I needed to do was transcribe the interview, but I couldn't. I think I'd find it easier to prostitute my body than my pen," he announced, thinking warmly of Paul Renault, "at least that's enjoyable."

She listened with amusement. However: who, other than Charles, knew Balzac well enough to think of the Alcalda in Seville to make their job easier? He went on:

"It was not merely a question of translating the nineteenth-century language into the modern idiom. The idea itself is not very original, what else are we doing when we clothe the gods of *Götterdämmerung* in SS uniforms?"

The gods or the Niebelungen? And wasn't it in *Rheingold*? Aline realized that she was allowing herself once again to get carried away by the conversation and tried to get a grip on herself:

"Fine. You know Proust and Balzac, the idiotic things they do with Wagner annoy you as much as they do me, but that doesn't tell me what you want from me."

"Are you bored with me?"

"No."

She had to admit it.

"But that's not the point. What were you doing outside my door yesterday evening, and later, how come you were in rue de Florence?"

Orlanda hesitated. In fact he did not really know why he was pursuing the woman he had run away from like this. But he had to confess that although he was enjoying his new life immensely, something incomprehensible drove him towards Aline and he felt happy with her.

"You wouldn't believe me," he laughed.

There was a hint of uncertainty in that laugh. In truth, Orlanda's current frame of mind is hard to describe – satisfaction and a certain childish conceit formed a screen, masking more complex feelings. He had approached Aline without any specific plan in mind. He had intrigued her with the double helping of chocolate sauce, convinced he was only trying to have some fun. The first time he had gone to place Constantin Meunier he thought it was for the pleasure of the walk, and yesterday evening he had no idea what he was doing, he ran without thinking and probably fell asleep in the street so as not to have to face up to awkward questions. Is it possible to be so unaware of what drives us? Or is it tremendously naive to believe that we know where we are going? When we think we are going out to buy a newspaper, do we always vaguely seek some hidden motive? Androgynes, broken by the anger of jealous gods, we are running after our lost halves, trying to reconstitute the original unity. Where is my other half? What has become of the exquisite oneness I remember, and in which life did I experience it? Aline and Orlanda pine when they are apart and want to find each other again, but when they are together, they hate each other. Subject to the envious will of Mount Olympus, they do not recognize each other, and fight. They cannot understand the blind attraction that draws them together. And even when I say Aline found Lucien attractive, I am digressing and giving in to common sense which is the enemy of the imagination. The fact is that each one wants the other and a battle is beginning.

Orlanda therefore replied to Aline that she would not believe him and she shrugged.

"That's the classic reply of the werewolf or the vampire in horror films. The audience knows the truth and laughs at the trusting hero who won't believe him and will get eaten."

"Do you believe in werewolves?"

"No," she laughed. "You win. I won't believe you!"

They had reached the ice cream place and went to sit down. It was not crowded, a waitress came over immediately and Orlanda ordered two vanilla ices with chocolate sauce.

"But I have to admit that you were in rue de Florence and although I can conceive of you digging up my thesis to read it, I can't see how you got there."

"I knew you were having dinner there."

"That explains everything!"

Orlanda felt puzzled. For the first time, he was able to visualize himself running through the streets and began to wonder.

"Perhaps I was missing you," he said.

"How could someone I don't know miss me?"

"I've already told you, I know you."

"Who are you?"

"You."

Aline stared at him in sheer disbelief:

"Or rather, part of you."

"As you predicted, I don't believe you," she said calmly.

That was when Orlanda understood what he wanted. He had enjoyed himself hugely since Paris, but that was not enough. Occupying Lucien Lefrène and doing everything Aline had forbidden herself were only a tiny part of it. He wanted her to know it, he wanted her to accompany him in spirit, if not in person. I want to rob her of her innocence, he said to himself, for a cynical thought verging on debauchery seemed to him more acceptable than the strange impulse that was driving him. He therefore set out to convince her. Strangely, if you think of it, nothing is easier than to prove to someone that you *are* them, you just have to list the things that only that person can know about themselves and that frighten them. The things I have never told anyone absolutely define me and isolate me, the things that I alone know about myself guarantee my boundaries. Here, this is me, there, is everybody else, the people who do not know the things I have never confessed. It was I who drank the chocolate that had been made for my little cousin, broke the jug, finished off the jam – petty crimes of childhood which we denied furiously without really knowing why. We probably told ourselves that it was for fear of punishment, but as adults! It would not have been the death sentence, for goodness sake! Mummy, who pursued me with daily vitamins and proteins was much too anxious about my health, at worst I would probably have received a mild scolding. No, it needs something else to explain the desperate urge to keep quiet, a more acute need. I wanted to create a barrier between myself and others, define my territory, say here, in this place, the only place in the world where it is known with absolute certainty who drank the chocolate. Here, is me.

So Orlanda told Aline that she had taken the packet of mints.

"But you can't know that!" she exclaimed, aghast.

"But you can see that I do know it."

She fell back on the rational explanation which also makes the informed spectator laugh:

"I must have told someone."

He laughed, mocking:

"What about the jug? You haven't forgotten the blue jug that mummy was so fond of, she said that the water turned sky blue and put summer on the table, you always thought it rather silly, but daddy was enchanted, which irritated you. I broke it, one day when she got on my nerves. You know very well you did it on purpose, when you walked past the little trolley in the kitchen, that I could very well have avoided knocking into, but I had had enough of her perpetual 'Don't run so fast! Don't wave your arms around!' and I felt like letting off steam with a vengeance."

Aline was transfixed.

"And what about Maurice Alker? I shan't be so unmannerly as to say everything about Maurice Alker, one should not offend a young lady's modesty, but you've never talked to anyone about that either, have you? The other evening I met a man who reminded me very much of him."

"He's dead," murmured Aline.

"I know. You even shed a few tears, he deserved more, but deep down, you've never forgiven him for not having seduced you. At eighteen, you were vaguely hopeful. He told you that you were pretty, but he didn't go any further. It never dawned on you that he was waiting for you to make a move."

"How do you know that?"

"It's obvious, he was over forty-five."

"No, that I was hoping."

"Because I am you."

She shook her head.

"You're mad."

"Of course," he laughed, "but it's not my madness that taught me those things. Don't worry about my mental equilibrium: yours is shaky right now."

Aline had been so numbed by these strange words that she felt she had forgotten to breathe. She made herself relax her shoulders, empty her lungs and try to recover her capacity for thought. I can usually cope when I'm confronted with new ideas, I sometimes have ideas, which I express, the other person replies, that's called thinking and talking, activities which I am familiar with. In a way, you could say they were the very basis of my profession. After all, this young man never does anything other than talk about things I know about, which are neither new nor crazy. I have always known that I broke the jug on purpose. Let's be precise: what he is saying to me is not surprising, what is surprising is that he knows it. That's the problem broken down into its components, now all I have to do is resolve it. She then remembered the science-fiction novel she had been reading in the train and regained her breath.

"So, are you telepathic?"

Orlanda, who had not read *Darkover Landfall*, opened his eyes wide in astonishment.

"Telepathic?"

Then he remembered the trip to Smith's bookshop and burst out laughing.

"That's an admirable explanation. The whole thing boils down to discussing whether we believe in telepathy, and then we could try to make the table revolve. Pity it's not round."

"You can't know all that, but you do."

"Therefore I am you."

Aline felt her soul cave in.

"If I was in rue de Florence yesterday evening, it's because

I remembered that you were going there for dinner. The Geilfus invited us two weeks ago, but you were going to Paris and it had to be postponed for a week. You knew that Jacqueline would be there, and you were thinking of her when you went into the English bookshop to buy a Marion Zimmer Bradley. She always complains that nobody shares her love of science fiction and you thought she'd be pleased. But in the train, it was you who had the book, so I haven't read it. You should lend it to me, I'm sure I'd enjoy that sort of story more than you, I'm less rational."

"How could you be me?" she stammered, horrified.

"It's the easiest thing in the world: by leaving you, while you were drinking your mineral water, for the handsome fellow you see before you and who came over and asked you for a couple of aspirin."

If a young man, no matter how attractive, were to come and tell me things that nobody could possibly know, I am sure I would be extremely disconcerted and that I would leave no stone unturned to try and find an acceptable explanation, but I would never subscribe to the idea that he was myself. I feel that Aline is not offering much resistance which strikes me as odd for someone who is so demure. I am wrong. We must not forget that it is in her that the separation took place, it is she who had this strange power and used it. She did not know it, and in fact she does not have it any more. Aline had felt the wrench at the station, when Orlanda left her to go down into the Métro and now, before the ice creams melting in their goblets, she is shocked and terrified, but the anguish that has been tormenting her for several days has gone. Even if she is not thinking about it consciously, this relief affects her mood. Beneath the panic there is a sense of relaxation, the delicious silence which the cessation of suffering always brings. So she carefully scrutinized the laughing face, the clear eyes with their dancing smile, and she tried to think.

She only vaguely remembered the aspirins. She concentrated her mind and recalled a boy who looked unhealthy, with a leaden complexion and stiff hair standing on end. Had she done any more than glance at him when *Orlando* had got on her nerves and she had sighed and looked up? Suddenly, he had been standing in front of her talking about a headache. She had not thought it unusual for a stranger to come over to ask a lady he did not know for an aspirin, and finally she realized that that was odd. It is certain that if I were to get up and go over to that man eating ice cream with his children over there and tell him that I have a headache, he would be astonished, but he wouldn't rummage through his pockets, he'd advise me to go to the chemist's on the corner. So did it seem natural for me to reply?

"Why did you come and ask me for an aspirin?"

"Because you always have some in your bag, Lili."

"What's this Lili? You're becoming rather too familiar."

"With myself?!"

"I don't understand," she said.

Orlanda sighed:

"To be frank, neither do I. I didn't know that it was possible, but as I did it, I accept the facts. I saw this boy sitting opposite me and, while you were engrossed in old Virginia Woolf, I thought I rather fancied him. So I left. You didn't seem to feel anything, because you didn't budge."

Memories came back to her.

"At one point, I had a strange feeling. It was indefinable, it reminded me of a minor earthquake."

"There! You were losing the most precious part of yourself."

"But I'm still me," she replied.

And yet there was a note of perplexity in her voice.

"As much as you ever have been. The best part of you is me."

"You're incredibly conceited!"

"I should think so! I lived oppressed, in the shadows, incarcerated in your fear, then I had a great burst of energy and I escaped. I have good reason to be pleased with myself."

Aline felt a rush of questions. Who was he? What was he talking about? Which side of herself had she neglected? But she ignored them because she realized that she was beginning to believe him. She was afraid. You can't accept a story like that without being mad, she told herself, but he knows I broke the blue jug. Unless this is all a hallucination, he never made mention of any jug and I'm raving mad. Whatever I want to think, I can't get away from the impossible. I've got to stop this conversation: if I haven't been suffering from delusions since the beginning, I will do if I stay.

She suddenly stood up.

"Don't follow me," she said.

And walked out without looking back.

Orlanda watched her leave. He knew that he would find her again when he wanted to and thought, most generously he felt, that perhaps he should give her time to digest all this novelty. He decided to return Paul Renault's book.

The impulse that had made Aline rush out carried her for a hundred yards, then she began to tremble and barely had the strength to get home. Albert was not there, luckily a meeting would detain him until ten o'clock. She took the rue Molière entrance and automatically went through the usual motions, hanging her jacket on the coat stand and putting her briefcase on the little table just inside her office. Then she just stood there because she could not think what else to do. Time stood still. After a long moment, a thought took shape: "Who am I?"

The simplest words: Aline Berger, had no meaning for she had to clarify who exactly Aline Berger was. Our century abounds in intense, lengthy discussions on the question of identity, a name and surname are not enough. The debate reaches such remarkable levels of subtlety that it is sometimes difficult to follow. When we say *I*, who do we mean? If someone else can say that he is me, where is *me*, here or there? Each of us is absolutely convinced that we are ourselves, and we rely on that assurance for our stability. Aline felt weak. She stepped back, leaned against the door frame and uttered the endangered syllable out loud. Nothing happened. She repeated *I* to the four walls, which did not send back an echo. Should she, in saying *I*, consider that part of this *I* was housed in another body? But surely, you can only say *I* from where you are? Lucien Lefrène claimed that he was *I* like her. But he uttered the word from a different mouth, not Aline's. She took a deep breath and declared: "I am me."

The words rang hollow to her.

He had said *I am you*, but never *I am me*. Who did he think he was? That's what I should have asked him. *I lived oppressed in the shadows, incarcerated in your fear.* She remembered those words perfectly. So did he claim to be a part of herself that she supposedly kept prisoner? Are we a prison for ourselves? I'm thirty-five, I teach literature, I live with a man called Albert Durieux, words suddenly devoid of meaning because a stranger had said that he was her.

Yes, but he knew that she had broken the blue jug and – she blushed – he had been discreet on the subject of Maurice Alker! Forget the jug, after all, it was conceivable, if not likely, that a servant hiding in the kitchen had seen everything and told, but the secret gestures in the dark, under the shelter of sheets and blankets, after locking the bedroom door, which mummy never noticed – I unlocked it again afterwards – and even if I'd forgotten that I mentioned the mints to someone, it's absolutely certain that I've never told anybody about that. I've only just remembered myself. Actually, I'd forgotten, because I was always careful never to think of it again, it was too embarrassing.

She realized that she was not feeling so dreadful. Thinking's always helpful, she told herself, and decided to run a bath. With a bit of luck, I'll fall asleep in it.

But she did not. Three quarters of an hour later, she was looking up Lucien Lefrène's telephone number in the directory. She dialled the number, but the line seemed to be engaged. After a dozen tries, she gave up.

Paul Renault had so carefully put Lucien Lefrène out of his mind that he was actually surprised to hear his name over the entry phone. He had just placed his dinner tray on the dining-room table – it was cold meat this evening – and so he added another plate.

"You'll regret it," said Orlanda cheerfully, "I eat like a horse and as you're very polite, you're likely to end up starving."

"People usually say: 'You shouldn't have!' or 'I was only dropping in for a minute!' "

"True. But over the last few days, I've given up hypocrisy. It's nice to be made welcome and I don't see why I should pretend not to be pleased."

"You are quite a strange character."

Orlanda agreed, but did not see much point in dwelling on a subject which was, in short, extremely complex. *The Rains Came* had surprised him enormously, he did not understand why such a bad novel had been so successful, and as he had all Aline's knowledge at his disposal, he spoke about it at length and in a way that astonished Paul.

"You seem to be something of an expert in literature."

"I love it."

He was surprised to note that on leaving Aline he had taken her likes and dislikes with him. What about geometry? I used to so love geometry! Have I forgotten everything? Could I go back to it, or to algebra? I haven't seen an equation for nearly twenty years, and Aline didn't have a mathematical mind, but I'm not forced to be like her, and there's no reason why I shouldn't go back to studying if I decided to. I'll have to find out whether Lucien Lefrène got his high school certificate, after all, I could use his money intelligently and go back to university. There's more to life than sex and hot dinners, the mind also needs nurturing. For the first time since the separation, he saw that he had a new life ahead of him if he wanted. This idea was so strange that he sat there with his fork poised in mid-air, staring into space.

"What are you thinking about?" asked Paul Renault, intrigued.

"About my life. What am I going to do with my life? I'm twenty, I'm free, I can choose."

Could he really?

"Do you know how long it takes to get a maths degree? Is it four or five years?"

At first, Paul had thought that he had to pay for his enjoyable night, then faced with a boy capable of dating a library, he had felt obliged to recognize his mistake. The maths degree caught him off-guard. Never had his partners in debauchery talked to him about a maths degree. He observed Lucien Lefrène closely and, of course, did not see Orlanda, but a young man dreaming. He had forgotten his cold meat, and seemed thrilled and overwhelmed. Paul was more sensitive than he would have liked to be, and was touched, not seeing that the maths degree was opening a chasm at his feet.

"I don't know. Would you like me to find out? The daughter of a friend of mine is about to finish hers, I can phone him."

This is madness, he said to himself, how can I explain my reasons for asking such a thing?

"No, I need to think. Oh! yes, you're right, it'll be easier to think if I have the right information. That would be very kind of you."

At least I'm going into another room, Paul groaned inwardly, I don't like lying in front of a witness.

"I'll be right back."

He quickly made up the fib he would need.

"A lady friend of mine wants to know how long it takes to get a maths degree."

"A lady friend of yours? Hmm . . ."

"Five years," he said walking back into the room.

"Five years?" echoed Orlanda, "with the money I've got saved, I'd have to live like a miser. It must be possible if you're passionate enough about the subject. The question is, can I revive my love of geometry?"

"But what have you studied until now?"

Orlanda checked himself just in time, the truth came to his lips spontaneously.

"Oh, nothing special. I was pushed towards the arts, but as I want to change my life, I shan't continue. Can you see me starving in a freezing garret for the love of algebra?"

Paul Renault knew himself well enough to know that normally he would have replied that so far, he had only seen him in bed, adding some flattering comment, but there was in this question a sort of childlike sincerity which defied his cynicism, and he simply smiled and wondered what was happening to him. For goodness sake, two evenings ago, this young man had brazenly picked him up!

"You might be able to get a grant," he replied.

"That's true! and even, if you're a very good student, there are some jobs going that help make ends meet."

Then Orlanda stared at his plate where his dinner was waiting:

"I'm forgetting to eat whereas, if I'm planning to go without, I'd better stock up! Can I have some more potato salad?"

To his utter amazement, Paul Renault heard himself saying:

"If you like, there'll always be a place laid for you at my table."

What kind of madness is this? He felt the whirlwind, he wanted to regain his balance and tried not to listen to Orlanda who was chirping away, commenting on his healthy appetite and the excellence of the salad. For goodness sake! The boy brings back a book, asks for nothing, and I go off and phone, I offer him half my dinner and next it'll be a roof over his head? Am I about to fall in love? It is clear that the notion horrified him. He examined his heart – and his feelings – without finding what is described as love, and which he was proud of never having experienced. Certainly, Lucien was still as good-looking, and Paul, a methodical man, looked him up and down attentively. There was no doubt that his mop of hair invited ruffling fingers, his generous, well-defined mouth evoked thoughts that Virginia Woolf etcetera, his nails had been cut short, you could no longer tell that they had been bitten, and his hands had regained their beauty. Paul remembered very well that they were skilful, everything was designed to arouse desire, but, at that moment, he did not desire, which annoyed him. Really, he said to himself, am I afraid of being in love, or of not being in love? And as he was no fool, he realized he wanted to desire Lucien so as not to love him. Love? Why the hell would I love this child whom I took for a prostitute? and why do I say this *child*? he's twenty, he is disconcerting, and I am disconcerted. The other night, in bed, there was certainly nothing childlike about him. But watching him, you saw his air of astonishment and delight as he seized an idea, leapt astride the first dream to come his way and grabbed at a coloured balloon. He laughed, his eyes shone, he was twelve years old and we who know that are not surprised. Paul Renault had never said to himself that in refusing marriage, or any long-term relationship, he had prevented himself from having a son, and did not say it to himself in front of Orlanda either: he felt himself plunging into confusion and saw in his duties as host his only defence:

"I think I have some cheese left," he said.

Orlanda ravenously devoured a huge chunk of gruyère, after which he helped clear up, then they both sat in the lounge and listened to the Schumann concerto interpreted in the way that Paul preferred. At ten o'clock Orlanda announced that he was dropping with exhaustion and returned to his flat in rue Malibran to sleep.

Lucien Lefrène, apparently muzzled, did not dream any more and Orlanda had the most peaceful sleep imaginable.

# SIXTH DAY
# WEDNESDAY

ALINE WOKE UP in excellent spirits, her sleep not having been disturbed by nightmares.

"This is the first time you've looked rested since you've been back from Paris. I was beginning to get worried," said Albert at breakfast.

"I must have been more tired than I thought."

And it was only after saying this in all innocence that she remembered her incredible encounter with the young man. She shuddered and, conscious that Albert was watching her with concern, pretended that the hot coffee had burned her tongue. He went to fill a glass with cold water, which he gave her, laughing: "You see, your mother's always saying you drink too quickly."

"My mother will kill me with her good advice."

She was astonished by what she had just said.

And goodness, so am I. It seems that such a comment would be more likely to come from Orlanda. Certainly the relationship between those two is not easy to understand, and I wonder what he took with him on leaving her. I have already discovered that he had her knowledge, but that does not mean that she has lost it: in short, it is not a division but a duplication. Orlanda has Aline's memory and her unwanted emotions, but he had not accepted the obedience that constantly tore the little girl in two. He had become the place to hide anger. But *My mother will kill me* coming out of Aline's mouth? It was Orlanda who felt he was being slowly killed, so how come Aline knows? When the boy is attacked, is the girl also affected?

She dutifully drank the cold water that she did not need.

How do we think when we are assailed by the impossible? By definition, this question has no answer, for the impossible is that which does not happen and which, therefore, has never happened to anybody – except in dreams, where we deal with the most incongruous situations quite naturally, unless we awaken with a start, like Aline when confronted with her half body. But she was not dreaming and therefore could not wake up. She had to eat her breakfast, get dressed and go to work – all mechanical activities that can be accomplished while thinking of something else. It was harder to pursue the conversation with Albert, an intelligent man who does not just exchange platitudes. The previous evening he had come home later than expected and had found Aline asleep – she had taken two aspirin – and this morning, he was telling her about Régnier's perpetual anxiety. They hadn't mentioned Hong Kong again, but that didn't mean anything, and she had to participate in the conversation. In fact, Aline is not a weak woman, Orlanda may well say that all the strength of character is his, but we should not trust his vanity. It was while he was relegated to the dungeon that she studied, worked tenaciously on her thesis and was appointed through her own merits to the position she currently holds. It was without him that the other evening she calmly lied to Albert and now she is resolutely putting her problems out of her mind. I'll think about them later, she said to herself, when I'm alone in the safety of my office.

She thought about them little, because she was continually busy. Her secretary brought in her typed article for checking, two students had an appointment to talk to her about their end-of-year assignments. Duchâtel was extremely agitated about the prospect of the faculty budget being slashed, and a girl who felt she had been the victim of a serious injustice burst into tears in the corridor outside her door. I'll see him again this evening, she thought, and I'll probably think he's mad.

Yes, but what about the jug?

On waking, Orlanda found an envelope that had been slipped under his door: "Mummy's going into hospital tomorrow. I hope you'll at least have the heart to go and visit her." *At least* was underlined twice and there was no signature. It's the sister, he said to himself. Then, as he was shaving, a new activity which he found highly entertaining, he pulled a face at Lucien Lefrène – it's time you behaved decently towards this poor woman. A bottle every day! You were killing her, you fool! Wherever he was, whether he heard or not, Lucien did not reply, but Orlanda was not disappointed because he had not been expecting him to. He was in a good mood, as he had been every day since the Brasserie de l'Europe, and impatient to see Aline again. He had no doubt that she was waiting for him and did not bother to ask why. We who are haunted by the legend of Tristan and Isolde know that the two halves are burning to reconstitute the lost whole. The gods, however, have been watching them since time immemorial; they sneer, their jealous vigilance is relentless and the love which is the fate of mortals is always defeated.

On the Sunday and the Tuesday, Albert's meetings with the Bordiers had left Aline easily accessible. They had been planned in advance and Orlanda knew about them, but this evening Albert was due home at the usual time and Aline would not be able to follow Orlanda to the café for an ice cream. She usually had lunch in her office, a tasteless sandwich from the cafeteria. Orlanda decided to join her, and went shopping. He bought some lovely crusty rolls, crab salad, slices of cold beef and her favourite mustard, then he went home, cut and buttered the rolls, made some very strong coffee and went back down to buy a Thermos, and even two paper cups and plates and a bottle of light wine. He was as happy as a child preparing a picnic. Soon he was ready, but it was a little early, so he decided to go via the Science faculty and pick up details of the maths degree course. He set out with a spring in his step.

He walked into Aline's office at half-past twelve, just as she was about to go out.

"No point, I've got everything we need," he said, placing the bag of provisions on a chair.

Then, to Aline's amazement, he began to clear a corner of the table, going about it exactly as she would have done herself. He opened the drawer where she kept the paper napkins and took out enough to make a sort of tablecloth, protecting the wood that was always inadequately polished by the university cleaners.

"Lunch is served!" he said when he had finished unpacking.

She looked: there were all her favourite things. That, combined with his knowing about the napkin drawer, was even more effective than the blue jug.

"It is true then!" she whispered.

"Weren't you convinced?"

As she stood there speechless, he took her by the shoulders and sat her down in front of her plate, where he arranged the beef sandwich:

"Save the best till last, right? As mummy always taught us."

"How can you be me?"

"I left you in Paris," he said, uncorking the bottle.

"But it doesn't make sense!"

He shrugged: "That's all I know. You were reading, I was bored, locked away inside your soul when it was a nice day and there were plenty of men who were very much alive, and who are not so unlucky as to have lost their sexual identity. This handsome young man you see before you also looked bored and I felt like going over to him."

"It's madness. You can't do that!"

And so on. I'll skip ten minutes of repetitive conversation.

"But *how* did you do it?"

The twelve-year old would have replied: Well I don't know, I just did it, but Orlanda, whatever he was, also had the ordinary knowledge of the twentieth-century adult, which includes no proof that souls can divide in order to migrate. He raised his eyebrows and opened his arms in a gesture of helplessness that Aline knew well.

"I haven't the foggiest idea. I wanted to, and it happened. How does it go: *There are more things in heaven and earth, Horatio, than are dreamed of in your philosophy.*"

"I don't know Shakespeare all that well."

"I know," he laughed, "so you say at least once a year, but you don't do anything about it. As I am less hopelessly rational than you, I didn't let anything stop me. I wanted to and I did. How many times did mummy bore me with her *you can do anything you want?* Well! I proved she was right. You always wanted to please her, you should congratulate me!"

"I always wanted to please her?"

"Don't you know anything about yourself? Ah! maybe not, and you are unaware that you made me."

Her eyes opened wide, she was utterly bewildered.

"I am everything mummy didn't want you to be. Each time you sensed her disapproval, you were afraid and you gave up, you wanted to remove whatever displeased her from yourself. But I must be the living proof that you don't get rid of anything, I slowly accumulated inside you over the years. You were always sad."

She could not deny it, she had thought it only too clearly in the train.

"Are you sad right now?"

She did not need to think about it to acknowledge that she was not.

"That's because I'm here. You were missing me dreadfully. Now

I'm before you, not inside, but I was more outside your grasp inside you than I am here, where at least you can talk to me."

"You're doing the talking."

"True, but when I tried to talk to you, you never heard me. Now you have no choice, unless you throw me out of your office and I think you know that you have no wish to do so."

It's true said Aline to herself, in a daze, it's true!

"Since I left you, I've had a whale of a time. But apart from the moments when I was in the arms of a man, something was missing. The first time I went home, I didn't even know what I was doing. And then, when you and Albert left for dinner at Denise's, I felt – I'm not quite sure how to describe it – a sort of panic. I wanted to join you. So I did, because I do as I please."

Aline vigorously shook her head. In the arms of a man! Went home! It was too much!

"In the arms of a man?" she asked, abiding by the rule that you break the problem down into its components to resolve it.

"Naturally! Have you ever found girls attractive? I'm like you, which means that, objectively, I am homosexual, whereas, subjectively, I still feel perfectly heterosexual," he chuckled.

"My head's spinning," said Aline. For the first time, there was a hint of laughter in her voice. "You're going too fast. And so I'm supposed to understand that since you left me – if I accept such a ridiculous premise, but I'm almost forced to: you know which drawer I keep the paper napkins in – you have homosexual preferences because I'm heterosexual?"

"That's right. I'm delighted to see that despite my departure, your mind is as sharp as ever."

She winced at the word departure.

"And what does *home* mean?"

"Well! My place. Your place. Our place. I'm staying in rue Malibran, in Lucien Lefrène's room which is, admittedly, bigger than the broom cupboards they call rooms in the student hostel, but it's hideously ugly, he must have bought all his furniture from the Salvation Army, except his revolver. I don't think he has any other weapons, and there's no bath tub, just a shower cubicle you can barely swing a cat in. Of course, daddy's flat in place Constantin Meunier was already much more habitable, but I loved what Albert did with it. And I'm going to tell you something you don't know: the idea of the walkway was mine. Do you remember when you thought of it? A sort of brainwave you were unable to repress and that surprised you? That was me."

She could not deny it. She had been flabbergasted and, yes, she had almost wondered where on earth she had got such an idea from and ignored a suggestion that she thought was eccentric. Albert however was enthusiastic. He forged ahead, brushing aside Aline's protests at the audacity of it.

"Mummy was horrified and you would have happily given up the idea, but she would have had to tear Albert away from it. She didn't dare contradict him and he didn't even know that he was defending you. That's what daddy never did, he left me alone with her, he thought it was a mother's job to bring up a daughter, and I was left without any support."

As he spoke, Aline who had never consciously thought those things, could not but admit that they were true. She realized that she was beginning to believe this unlikely young man who was determined to tell her things that she had never said to herself, and refrained from repeating the *How do you know that?* which was going round and round in her head. Orlanda saw her waver and pressed his advantage:

"After all, the idea isn't new. Julien Green writes about it in *If I were you.*"

And, what was more, he had the same literary references as her!

"But what about Lucien Lefrène?"

He indicated his physical person with a sweeping gesture:

"He's cute, isn't he? I love his blond hair. He covered it in some foul muck that made it stiff, I had a hell of a job getting rid of it, but now, all tousled, it's gorgeous. And my broad, muscular, shoulders, straight back, slim hips – he's a real beauty this boy! People find me attractive, you've no idea how nice that is."

"That's not what I mean. Where is he?"

"I don't know. I pushed him out and he didn't put up any resistance. He probably had a weak character, or he was so fed up with himself that it is as though he committed suicide on my arrival."

"But what about his past, his memories, his life?"

"Nothing. In the first seconds, when he had a headache and I came and asked you for some aspirin, I barely heard that he didn't like medicines, and at night, he has nightmares. Then silence. Perhaps he's delighted at my arrival, I've relieved him of his existence, which must have been a burden to him. I even wonder if he wasn't contemplating suicide."

He briefly told Aline about the savings and the bottles of whisky.

"Life is painful when you are torn between such conflicting demands, I know all about that."

"Why are you talking about suicide?"

"Because of the revolver. Apart from gangsters, who has a revolver other than people contemplating suicide? Imagine my surprise: dirty dishes, three shirts, no more, piled neatly one on top of the other, and a Colt underneath! I was so shocked to find it in my hands that I gently put it back."

"Has he got a gun licence?"

"Goodness, I've no idea what one looks like and I can't have seen one because I only found ordinary papers: bank statements, a cheque book, insurance policies – only the usual."

Aline forgot Lucien Lefrène and remained pensive. So, part of her was in this young man and, clearly, he was enjoying it immensely. Really! How was it conceivable? She tried to imagine that she lived in that body, thought inside that head and saw through those eyes. It was in vain, she used words, but they lacked substance. And as for me being dispossessed, she said to herself, but she did not dwell on that thought which sensed that it was untimely and went away and lodged itself somewhere in its owner's mind, for, even though Aline had been diminished by half, she still had her orderly habits. Orlanda, who had to be called Lucien, as he was by Paul Renault, helped himself to the second sandwich. Aline recalled him finishing off her ice cream and her quickly forgotten shock at such an incongruous gesture came out of the dark recess to which it had been relegated. She now understood that he enjoyed a total physical intimacy with her, and this imbalance bothered her. She carefully studied the boy's face, the tousled hair which he was so pleased with, and admitted that he was indeed attractive. The inconceivable was happening before her. He knows me from inside, he knows the sound of my voice when I speak, which is so different from what I hear when I listen to it recorded, he knows the taste of my mouth and my most intimate smells. When I see myself on film I don't recognize my gestures, he sees them from outside and what's more he knows what I feel when I move. Unless he has already forgotten. How long do you remember yourself?

"Do you remember the sound of my voice inside my head?"

"Haven't you noticed that I've got the same intonations as you? When you speak, I hear you as if I were listening to a recording of myself before leaving you, but when I talk I hear myself as you hear yourself, except that the timbre of my voice is different, because it's a different larynx. You made me think of it: from inside, it's amazing how little difference there is."

"What about your gestures?"

"They're the same. My hand is bigger than yours, but it moves in the same way. Aha! So that's why men so quickly identify me as a potential partner: I must have preserved something feminine in my movements, which show that *I'm one of them*, as the dear Baron de Charlus would have said!"

She was not in the mood to be drawn into Proust. That hand

was animated by a spirit which was partly hers. She experienced a strange feeling: she was entitled to that long, strong hand that was opening the sandwich, and to the other hand too, that was picking up a knife, cutting the bread and spreading the crab evenly on the two halves, exactly as she would have done herself, so that the mayonnaise did not dribble. Then Orlanda started the same operation with his own sandwich. Aline was fascinated, she could not contain her excitement: she placed her fingers over those of the youth, felt them up and down, moved up towards the wrist, then turned the hand over and explored the palm, which was more muscular and not as soft as hers. He watched her.

"Careful," he said, "that's mine."

"No, it's Lucien Lefrène's and if you're me, it belongs to me as much, or as little, as it does to you."

"I'm the one who left."

"What does *I* mean when you say it?"

"My dear, volumes have been written on the subject. What is the sense of identity? Who says I? I'm sure you remember as well as I do Orlando calling Orlando at the end of the book, when she goes home with her sheets for a double bed, for her present self irritates her and she wants to invoke another, more amusing self, and is unable to. She calls up all the I's of her soul and none of them is to her liking. I am me. Part of me is also you, I know you like the back of my hand but only up until one o'clock last Friday afternoon. Since then, each of us has experienced things that the other knows nothing about, although I can probably imagine more easily what you have done than you can imagine what I've been up to. I've changed. Now I am a man."

She looked. She blushed.

"Yes! It's a wonderful experience. You touch my hand, you say you have a right to, that it's also yours: but I've got a dick."

The word shocked her.

"Still as prudish, aren't you? I certainly had no reason to take your modesty with me. I bet you've managed not to think about it even once."

There was a stir in the recesses where Aline stored cumbersome objects.

"I don't know," she said. "In any case, I don't remember."

"I believe you. You have an extraordinary ability to put to one side anything that you find awkward, my very existence is the proof. Aren't you eating?"

She had not touched her sandwich.

"I don't think I'm very hungry."

"It's the emotion. Drink your wine, that'll relax you."

"It'll send me to sleep. If you're me, you know that all too well."

"That's one way I've changed. Wine doesn't make me sleepy any more, on the contrary, it makes me livelier and happier. You only fall asleep because you're afraid of your vivaciousness. I'm sure you're hungry, and you love crab. Eat and drink and try not to be so afraid of your thoughts. I'm not mummy, I'm the part of you that couldn't stand mummy's constant fretting. You're safe with me."

This idea astounded her.

"How can I be safer with you than on my own?"

"Because I'm not afraid of you. You know very well that people are like dogs, what frightens them is the fear they provoke. Mummy's anxiety made you fearful, but it made me furious, though you would never listen to me. Think hard and you'll see that you couldn't stop yourself thinking about it."

"About what?" she asked, honestly, for she was so confused that she kept losing track of the conversation.

He merely laughed, which jogged her memory, and she turned crimson again. But her curiosity, clearly irrepressible, got the better of her modesty.

"What's it like?"

"Amazing! The difference is incredible."

"Better?"

"It's as different as chalk and cheese. I feel better as a boy than I did shut up inside you, but it's because of mummy. *Aline! A young lady doesn't do this, doesn't do that* all day long, all year round, she cramped my style, my thoughts and my plans. Just look at you, repressed, timid, a real lady, what a credit to your mother! It's because of her that you never tried to have Maurice Alker, you are incapable of provoking a man. I can, and they like it."

"Not all of them, for goodness sake!"

"You'd be amazed. Many more than you think, and more than I'd expected. And then this," – he pointed to his flies – "reacts much faster. Where you blush, I get a hard on."

"Please," she said, almost mechanically.

"I ignored mummy's precepts, or rather it was you who sheltered me from them by shutting me away in the dungeon, without realizing it, for you certainly had no such intention! So I remained a lot more natural. The upbringing was aimed at the girl, it affected the girl but didn't touch me."

"You remained a half-wild little animal."

She was disconcerted to find herself, after keeping her distance all this time, now speaking to him with such intimacy. Orlanda was delighted.

"I see you recognize the obvious."

Aline pensively ate her crab. Orlanda continued chatting, she no longer listened. Her world had been turned upside down, but she did not feel the turmoil she had felt the day before, staggering between Molière and Constantin Meunier. I'm getting used to the idea, she thought. I must be one of those people who always adapt to any situation because it's easier than resisting. In the past, I complied with my mother's demands, and now this young man is confronting me with the impossible, and I'm getting used to it. Maybe I have no personality? Or, maybe I'm a nexus of ambivalence, maybe I have too many personalities, one of them can leave without my noticing. I am like a mother with too many children who leaves one of them in a supermarket. It's only in the evening, at bed-time, that she notices one of the beds is empty. Oh well, I expect they'll have taken her to Lost Property, I'll go and pick her up tomorrow. And then the next day, overwhelmed by nappies and washing up, she allows the missing child to slip her mind. Oh my God! I've forgotten again! At dinner, the husband counts the daughters: strange, there are only six. Haven't we got seven? Do you think so, she asks, reddening a little. He counts his offspring on his fingers, in order of arrival: Caroline, Annie, Claudette, Gisèle, Isabelle, Françoise, that's it, Myriam's missing!

Orlanda, frowning, watched her laughing.

"I know I've got a brilliant wit, but I don't recall saying anything that funny."

She could not refrain from telling him her fantasy.

"I find you extremely disrespectful. Mothers overwhelmed by the fruits of a happy marriage aren't funny, you should sigh and say something ought to be done. Besides, you haven't forgotten anybody, I left. And I wasn't a girl."

"So, when I talk to you, am I talking to myself? Like madmen who mutter at you in the street or drivers who are bored alone at the wheel?"

"But are they talking to themselves? When I was still living inside you, you never deigned to talk to me. And yet I could have given you some excellent advice. Besides, you admit that I came out of you, but you simplify things. Since Friday, I've had other experiences, we've gone different ways."

Aline sighed. She had to admit it, she no longer had any doubts. Maybe having no doubts means that I've gone completely mad? She shrugged: it would also be mad not to accept the obvious, even if the obvious seems crazy. I dived into a sci-fi adventure, and if what this young man is made up of was part of me before the separation, I have to admit that it was I who took the plunge. I would not have believed myself capable of such a thing! There are more things in my soul than are dreamed of in my philosophy. Well, *there were*, seeing as he claims that the whole thing was his idea. But then he appears to have taken away the most interesting side of me? Damn it! who was I? So I only start to discover who I am when half of me has been removed?

The next thought that began to take shape in the recesses of her mind was, of course, "how do I get myself back?"

She stared pensively at Orlanda. *We've gone different ways.* True. But how far? What was the part of her that had left her made of? I don't believe in souls, she said to herself, but am I saying anything different if I ask myself what makes up the psyche? Thought is the product of cerebral activity, isn't it, and your daughter is dumb because she doesn't talk. But in leaving, what did he take with him? and what have I got left?

There were no answers to all these questions, and it was one thirty – she had to go and lecture.

"Since you are so familiar with my office, perhaps you would be so kind as to clear up, I have to leave you," she said.

He laughed.

"It will be as tidy as when you do it yourself!"

Of that she had no doubt.

The situation between those two was extremely curious. When I say those two, I hesitate: are they really two? Orlanda is convinced they are, but I sensed doubt creeping into Aline's mind. I watch her leave, with a hurried step because she is slightly late. Not the repressed strides of before, but I do not think she had such a confident step in Paris, as she made her way across place Napoléon III towards the station. She amazes me. It is not the first time – I was as astonished as she was after the first encounter with Orlanda, to hear her lying to Albert with the aplomb of a seasoned fibber. The fact is, she is not easy to follow, for she constantly deludes herself and similarly deceives those who are watching her. I only met her at the moment of the separation, when she was struggling with the Ladies of Purity and Chastity, and now it seems to me that I was too quick to sympathize with the point of view of Orlanda, who did not like her. Is there not a rather admirable flexibility in her willingness to accept the impossible? I can imagine that weaker characters would be thrown into turmoil: she bends but does not break. We must not forget that she was the author of this impossibility, which makes it easier to understand why she does not put up too strong a resistance.

Orlanda tidied everything away, as promised, and then went into a bookshop and bought six years' worth of geometry and algebra and spent the afternoon revising. He was thrilled because the theorems came back into his head as if they had only left it the day before. Yes, he said to himself at seven o'clock, as he closed the textbooks, but what about my wonderful idea of buying up old mansions and renovating them? I can't do both. He pulled a face at the realization that he would have to choose. Already! Aline has spent her life making sacrifices, and now I'm doing the same? He wanted to talk it over with someone and, thinking quite naturally of Paul Renault, he set off for avenue Lepoutre.

Paul, panic-stricken at his own impulsiveness, had decided that, for a few days, he would not be at home between six and seven. He had never had to resort to such manoeuvres for he was in the habit of controlling his feelings, but he was a realistic man and, after the telephone call about the length of the degree course, and the offer of a place at his table, he felt that it would be wise to be wary of his feelings and to take precautions. So, on the Wednesday, on leaving the office, he studied the cinema listings, but nothing appealed to him. There was a concert of baroque music at the Conservatoire but he did not feel like baroque music. He flicked through his address book and decided that nobody would want to see him, but, refusing to be fooled by his eagerness to limit the number of options, with a sigh, he sought out a pavement café where he would read his newspaper until eight o'clock. No! Seven thirty, he said as he purchased *Le Monde*, *Le Soir* and *Time* magazine, which he was unable to spin out for three quarters of an hour.

So on arrival at avenue Lepoutre, Orlanda bumped into him outside the door.

"I've brought dinner," he hailed him cheerfully.

He was feeding everyone today!

Paul watched him unwrap some smoked salmon, trout in aspic, calves sweetbreads in sauce that needed reheating and two bottles of Pouilly.

"You've robbed a delicatessen! There's enough food here for three days!"

"Don't underestimate me."

Aline found Albert grumbling and groaning: there was no avoiding Hong Kong and as there were no direct flights from Brussels, they would have to go via Paris, he would be leaving on Saturday and would not be back until the following Thursday.

"The old chief has never been able to get over his fear of flying and prefers to avoid planes if he can, so we'll be on the motorway first thing in the morning, five of us sandwiched into one car. And I know he hates going at more than sixty miles an hour which means four hours of inane chit-chat. I say four hours because you have to include the prostate stops. The architects aren't invited, so they're furious and are in a huff with us, but I phoned them and they agreed to save all their anger for Bordier. Meanwhile, I've got no choice, I'm going and I'm fuming. My only consolation is that we'll be away on Easter Monday, so that's one less day lost."

You should hear Aline's sympathetic murmurings in response to this outburst.

Does Aline love Albert? She is not consumed with passion, that is certain, but she is fond of him and she commiserates with him.

There is no ardour. Right now, Orlanda is enthusing about Euclid's postulate to Paul who can feel himself being swept along in a torrent of parallels. But, last Sunday, had not Aline been passionately engrossed in *Orlando*? Why does Albert's frustration not affect her? She takes the meat out of the refrigerator and asks the right questions, taking care not to exacerbate his anger. He paces up and down the spacious kitchen and starts to prepare the salad dressing almost mechanically as she rinses the lettuce. As they sit down to eat, he is beginning to wonder whether, apart from the tower, there is anything worth visiting in the area.

"May as well," he sighs, "if I have to bow to the inevitable, why not try to make the most of it?"

By the time they got to the dessert, they were laughing.

Orlanda had not brought a dessert. Paul was listening to his account of the house in avenue Winston Churchill.

"The most amazing thing is the library. You find yourself on the ground floor, in a huge, rather strange room, very ornate with panelling and gilt, but you don't know if it's a hall or a reception room because there are four or five doors. The estate agent opened one, and at the end you could see a narrow, well-lit staircase, and the wall on the right, which overlooks the courtyard, is all glass. You go up towards another door. It's an odd feeling, being on a staircase that's closed off at the top and at the bottom, it's like a tiny, long, narrow room which has been built solely to house the staircase. There are around fifteen steps, made of beautiful wood, I think it's polished mahogany. Mahogany is always polished, which makes it look artificial, like those society women who are so smooth and dazzling that you wonder whether they are really the product of ordinary biology. Natural mahogany has a slightly thick fibre which gives it strength and the steps are a good size, which makes them pleasant to climb. Open it, open it, says the estate agent when I get to the top, and I open it: it's incredible, fifteen metres long, ten metres high, two galleries of shelves, and not a single book! The effect is hard to describe, a room with no furniture is empty, but a library with no books is emptier than nothing. I went closer: it couldn't have been cleaned for ages. When they removed the books, there were two thicknesses of dust, showing where the books had been. Their ghosts are still there."

"You really love them."

"Do you think so? I don't know. I think they're restricting," he replied absently. What would become of that room? It would need thousands of books. It would be demolished, turned into a bar, a children's play room, a discotheque . . . anything would be a crime. "I'll buy the house, restore it and sell it to a wealthy book-lover, but what about my maths?"

"You can't do everything."

"That's what's so terrible. I want to do everything," he retorted with the vehemence of a frustrated child.

Then he laughed, and there was something childlike too in his rapid mood swings.

"I'm unbearable. I always have been."

"You're delightful," replied Paul, in spite of himself.

Albert and Aline cleared up the kitchen together and then Albert, exhausted by his emotion, suggested turning in early and reading in bed. They took the walkway, pausing to check the soil around the bougainvillaeas and to water them.

"It's been very hot," said Aline.

"Yes, but soon we'll have to let them go thirsty, or they won't flower."

When they were in the bedroom:

"Oh! By the way, who's that young man with whom you've been seen eating ice creams on the corner of rue Vanderkindere?"

Aline froze. Her heart missed a beat.

"Who told you about that?"

"I can never remember his name. That man who walks his dog and gossips. He keeps the neighbourhood informed of the marriages and deaths of people one's never spoken to."

"The old bore opposite," breathed Aline.

Had he been at the ice cream parlour?

"He stopped me this morning. He was very keen to know whether this young man is a nephew or a cousin. As neither you nor I have any nephews or cousins, I told him he was a student, but as far as I know, you never go for ice creams with your students."

She was so pale that Albert frowned.

"You look terrified."

"I am," she murmured, in no state to pretend.

He had begun to remove his tie: he stopped in mid-gesture and scrutinized this woman with whom he had lived for fifteen years. He had always had the vague feeling that she would not allow him to get to know her too well.

"Then I'm going to be terrified. Who is he?"

Neither nephew, cousin, nor student – having eliminated the harmless options, the only one left was the lover.

"It's not what you think."

"I don't think anything yet."

"Maybe, but you soon will. A young man I haven't told you about, twice since last Sunday. I presume our charming neighbour was specific?"

"Yes."

As the truth was impossible, she had to make something up, and quickly. Earlier, when she felt safe, I hesitated, I wondered whether she loved Albert: it is when our relationships are threatened that we become aware of the strength of our affections. Aline, gasping, knew that she would not let anything in the world jeopardize her relationship with Albert. She sat down on the bed.

"I didn't want to tell you about it."

"Why not?"

Then, it came to her. It was so brilliant, such a relief, that she nearly burst out laughing, and only just managed to control herself.

"Because I'm not the only one implicated."

"What on earth are you talking about?"

She hung her head, which always gives an impression of confusion, and in this instance concealed the expression on her face which she was certain displayed no confusion whatsoever.

"Well, I think it's what's commonly known as a skeleton in the family cupboard. You know, the sort of thing people are anxious to keep secret and only reveal on their deathbed."

"What are you talking about?"

"Nothing yet. Can't we leave it at that? After all, you know me, you could trust me."

"In theory, yes. But I'm not perfect."

Have I hesitated long enough, she wondered.

Goodness me, she's crafty! I had not expected her to be so devious.

"I told you, I'm not the only one who's implicated."

"Stop beating about the bush. Even if we're not married – I know you too well to have risked asking you to marry me – after fifteen years one could say that I'm part of the family. And we're a long way off from our deathbeds. At least I hope so."

"That young man is my brother."

"What?"

"It's an absurd business, which I knew nothing about until last Sunday. His name is Lucien Lefrène and he's the result of a lapse which my father was the victim of twenty years ago. Well, victim or perpetrator, depending on where you stand. Mummy has no idea, of course."

The tale was taking shape so clearly in her head that she began to experience the euphoria of the inspired storyteller. She hid her face in her hands for a moment.

"And Lucien himself has only just found out. His mother died a few months ago, and he had to sort out her papers. That's how he discovered his father was unknown. He had not got over the shock when he came across eighteen years of monthly payments made by a certain Edouard Berger whom he had never heard of. His mother worked, but didn't earn much. He had never thought about their relatively comfortable circumstances which is natural in a teenager. He saw that the payments had stopped at the very time when he himself had started working. The Ohain address was on the cheques, and he went there, but did not show himself. It was one Sunday, last summer. He saw daddy mowing the lawn and mummy laying the table for tea. He thought how that man had scrupulously paid up to spare his family, and he could not condemn him for it. You and I arrived. He hesitated for a long time, but this half-sister intrigued him, and he wanted to meet me."

She paused, and mulled over her story. There were a lot of gaps but she felt confident she would be able to bridge them when necessary.

"So he hung around our district for a bit. He was unsure what to do. Understandably, don't you think? On Sunday, when I went out to get a breath of air, he approached me."

The astonished Albert still had his hand on his tie.

"Your father! Your father and a mistress, an illegitimate child!"

"Adulterine. Lucien knows nothing about their affair. He assumes it was brief. His mother had told him about a husband who had died in an accident at the beginning of her pregnancy, but the marriage had already broken up and she had no wish to remember him. It sounds as though my father quickly came to his senses, but he paid, so he knew."

"All this is unbelievable."

"Of course it is," said Aline who was so caught up in her story that she was beginning to believe it. "That's how I've got a half-brother. He describes his mother as he sees her, but you know how people can say one thing and suggest another. He describes her as rather dull. She didn't have an abortion because she's a Christian, and yet she had my father all hot under the collar, even if it was only for a week!"

Albert finished removing his tie at last and sat down beside Aline.

"And what does this brother want from you?"

"Nothing. To get to know me. Naturally, because we don't have any mutual acquaintances, he had to tell me the truth so that I would allow him to talk to me, but he doesn't want to bother my parents. My brother's a very nice fellow."

An only child, Aline derived enormous pleasure from saying my brother.

"Do you believe so? It could all be pure fabrication."

"Undoubtedly, and that had occurred to him."

After this, I don't see why I shouldn't write fiction, she thought. I must have developed a talent without realizing it from reading so many novels and talking about them!

"He had eighteen years' worth of deposit slips signed by my father. I looked at them all. You can imagine how hard I found it to believe, and then he burned them in front of me. Not in the ice cream parlour. Eighteen times twelve, work it out, a fat bundle, but ten at a time over a drain. The neighbour must have been out, or he'd have told you. Now, there's no trace of them. But my father knows. It upsets me to think he has a child he's never seen."

"The most trustworthy man you could imagine!"

"Yes. I'm not in a hurry to see him. I need to get used to the idea. There's no way I can talk to him about it. If he'd wanted me to know, he'd have told me. I'm relying on you to keep quiet about it too."

He shrugged: "You don't even need to ask. But it's true that it'll take a bit of getting used to."

Poor daddy, she thought.

* * *

Well! I need time to get my breath back! Honestly, Aline keeps taking me by surprise. I thought she was an unadventurous creature, I was not expecting her to show imagination, in other words, to tell lies. The fact is, I accepted her own view of herself, forgetting that she created Orlanda. Human complexity sometimes catches the storyteller out. The thing that bothers me the most is the extraordinary dishonesty of this charming young woman who calmly accuses her father of adultery and of abandoning his child, and derives great pleasure from inventing a scandal of which she alone is the author. True, it is hard to see how else she could have wriggled out of the awkward situation her nosy neighbour had put her in, although she could have claimed that the young man was one of her students. The girl bursting into tears outside her office could have provided inspiration. He's a young man who's writing his thesis and wanted to talk to me about mine? But she thought faster than I am doing here, she remembered her panic-stricken expression and her sudden departure, and said to herself that an academic conversation did not justify such emotion, which was probably very obvious. She did not know precisely what the neighbour had said. *What did he tell you?* might perhaps have increased Albert's suspicions, she needed some explanation that would justify her disarray. So when all is said and done, she deserves credit for her quick-wittedness.

All the same, she is outrageous, and I wonder just how far she will go.

Paul Renault watched the sleeping Orlanda and found his beauty angelic. What strange ways Venus employs to ensnare her prey! Picked up at the concert, Paul paid and thought no more of it, but *The Rains Came* and then the maths degree had flummoxed him, and the empty library in the house in avenue Winston Churchill was the last straw. All his life, he had triumphed over love and now he saw himself defeated by a laughing boy who had no ulterior motives. Right now, he is thinking only of the pleasures he has just tasted, but he is not a man who lives only for the moment. As he contemplates the fair hair spread over the pillow and the graceful lines of Orlanda's cheek seen in soft silhouette, he is thrilled and moved by the gentle, almost imperceptible breath passing his lips, but he knows that dread is not far behind. He has created a persona that is important to him, he is the bachelor with a slight aura of mystery, sought after for his charm. Women like him and he has never disclosed his preferences, which would disappoint them. People appreciated his availability, which he felt was in jeopardy. He has constructed his lifestyle like a stable edifice, and he cherished it. He believes he is happy. Orlanda terrifies him. There is something about him that he cannot grasp. He seems completely spontaneous, as though he is hiding nothing, but Paul senses contradictions in him that he could not put his finger on. He wants to think that the young man gives nothing away, but has to admit that he has not asked him for anything. I don't even know his address, he said to himself, but I haven't asked him for it. Would he give it to me? In fact, I don't think I've ever asked for anyone's address, and here I am judging him for not answering a question that hasn't been asked. Damn it! If I'm going to break all my own rules and fall in love, couldn't I choose someone who gives me a sense of security? Must I be so crazy as to fall for someone who is going to make me suffer? This charming lover does not seem to have any plans involving me, other than having dinner and making love, and here I am, anxious, questioning my emotions, I'm just like everything I've always rejected. I'll soon be gazing at him before holding out my arms, hesitating and saying: "If you don't mind?" and asking him when I'll see him again in that tone of voice that makes people reply I don't know! He found the idea so repugnant that he resolutely wakened Orlanda, and in a manner which left no doubts as to his intentions. Orlanda responded enthusiastically, which did nothing to allay Paul's confusion.

* * *

Agitated by his fury over Hong Kong and the incredible revelation about the half-brother, Albert was unable to read as he had planned, or to go quietly to sleep. Aline's mind was still racing, she was still feeling inspired, and continued the story, inventing hundreds of additional details. Separately, they both tossed and turned, and two restless people in a double bed usually end up tossing and turning together.

Thus Aline and Orlanda, although apart, were simultaneously transported, something, according to hearsay, that poor Virginia never experienced.

# SEVENTH DAY
# THURSDAY

ORLANDA SPENT THE night at Paul Renault's and woke up at the same time as he did. They ate breakfast together.

"But," said the young man amiably, "I remember you said you don't like long-term relationships. Do tell me, if I'm in your way. I won't be offended."

"Don't worry about that," replied Paul so hastily that he gave himself a fright. So he went on: "For the time being. Two nights don't make a relationship and you are a delightful companion."

"You're too kind."

He looked content, which made Paul happy, then furious at being happy. He groaned inwardly.

They left the apartment at the same time. Orlanda, after a moment's hesitation in front of *Mrs Parkington*, had decided to spend the day studying.

"Would you like me to drive you home?" inquired Paul, opening his car door.

"Oh no! I like walking. I think the weather's going to change, look at those clouds. I'll make the most of the last of the sunshine."

Was he trying to keep his address secret? wondered Paul, driving off.

Yes, but not from you, Orlanda could have replied, on arriving home twenty minutes later. A young woman was leaning against the door. Catching sight of him, she drew herself up and confronted him angrily:

"So there you are! What on earth are you up to, Lucien? You've taken your phone off the hook, you're never home, you've left your magazine. It's impossible to get hold of you, mummy's moaning, Marie-Jeanne keeps pestering me, Jacques was expecting you at the baby's christening and he's furious, he had to find someone to take your place."

And so on. Georges, or Gérard, I didn't get his name, wasn't exactly thrilled to be a second-choice godfather, there was also a certain André whom Lucien was supposed to have accompanied, as he did each week, to a junk shop, a whole army of friends and relatives complaining, grumbling, fuming. Orlanda pictured them in imitation-leather jackets covered with zips.

He sighed, opened the door, and she immediately noticed the schoolbooks lying open on the table.

"What's all this then? Are you doing geometry?"

Lucien Lefrène's sister was bound to know whether he had finished high school. How could he obtain such a vital piece of information? He stared at Annie. She wore no make-up, and her light chestnut hair was drawn up in a bun. It looked as though it was as thick as her brother's, but was kept under control. Her skirt was plain and her little blouse clean and carefully ironed, no imitation leather, a knitted cardigan and a large shoulder bag.

"Aren't you at the hospital?" he ventured.

"It's my day off."

He had not been mistaken, she was a nurse.

"But I'm going to see mummy later. And it would be a good idea if you came with me."

"I'm not free," he replied, shuddering in horror.

Annie looked around the room: "It's blindingly obvious you don't live here any more. There are no dirty dishes, the bed's made, everything is clean and tidy. So Marie-Jeanne was right, there's somebody else."

That could not be denied, but it was not what she thought.

"Yes, I'm a different man," he said, trying very hard not to laugh.

There was absolutely no reaction from the real Lucien who, from the depths where he had been relegated, did not feel the slightest need to protest.

"So it seems," retorted Annie. "But you're still our mother's son, and I demand you do the right thing."

He sat down on the bed and stared dreamily at the young woman. *I demand.* There was a word that is not always uttered, but is often implied. Aline had spent her life in thrall to the demands of a mother who had never said the word. I suppose poor old Lucien did the same thing, he thought, and was unable to stop himself rushing to the hospital, hating himself all the while for obeying. But I have no connection with this girl who manages to remain calm when she's angry and, in spite of her discreet *I demand*, I have no difficulty whatsoever in refusing to comply. We destroy our lives without realizing it, to please people who irritate us but whom we are unable to say no to, and I'm going to say no to poor old Annie without the slightest remorse. Actually, it's not fair, it's Lucien who ought to say it and relish his new-found freedom. Or, supposing I tried, out of pure altruism, to help the girl break away from her repulsive, bald, gouty mother?

"Annie, I'm not kidding, suppose you just forget it? Your mother disgusts you as much as she does me, but you're making a rod for your own back. They'll dry her out, she'll leave in better health than when she went in, and then she'll start drinking again, you know that's what always happens. You've got your own life to lead, in ten or fifteen years' time she'll be dead and it'll be too late for you."

She looked as though she would choke with shock:

"How can you talk like that? She's your mother!"

Orlanda said nothing. Annie was gasping, she made a slight

gesture with her hand and seemed to lose her balance. He rose and helpfully pushed a chair towards her. Mechanically, she sat down. When she was able to breathe again:

"I don't recognize you, Lucien, honestly! I don't know who you're seeing, but they're a bad influence on you."

That's families for you, he said to himself, you're not supposed to have your own opinions, and if you change, it's because you're keeping bad company. It goes without saying that a mother's influence on a young man's upbringing cannot be damaging, even if she's an alcoholic. Shall I try again?

"Think. Have I said anything that is not absolutely true?"

Getting into his stride, Orlanda took another risk:

"Didn't you yourself explain to me how useless detox treatment is?"

"That's not the point."

Whew! She had talked to Lucien about it! Aline knew what she did from Jacqueline, but Orlanda had no idea what kind of conversations Lucien might have with his sister.

"We must do everything we can, but you want to abandon her."

"And you should do likewise, for your own sake."

"You are contemptible. You were contemptible in keeping her supplied with as much booze as she wanted, and you are even more contemptible now you no longer want to play along."

"But if you admit yourself that she'll start drinking again, what's the use of your devotion? Isn't it purely to satisfy your own conscience?"

"I never want to speak to you again, Lucien. Never. You've gone too far."

She left the room. Orlanda admired her resolve, she did not just make empty threats but carried them out. But he was worried about Jacques and Gérard or Georges, and told himself that they would turn up and scold, lecture and aggravate him. I can't stay here, they'll never leave me in peace, I must get out of their reach. Lucien, my man, you're going to have to move!

Yes, but not without thinking, he added. It's time I organized my new life. I jumped into Lucien Lefrène as if I had run to the station and bought a ticket for the first train, and only learned where it was going when I got there! I was thirty-five and now I'm twenty, I've got a whole new future to build and I don't want to be disturbed by anyone. Marie Berger, Aline, Jacques, Georges and Annie will be powerless over me, but whether I decide to go back to university or to recycle myself as a property developer specializing in empty mansions, I'll need money. Until now, I've spent recklessly, because I hadn't made any plans yet.

He laughed softly. Since the bourgeoisie had emerged from feudal society, the Berger family had been part of it. He could live from day to day for a week, after which several centuries of providence and thrift regained the upper hand. Well, he thought, and a good thing too. I'm a happy-go-lucky young man, I don't fancy finding myself penniless and homeless. I need to find my landlord's address so I can give him my notice and find somewhere else, but I'll do it in an organized way, without rushing into things. Let's go through my host's papers again, perhaps he's got a lease.

He then spent the day visiting ugly apartments that were within his means, and by the evening was in a thoroughly bad temper. This had not yet happened to him since the separation, and, as Orlanda, he had no defences against such an inconvenience. What would Aline have done? He consulted a past which he was not very pleased to acknowledge as his own and realized, to his surprise, that Aline did not allow herself to give in to ill humour. She might be sad, tense or anxious, but not angry. When she clattered her heels on the pavement, she was not aware of it and was already thinking about something else. But what could I think about? wondered Orlanda. He walked past a shop window and saw the reflection of his attractive body. He need look no further for inspiration: he'd go cruising.

* * *

So we will leave him to it, and go and join Aline, who is having friends to dinner this evening.

She had to confess that she was vaguely disappointed not to see Lucien Lefrène at lunch time. She left her office as early as possible, did some last-minute shopping and when she was weighed down with purchases dashed into the lobby of place Constantin Meunier, for she did not have much time and was afraid of allowing herself to be distracted by the young man. But he was not there. Why wasn't he there?

Albert was slicing vegetables while waiting for her. They had two hours to cook a complicated meal. Such marathons did not dismay Albert who, as an engineer, had a highly developed sense of organization and planned everything meticulously. So there was little time to talk about Aline's brother:

"I've thought about it over and over again, I'm still speechless."

Or about Hong Kong: "As old Bordier hates being rushed, we'll be leaving Brussels at nine o'clock and have lunch at Roissy where Régnier claims you can eat well. Unfortunately, you know him, he's got no idea when it comes to food."

"With Olga's talents, that's just as well."

"My dear Aline, that was a spiteful thing to say."

It's strange, she thought, I don't think I could have said that last week.

Then she started making a hollandaise sauce and put the matter from her mind.

But, when everybody had arrived, the conversation immediately turned to Hong Kong, and Albert had to make a huge effort not to complain about Régnier. Olga was thrilled at the thought of rickshaws, silk and sampans: "You mean crowded avenues, traffic jams, and a tower block crammed with computers and programmers!"

"What about the bay and the sky of China!"

"Balmy nights," grumbled Albert.

Aline saw his expression cloud over and thought of typhoons: "Come and eat. A soufflé waits for no one."

Now it was Albert's turn to come to her rescue: Charles wanted to get back to Virginia Woolf.

"Have you read the whole *Diary* closely?"

Albert cut in: "Aline, have you told Jacqueline that you read her beloved *Darkover* whatsit?"

"No, we haven't seen each other since."

"You've read it? Does that mean I'll no longer be the only science-fiction fan, at last? I know a lot of people who love thrillers, why doesn't anyone want to go off into space?"

"Ah! A grisly little murder, at night, in the security of your own home, after a day in court defending the innocent!" mused Louis Lardinois.

"If that's what you want, I promise you there are plenty of massacres in science fiction. John Wyndham never begins a story without destroying nine tenths of the human race."

"Nine tenths is too much. It becomes anonymous. Besides, how do you find the culprit when it's nine tenths!"

Charles persisted: "In the *Diary*, it's obvious that Vita . . ."

And was tactfully interrupted by Denise: "Jacqueline, I promise I'll read one of your awful books if Aline managed it."

"I liked it," said Aline. "It's badly written, the plot is full of holes, the characters are one-dimensional, but it has a certain appeal."

And, it will not surprise us to hear that she uttered exactly the same words as Orlanda: "I don't think I've ever come across such dreadful literature."

Then added: "But I became intrigued when the telepaths started resonating."

After five minutes, the conversation was in full flow, and Charles had no choice but to join in or keep quiet.

"In actual fact, there are few people who haven't had a paranormal experience," Jacqueline was saying. "It all depends what they make of it. One of my friends told me that one night, she woke up at four o'clock, terrified by a horrendous nightmare. Her son was standing in front of her, covered in blood, and said to her: 'Don't worry, I'm fine, but there's nothing left of the car.' She couldn't get back to sleep. At five o'clock, she heard the young man come in, and rushed out to meet him. He was covered in bandages, his clothes were soaked in blood, he told her he was fine but the car was a write-off. And she's never gone in for seances."

"Pierre read Henry Van de Velde's papers from start to finish, and in manuscript, which is a feat in itself. In '42 or '43, I can't remember, Van de Velde saw, in a dream, his daughter who lived somewhere in Asia. She was very thin, pale and dressed in a shroud. In the morning, he said to his family, who have always confirmed it: 'Anne's dead.' It was that very night that the young woman had died of exhaustion in a camp."

"I've got a story too," said Louis Lardinois. "You know I hardly ever travel, well, for years, I dreamed I had to take the five o'clock plane to New York, but every time I missed it, because all sorts of hitches cropped up. In the morning I would complain that it was exasperating to keep having the same exhausting dream. In this dream, I had to run like mad, which is quite tiring for a man of my size, and I was worried sick! Then, one day, I took it into my head to go to New York for a conference and, naturally, I didn't notice that the plane left at five p.m., just like in my dream, because I had to leave Brussels at three to get the plane from London, which is much cheaper. With the time difference, it would be six o'clock by my watch, whereas in London it was five. My father died unexpectedly the day before, in the early afternoon, and I still haven't been to New York. I don't think I dare. I've never had that dream again."

"Freud admitted the possibility of telepathy in his article entitled "Psychoanalysis and Telepathy". He even went so far as to say that psychoanalysis prepares us for this type of phenomenon, I can't remember how he substantiates it."

Aline listened to all this remembering that she had asked young Lucien if he was telepathic.

"Fine," she said, "but if telepathy existed, what would be its medium? How would a thought travel from one mind to another?"

Albert turned to Jeannine Lardinois: "Jeannine, you're a scientist, the only one of us who's really qualified, what do you think?"

"You're too modest, I have enormous admiration for engineers. Anyway, I've never thought about it. I'll have to improvise."

"Louis, as she's got to improvise, give your wife a drink."

"I'm a mere secondary-school physics teacher, I'm neither a scientist nor a poet. You're asking a lot of me. I can tell you that they discover new corpuscles every day, and if they can't see them, they guess at their existence and then invent experiments to prove they do exist. I've even read, in *Scientific American*, that time travel is not incompatible with quantum physics, and that telekinesis is not impossible. But we won't travel like the heroes of *Star Trek* – that privilege will be reserved for photons."

"For photons?" queried Olga.

"They're the particles that carry light. They belong to mechanics and electromagnetics."

"Of course," said Olga.

"As far as I understand from the article, sometimes an excited atom sheds its excess energy by emitting two photons at the same time, whose properties are not independent, but necessarily correlated, and quantum physics says that they can, after separation, remain correlated for ever."

Aline was immediately intrigued. Was that how Lucien had left her?

"Give me some more wine," clamoured Jeannine gaily, "I can feel the oracle stirring. The gravitational field has been defined, which means that when we stumble, we fall, like a ripe apple under Newton's nose, now there's talk of a quantum space, governed by Planck's constant . . ."

She looked at Olga and smiled: "Which is, as you are no doubt aware, a fundamental constant equal to the energy of any quantum of radiation divided by its frequency. It's symbol is *h*, always in italics."

Régnier frowned, but Jeannine went on without giving him time to wonder whether she was making fun of his wife.

"Physics is becoming increasingly poetic. I read an article entitled *Elementary particles that have charm*, just like you and me, my dear. One of these days they will define a psychic field, why not? The particles in it would be called psychotrons, and they would move at the speed of light. Since we're talking about psychic phenomena, which is not my field, as Jacqueline will tell you, it's not my job to invent the laws that will govern it, but with the help of the wine, I'll tell you this: from time to time, I imagine it's under the influence of a powerful emotion, a group of these strange creatures break through the barrier of the skull and behave according to the wishes of their owner. Anne Van de Velde, dying and destitute, thinks in desperation of the father who loved and protected her, setting off the psychotronic wave. Under the impulse of a tremendous force, it finds its way to the soul she is seeking, flies over continents and penetrates her father's sleeping brain. Henry sees his pallid daughter looking at him as she breathes her last. He reaches out to her, she reaches out to him, a nanosecond more and, all the laws of physics overcome by love, the daughter would have joined her father, but it was the last gasp of a life that was over, Anne died and Henry woke up in tears."

Everyone clapped softly. Jeannine acknowledged their applause with a modest nod and went on: "We know that there are electric charges running along the neurones and jumping across the synapses."

She shot a glance at Olga, who was listening without comment.

"But what does that mean? Current scientific practice is not to claim that things don't exist until their existence has been proven, but to try and find a proof. If one day physicists decide to defend the hypothesis that telepathy exists, they'll come up with theories, they'll invent experiments. We probably won't be any more capable of reading each other's thoughts, but at least we'll know why."

That's what he did, thought Aline. Then she corrected herself: that's what *I* did, because, just before the separation, the initiative came from me, even though it's now part of Lucien Lefrène. I applied laws I didn't know existed, but the earth revolved around the sun well before we poor humans found equations to express gravity. I haven't accomplished the impossible, only the improbable. That's not much comfort, for the improbable doesn't happen twice in a row, and I don't see how I'll get back what I've lost.

It was the first time that such an interesting thought had occurred to her, and for a moment she sat there awe-struck.

At that very moment, Orlanda, content with his evening, came to sit in the square. The windows on the third floor were lit up and, although it was cooler than it had been over the last few days, one of them was open. It was nearly midnight, there were few cars in this quiet district, and he could hear laughter and exclamations. Amid the din, he could distinguish the smoothness of a sonorous bass and the mellow tones of a rich contralto. That must be Louis and Denise congratulating Jeannine. Albert opened a bottle of champagne, Orlanda heard the cork pop, or thought he did, and pictured the cheerful gathering, the large table cluttered, Aline hastily getting the goblets out of the old sideboard she had brought back from Ohain, Charles, a little flushed, saying that if they carried on like this they'd have to walk home or get someone to drive them, and Olga, as silly as ever, replying "But you only live across the square!" All the complicity of old friends from which he suddenly felt excluded, and, for the second time since the separation, he felt a wave of nostalgia, which made him furious. I don't give a damn for Aline's friends! But Jeannine's imaginative account and Denise's smile haunted his half-soul. Louis had probably got up to open the other bottle, saying to Albert that there's a technique for opening champagne bottles so that the cork doesn't fly out. He could see him in his mind and was overjoyed to discover that he did not see him through the same eyes as the demure Aline. He was not corpulent, but had a muscular frame and his slight portliness only emphasized his vigour. Orlanda thought of his large hands, made for generous caresses. He felt a thrill of desire which Aline had always repressed and pictured himself crushed against the broad chest, seeking with his belly the ardent response, and had no idea that, at that moment, he thought of his body as a woman's body. Just then, a lady out walking her dog came within inches of him scolding "Kiki! this has been going on for ten minutes, do your wee so we can go home", but Kiki, who was a sharp little mutt, ferreted, sniffed and made a beeline for Orlanda's leg. Rudely awakened from his reverie, Orlanda started. The front door was opening, the Lardinois, Denise, Charles and the Régniers came out chatting, and, curiously, Orlanda withdrew to the shadows as if he were afraid of being seen. He listened to them saying their goodbyes and watched Charles walk past within inches of him. Using my privilege, I shall eavesdrop for a few seconds on the thoughts of this faithful friend: he is going to go back to the key passages from 1926 and 1927 in the *Diary* and photocopy them to send to Aline. It is pure concern, she'll have them to hand and will be able to consult them when she likes. Gauche as he could sometimes be, Charles remained unswerving in his affection.

Upstairs, Albert was telling Aline to leave everything, the cleaner would clear it all up in the morning, and he led the young woman into the bedroom where, Orlanda being close by, she enjoyed more intensely than usual the pleasure of being borne by her lover's calm confidence.

# EIGHTH DAY
## FRIDAY

ON AWAKENING, ORLANDA inspected his possessions. The move due to take place in two weeks' time would not involve too many things, there were no preparations to be made. He checked that the door was properly locked and the telephone off the hook, and plunged into his textbooks. At half past twelve, carrying a picnic, he joined Aline.

"It's odd. I didn't know you were entertaining, yesterday evening."

"It was a last-minute arrangement, to console Albert for having to go to Hong Kong."

"Hong Kong?"

She told him about the trip. And then, getting carried away, she found herself telling Orlanda the story she had made up about their kinship.

"Daddy? You accused daddy?"

He laughed until he cried.

"It's not funny."

"It's hilarious!"

"It makes me sick with dread. Supposing he got to hear about it."

"Don't be silly! Don't you trust Albert?"

"The fact is, this situation's impossible. You're making things difficult for me. Here too, people are going to start wondering about this young man who comes to see me at lunch time."

"Well you've accepted me, haven't you? Haven't you noticed how you've started being quite familiar with me?"

She had put her hand on his arm without realizing, and blushed deep red.

"My dear Aline! What could be more natural than being so at ease with yourself? Anyway, I could be your cousin."

"I don't have any cousins."

"Neither Duchâtel nor your colleagues will go and check up."

"If you left my soul," she stopped short – putting her hand on his arm had been dictated by some greater force. She sighed and went on: "If you left my soul, why are you coming back into my life like this?"

"I don't know," he replied. "I have no choice."

They stared at each other in silence.

"What about you? You can't turn me away, can you?"

She could only shake her head.

"We're caught up in a very strange adventure. You and I don't understand the rules. We have to accept them, and, eventually, maybe we'll define them."

"The adventure you caused," she said, with some dishonesty, because the previous evening, she had admitted that, at the moment of separation, whatever it was that had separated them was still part of her.

Orlanda, in his complacency, did not protest: "Fair enough, but it was your fault. If you had listened to me, if you hadn't meekly obeyed mummy, I wouldn't be here."

"That's the second time you've said that. I don't recognize myself."

"Of course not. I disappeared from what you called you as you created me and that is a bond between us which can't be denied, even though you don't like it. You made me without being aware of it, but I remember every second."

She remained silent.

"Actually," he added, "of the two of us, I'm the better off, because I know everything about you and you know nothing of me."

For the time being, she thought, without really understanding what she meant by that.

But what will be the outcome of this affair? Where are we going? It was clear that Orlanda, who lived for the moment, was perfectly content to see her when he felt like it and that was it. She shuddered.

Someone walked over my grave, grandma used to say.

Albert's leaving tomorrow? Orlanda finished his lunch in a dream. Plans were forming in his mind, which he thought it best not to share with Aline.

That Friday morning, Paul Renault had awoken feeling pleased with himself. He had spent the previous evening with friends and thoroughly enjoyed himself. Several times he had noticed that he was no longer thinking about the delightful Lucien at all. He had replied lightheartedly to the friend he had consulted about the maths degree and had not felt awkward, honestly! His friends had invited a charming young lady who lived alone since a painful divorce, barely concealing the fact that they wanted him to meet her. He had spoken to her with just the right degree of courtesy, showing that he was a sensitive man of the world with indisputable charm, but at the same time he made it clear that he was unavailable. Why was I so afraid that I had fallen in love? he wondered while shaving and, naturally, did not realize that in thinking that he was not in love, he had Lucien constantly on his mind. He returned home at the usual time, began preparing his dinner and saw to his astonishment that he had laid two places.

He did not have time to get annoyed. Lucien was ringing the bell.

"Well, aren't you going to introduce this brother to me?" asked Albert.

"When you get back, if you like," replied Aline.

# THE SECOND PERIOD

AT NINE O'CLOCK, old Bordier's huge car pulled up outside the door. Albert climbed in with a sigh, and left.

At ten, Orlanda rang the bell.

Aline was expecting him.

"Whew!" he said, striding up and down the apartment, "it's good to be home!"

She did not respond.

He flung his jacket onto a chair, the briefcase containing his textbooks onto the table and himself down on the sofa. Aline, watching him, felt something shudder inside her, it was strange, a storm with no wind, a soundless cry, a memory with no images.

"*You're such a tomboy,*" she whispered.

He looked at her, laughing.

"Oh, so you do remember!"

She shook her head: "I don't know why I said that."

"Because that's what mummy said to you. It's a pivotal moment in our past. You recognized me."

Aline felt giddy. She sat down facing Orlanda and tried to steady herself.

"You walk into my home as if you own the place, you go into all the rooms and you throw your things down anywhere."

He interrupted her: "You're cheating. You don't believe a word of what you're saying. I'm just as much at home here as you are, even if I do live inside the body of someone who's never been here, and you know it. You had no hesitation in letting me in. Admit it, you were expecting me! Albert's absence is very convenient for you and it suits me fine."

Aline is shaking. I know there is something strange going on inside her that I cannot put my finger on. I had better stay a while. I think she is afraid, but she cannot be frightened of Orlanda. There is nothing scary about this joyful young man with tousled hair. He just wants to have a bit of fun, even if it is at the expense of his former gaoler. Besides, the word gaoler is not appropriate any more, he no longer bears a grudge. Sitting on Aline's sofa, he sees her as the ideal companion for the games he has in mind. He is anxious for her to relax so they can have fun together. Orlanda is the simplest creature imaginable, he lives for the pleasure of the moment, whereas Aline is much more complex. I had thought that she was utterly predictable, I saw as little mystery in her as in a plain stretching monotonously towards the horizon, and I thought that in losing Orlanda, she would become even simpler, but, as I have already said time and time again, and I keep forgetting, it was she who created Orlanda. He is standing before her, Albert has left, and she is terrifyingly free. To be honest, I had not got the full measure of this woman, even though I had all the facts at my fingertips. Would somebody with a rudimentary mind study Proust so closely? To perceive and communicate the richness of a work of literature, you need to be able to respond to all its complexity from within yourself. Understandably, she is less afraid of the depths in Proust than she is of her own. Something I had not realized, and which is beginning to become clearer, is that while she is trembling, she also feels appeased. She felt a tranquillity come over her the minute Orlanda arrived, and she is conscious that it is not the first time. As soon as Albert left, she once again experienced the tension that has become so familiar to her since the Brasserie de l'Europe. She paced frantically up and down between Constantin Meunier and Molière, biting her lips, her heels striking the parquet floor, when, suddenly, her restlessness abated, she breathed deeply and realized, a second before he rang the bell, that Lucien was there. So, he calms me down? She thought, in front of him, about Jeannine's correlated photons. If we are one and the same person, how can he manage without me? Then, she pulled herself together: Am I going to be less perceptive listening to him than I am when I read *Orlando*? If the truth is in the writing, then it is also in the words he uses: *Whew! It's good to be home!* Home for him is with me. I feel calm before he rings the bell. He comes, and he rings the bell. He's the one who made himself known to me, he can't do without me and won't recognize it. That's his problem.

Then a daunting and brutal thought occurred to her: that puts him at my mercy.

But where is all this leading to? wondered Aline. She could no longer deny that Albert's absence suited her. Fine, I must take things exactly as they are at the moment and allow myself to go with the flow.

"Do you want some coffee?"

"No thank you. I've just had a huge breakfast. Paul Renault makes English breakfast with fried bacon and eggs and mountains of toast and tomatoes that have been plunged in boiling water for a few seconds. I love it."

"Strange! I'm never hungry in the morning."

"Yes, but I'm twenty!"

It was a bit irritating the way he went on and on about his age! Aline tried to sound indulgent: "Of course. As you were thirty-five before you left me, that must be very nice."

"Actually, I wasn't thirty-five like you because I'd never lived my own life. Let's say I was locked up inside you for thirty-five years."

She clung determinedly to her duties as hostess.

"Would you like anything else?"

"A bath!" he retorted enthusiastically. "I love my new life, I'm thrilled with everything, except the bathrooms, which don't always have a bath tub, and when they do, they look as though they've been designed for a midget, sometimes I can barely sit up in them."

"Make yourself at home."

"Thanks a million," he said, laughing.

And, as though it were the most natural thing in the world, Aline and Orlanda went into the bathroom together.

She perched on the edge of the bath and turned on the taps, regulating the temperature with precision, because she knew, of course, exactly how hot it should be, while Orlanda undressed in a leisurely fashion, delighted to be in familiar surroundings. He paused in front of the dressing table: "Christ! It's true, all those beauty products, make-up remover, moisturizer, day cream, night cream, eye contour cream, foundation, mascara, nail varnish, nail varnish remover, what a bind – I'd already forgotten all that!"

"I suppose you shave."

"Yes, but it's a lot less demanding. That reminds me, I didn't have time this morning."

He leaned over and looked in the mirror above the washbasin: "The good thing about being fair is that you don't get a five o'clock shadow. Albert's chin would already be black. I like hairy men, and I'm hairy, I really have been very lucky with Lucien!"

Aline went to get bath towels and a bath-robe from the cupboard. When she turned around, Orlanda was naked, admiring himself in the large, three-sided mirror. The young woman automatically looked away, but he was exclaiming jubilantly:

"Wow! It's the first time I've seen all of me. I'm even more beautiful than I thought! Look at that! What a superb long, straight back, the small of my back is nice and slender and my buttocks slim and taut, and look at the way the sun catches my blond down! I adore my body. I bet you fancy me."

He turned around, giving her a full chance to admire him. He had shied away from Marie-Jeanne's gaze, but he did not have the same relationship with Aline, did he? Orlanda did not feel the least embarrassed by the slight erection that the sight of his many charms produced.

"I'm beautiful, aren't I?"

As they shared an aesthetic sense that had been forged by the same influences, Aline had no option but to nod her agreement.

"But you are also incredibly vain."

"Not at all. You forget, I'm admiring Lucien Lefrène. He's in much better shape than when I took over, that's for sure. He was lacking in confidence, but I had spent too long stymied by your coyness and I wasn't going to make that mistake again. You could be a lot more beautiful than you are, all you need to do is look at yourself objectively, the way I look at Lucien. Because I haven't spent my life inside him, I have no idea of his uncertainties, whereas I was present at the birth of yours. Why the hell should I imitate your qualms, when I've got such a superb body?"

Uncertainty, qualms? He climbed into the bath and immersed himself, while a baffled Aline studied her reflection in the big mirror. She thought she had a fair appreciation of her physical attributes while being aware of her shortcomings, so what was this naked young man talking about? That morning she had put on a pair of grey slacks which suited her very well, she was convinced, and a matching sweater. She looked attractive, but maybe she lacked a certain radiance as she had not put on any make-up. She sat down at the dressing table while Orlanda floated, and reached for the mascara.

Looked attractive? She stopped in mid-gesture: she had thought about her clothes, he about his body. Well, his body? Anyway, she said to herself, let's be honest, I mean I thought about the attire in which I clothe my person, not about the person herself. It's true I know myself inside-out, whereas Lucien – Lucien? he's only Lucien physically, when I think of him, I should almost say *me*! – well, the point *he's* at with the person he inhabits is like getting to know someone you're attracted to. He's right to find him handsome, that I can't deny, but that said, I don't see how I could stand in front of the mirror and get excited about something that is as familiar as a well-worn coat!

Even when she talked to herself, Aline remained prudish. When she said *excited*, she thought of the young man's mild erection.

He admires the back and hips that he's been sporting for a week, I'd do the same with a new dress. Maybe I'm wrong and I've allowed myself to be sucked into a routine? She studied her face carefully. Let's have a look. My eyebrows are well-defined, my eyes . . . what can I say about my eyes? Albert says they've got a charming slant, fine! What about my mouth? Oh! I find this really irritating! I'm not going to go over my features one by one, I know myself, I don't find myself exciting, but anyway, I'm a woman and women don't get excited!

Am I being honest? Orlanda's words of the previous day came back to her: *I disappeared from what you called you as you created me.* An image came into her mind which she realized, a few days earlier, she would have dismissed. Jeannine, all dressed up, ready to go out, spinning round on catching sight of her reflection and saying: "This evening I really am being dreadful! You see, when I look this stunning, I wish I could be a man for an hour to appreciate myself!" Aline had not understood and had not hung around. All the same, she said to herself in front of her dressing table, I have to admit I haven't forgotten. Jeannine found herself attractive, but could not imagine any other way of enjoying herself than turning into a man? I don't think I ever love myself that much. Is Lucien right? am I so obstinately heterosexual that I can't even find myself attractive? She found this idea amusing, and turned round to watch Orlanda who was floating, his face underwater, his eyes closed.

From time to time he had to come up for air, as she did when she immersed herself. He was happy and did not look as if he were ready to curtail his enjoyment. If I put aside my annoyance and try to be honest, I must admit that he is very good-looking, but I'm not used to looking at boys of that age with desire – they're students and I'm a lecturer. Come on! I was twenty once! If it's true that Lucien is made of something that I locked up inside me, then the twenty-year-old me must be in there somewhere, and fancy young men, so it would be quite natural for me to be filled with desire too at the sight of this delightful body. She concentrated: shoulders, taut stomach, long legs with a generous covering of blond hairs. Nothing. At the very most, if she paid careful attention, she was aware that her gaze tended to return to his penis floating gently from side to side in the water, and she remembered how, as a little girl on the beach, she had been so interested in boys' underpants that her mother had scolded her, but oh so very gently! Haven't I changed at all? she asked herself, vaguely irritated.

They are together. What on earth are they going to do together? I am enormously intrigued: here they are, thanks to Régnier's anxiety, facing the prospect of several days' freedom. Orlanda has brought his maths books – does that mean he intends to stay in the apartment? Will Aline let him? Where is the young woman who was so prim and proper that it was astonishing that she allowed a stranger to speak to her in the first place? She is changing quickly, but the adventure befalling her is too unique to think according to the usual criteria. As nothing comparable has ever happened, as far as I know, I am prepared for the unexpected to happen at any time. But I have often seen Aline restlessly pace up and down the apartment, seeking in vain for something she could not articulate, agitated, tense – anyone else would have chewed her nails – and I imagine that she will allow the young man to have his way. Besides, the moment I take my eyes off her to think, there she is in the kitchen, rummaging around in the freezer and contemplating lunch! Soon, Orlanda comes in via the walkway, rubbing his hair. She asks him why he did not use the hairdryer, and he replied that since Paris, he had got out of the habit. What do you expect, he laughed, Lucien Lefrène lived like a pauper, and hoped to grow rich on his savings. She laughed too, then showed him her trophies. She could not make up her mind between a little joint of beef and a roast made of young turkey legs that had been boned, rolled and tied up with string. Orlanda said that Albert was the one who preferred beef and that they liked turkey. He fetched some potatoes from the pantry and began to peel them to make a potato gratin. They joked all the time. I have never seen Aline so light-hearted, so cheerful. She washes a lettuce and now they are reminiscing: mummy's inability to decide whether to have peas or beans with the lamb, Aline's appetite when she was still striding around and when, passing the kitchen, she would shout out: "Do both!" And, do you remember, that time when I twisted my ankle rushing up the stairs, and the other went on: "It was awful, I was going to miss the gym exam!" They could have been, as Aline had got Albert to believe, a brother and sister evoking their childhood, but it was strange because they both said I. When it came to making the salad dressing, Orlanda taught Aline Paul Renault's recipe. You whisk together the mustard and oil, there's a knack to adding the vinegar very carefully. Aline was thrilled and said she thought she knew all there was to know about making a vinaigrette and this made them both giggle hysterically. Orlanda's youthfulness is contagious, he is able to make Aline live the present moment, he has awoken the child in her. She is playful, as though she has suddenly forgotten her character. She is no longer the level-headed woman who goes from one task to the next without dithering, she dances, she leaps around and she flings herself down in the grass and daydreams as she watches the clouds being buffeted by the winds.

* * *

After lunch, Orlanda yawned and announced that he fancied a siesta.

"We've drunk far too much wine," said Aline, astonished at the two empty bottles and a third one that was significantly diminished. We'll keel over."

"So! The bed's not far away."

They lay down side by side under the big duvet and giggled a bit more before falling asleep.

At Roissy, Albert received the depressing confirmation that he was right: Régnier was not a good judge of food.

In avenue Lepoutre, Paul Renault was thinking about Lucien Lefrène. He had no means of getting in touch with him and was perfectly aware that he felt like waiting for him. I have a choice, he said to himself, between giving in to what I've always avoided, waiting, listening for the door bell and the telephone, the ache of disappointment if it's not him, feigning surprise and tempering my delight if he does come, or fleeing. He was so afraid that he did not hesitate. He threw a razor and a shirt into an overnight bag, threw the bag in his car and set off. Paris or Amsterdam? A lorry prevented him briefly from turning left, so it was to be right, and Paris. There were a few young people hitch-hiking on the motorway sliproad. He opened the door to a swarthy youth with such black hair that he assumed him to be of Mediterranean origin, and was surprised to hear a strong Canadian accent as soon as the boy opened his mouth.

Despite the specialists' skills, weaning Madame Lefrène off the bottle had not gone smoothly, and she was fighting for breath in an intensive care unit. Annie, sitting beside her, watched her soul hovering between life and death and thought ruefully of her brother.

* * *

Marie-Jeanne, disgusted that her savings and her sacrifices had not secured her happiness, was also sitting down, but at the hair-dressers' where she was recounting her woes while the stylist employed his talents to change her hair from natural blonde to honey, saying that it was so much sexier.

Georges – or Gérard – dropped by Lucien's flat in rue Malibran for the second time that day and found nobody at home.

*Animula vagula blandula*, each one of us, little wandering souls seeking a share of happiness and always disappointed, as we go from dawn to dawn, our hearts torn, brave and pathetic, desperately trying to behave with the dignity required by our human condition. Clumsy, disconsolate, tenacious, our mistakes teach us nothing about ourselves or about others, and when, rounding a bend in the path, death stares us straight in the face, we stammer, we say it is too soon, that we had nearly succeeded, but death sniggers, replying that we have had all the time we needed, that three seconds more would make no difference, because we never learn. We mistake good manners for morality, our own lies for the truth and life for a fool, after which it carries us off howling to the dismal cauldrons of eternity.

Madame Lefrène died a little short of four o'clock.

Aline awoke first. Orlanda and she had slept in capital V formation, head to head, their feet separated by the full width of the bed, and she felt wonderfully well. She yawned, stretched and went to clear up the kitchen. Orlanda soon joined her.

"I've got work to do," she said. "I've got to mark the students' essays."

"I'll help you, you'll get it done quicker."

"But how could you . . ."

She cut herself short.

"Of course!"

"You'd nearly forgotten again that I am you. Mind you, I think my writing's changed a bit, it's bigger and bolder than yours. But if I'm careful, and control my pen, I should be able to ensure that it's not noticeable. I presume it's a comparison between the two maternal kisses, in *Jean Santeuil* and in *Remembrance*?"

When, a little later, she glanced at what he was doing: "I think you're a bit stricter than me."

"You get softer with age. I still have the implacability of youth which you've allowed experience to erode."

They marked half the essays, then Orlanda stretched, saying that he had had enough and that they would finish them tomorrow.

"What do you want to do?"

"Go cruising," he replied.

And left her on her own.

As decency deters us from following him, we shall have to stay with Aline, but Aline wants to go with him, which she finds rather shocking. Besides, how come she allowed him to sleep at her side, on a bed which, even if she did not wed Albert, is to all intents and purposes their marriage bed? She cannot recognize herself. She would like to appeal to her ordinary nature but seeks it in vain. Where is my sense of propriety, where is my common sense, where are the respectable prejudices that make me a decent woman? But, to my utter amazement, I see that she is smiling. Orlanda's influence really has transformed her! I shall echo her words: where is Madame Berger who was bored with her book at the *Brasserie de l'Europe* and did not hear the subterranean river of hidden thoughts? For a week, it has been flowing above ground, and she is fascinated by it. How does a man go out looking for sex? She thought of Paul Renault, who intrigued her, and remembered Maurice Alker, who only looked at her covertly. She was twenty-five when he died, very suddenly, of liver cancer. If I had seduced him as *he* – she still hated calling him Lucien and I cannot whisper Orlanda to her – claims I could have, it would inevitably have led to marriage. An old friend of the family doesn't approach the daughter unless he intends to marry her, and I would soon have found myself a widow. Would I have finished my degree? I wouldn't have met Albert, as we have no mutual acquaintances, it wasn't until I lived on the same floor as him, and I would have lived in the house in Linkebeek, which I would have inherited. What kind of life would I have made for myself? I suppose I would have married again. She pictured herself with two children, a husband in business, little Chanel suits, and shuddered. Actually, I like my life, she said to herself, amazed because she remembered the perpetual sadness which, a few days earlier, she had still been lamenting to herself. I certainly love literature. She remembered the delight she had taken, on Wednesday evening, in inventing a brother. Maybe one day I'll even write? But that thought seemed too daring to contemplate and she pulled back. She decided to go and see Jacqueline, who was on her own at the moment as her husband was also away on business and so she picked up the phone to call her.

"You've saved me!" said Jacqueline. "Olga is so lost at having to live without her Régnier for a few days that she's invited me to dinner. I avoided the worst by suggesting we go to a restaurant but I was panic-stricken at the idea of a whole evening on my own with her."

"Er . . ." replied Aline.

"Don't try to wriggle out of it! You owe it to me as a friend to be there in my hour of need. She's coming to pick me up at eight. If you come over straight away we'll have a good hour's worth of intelligent conversation to fortify ourselves."

"It's not fair to appeal to my finer feelings to gang up against Olga."

"You're right, but it's very useful!"

* * *

It was past ten o'clock when Orlanda came down from the heavens where he had joyfully been transported and landed on the uneven cobblestones of Brussels. Paul Renault had done well to leave, the ungrateful young man did not think for a moment of walking in the direction of avenue Lepoutre. He dropped into rue Malibran, cautiously, because he feared someone would be waiting for him there, put some toiletries in the overnight bag and left for place Constantin Meunier. He did not need to ring the bell to sense that Aline was not at home, and stopped in the middle of the street, puzzled. Where was she? How could he find her? He found it perfectly natural to stay in the apartment during Albert's absence and it had not occurred to him that Aline, deserted in favour of depravity, would go out. At first he planned to wait for her, she was not in the habit of coming home late, and he stretched out on one of the benches in the square using his bag as a pillow, but he soon felt jittery and jumped up. Where was she? He pondered, did not have the least idea and yet set off as though his body could supply the answer his head could not. A quarter of an hour later, he was watching Olga, Aline and Jacqueline leave the little restaurant where they had had dinner, wish each other good night and make for their cars. He stationed himself near Aline's little Citroën, and she slid behind the wheel pretending not to have noticed him. Olga was a slow, clumsy driver and Aline had to wait until she had driven off.

"You're crazy! I don't want anyone to see you!"

"Even though I'm your brother?" he laughed.

"It's a story I don't want to get around."

Orlanda knew, of course, that Aline's parents and friends hardly ever met. He shrugged.

"When Albert gets back you'll have to find me an official place in your life."

She nodded in silent agreement, enough to make me goggle: so they admit as though it were a foregone conclusion that they will continue to see each other and develop their strange relationship, build it into their day-to-day lives?

"If not your brother, you could say I was your cousin."

"You know full well that mummy and daddy are both only children."

"Impute the crime to your grandfather. I could have gone looking for my roots, exactly as you said when you blamed me on your father, but traced them back to Léon Berger."

They thought of the worthy notary who had led an entirely honourable and respectable life and they both began to giggle uncontrollably.

When they arrived, Orlanda impatiently demanded the keys and ran up the three flights of stairs to rediscover the joy of coming home all the faster. By the time the lift had made its deliberate way up, hindered by the burden of age, and Aline stepped out, the young man had walked in a complete circle round the apartment and was making for the refrigerator.

"Haven't you had dinner?"

"Yes, but it wasn't very good. I was sitting by the window, in a rather boring restaurant, and I was about to tuck into a steak that was clearly overdone, when the sort of man I fancy crossed the street: fortyish, very well dressed, a little bit too sure of himself . . . ah! that type can't resist me! But I was hungry!"

He rummaged energetically: "Haven't you got any cold cuts?"

"Top shelf. They're not unwrapped yet."

"*The lions had not eaten for three days*," he said, finding the bulky packet.

Just as when he had repeated Madame Berger's *You're such a tomboy*, Aline stood there dumbfounded. This iambic pentameter reverberated inside her, awakening distant echoes. *Dishevelled all and wan amidst the storms!* It was the poem that followed *The eye was in the tomb, 'twas fixed on Cain* in the *Légende des siècles* unless there was one that came between the two? The French teacher tended to turn her nose up at Victor Hugo as she found him a bit *infra dig.* and only cared for the symbolists, so she had not asked them to read further than *Conscience*, but Aline had gone to look it up. *The Lions!*

"*The lions in the pit were nearly starved*," she whispered.

"*Their tails sadly whisked their hollow bellies*," continued Orlanda as she admired the slices of cold beef.

The words were coming back to Aline but not their context. What the hell were these lions doing in the den? Daniel? A Christian is thrown to them, *The man addressed them: Peace be with you, beasts!* and the mystical splendour of such a soul makes them forget their hunger. Aline, still irreverent, had laughed to the point of tears. At dinner time, she had come to the table with the beautiful Pléiade edition – Aline, don't get it dirty! – and at each course declared that the lions had not eaten for three days. Her father had laughed, but Marie Berger wondered whether it was proper to make fun of Victor Hugo. Hadn't he been a member of the Académie Française? During the meal, Marie had become increasingly uncomfortable and when Aline got carried away and improvised a sacrilegious ending with hunger winning and Daniel being gobbled up, and here are the wild beasts who *Lift their mighty heads to belch at will, / For these are lions that have had their fill*, Edouard, who was always alert to his wife's sensibilities, had hesitated. Aline described *The shivering moon all pale against the night*, in the same blasphemous vein, but at *God looked at Daniel and observed as follows: 'Tis nothing – all my thunders sound like belches*, he had stepped in to stop the girl.

"Christ!" exclaimed Orlanda, "I was something in those days! *A Titan burping does not sound more dire!*"

"*Nor belching Etna's leaking surplus fire!*"

"So you can imagine my agony faced with the steak! Think of the dilemma my instincts caused me. I had hunger in my belly but my cock had its own agenda. Oh! the terrible struggle between conflicting appetites. If I lingered at the table, I'd miss a wonderful chance, but I'd have to go without dinner if I followed my sexual urge! They are fleeting moments, the soul is torn by titanic forces, it pants, *dishevelled all and wan amid the storms!* It is now or never, you can't feast and fuck both at once, forgive my language – the young man rises up, flayed alive by the storm, and his brow's incandescent from flashes of lightning. Where's the mustard?"

"In its usual place. So which did you choose?"

"I slipped some money under my glass and walked out, steak in hand."

"Don't tell me you went up to the object of your desire chomping on a piece of steak!"

"But a mere hundred yards and the steak was devoured."

He finished making his sandwich, laughing while she made her way towards the bathroom.

"A steak that thin took four mouthfuls to eat, then was I ready for the amorous fray," he said, joining her.

"I hope you're not pretending that was a pentameter, it's simply not on."

"Oh dear, I'm afraid we're both the same, rhythm's our thing, not rhyme."

The bath ran while Aline finished undressing. He sat on the chaise-longue and watched the young woman.

"You are really pretty, you know."

She suddenly switched back into her usual manner: "Come, a little discretion, please!"

Orlanda burst out laughing: "But Aline, I know your body better than the one I'm in. Except from behind, of course, and there I am most agreeably surprised. I had no idea that I had such a long and graceful back, or that natural sway which gives a spring to each step."

She immersed herself in the hot water.

* * *

But where on earth are we? I can picture Aline, standing on the pavement in confusion the first time Orlanda spoke to her, or even this same morning, half shocked when he walked into the apartment and made himself at home, and here she is, naked in the bath while he perches on the side chatting happily as he wolfs down his huge sandwich and she shampoos her hair! And what about Orlanda? Orlanda, who left her in a fury, like a prisoner leaving his gaol, but is constantly seeking her out. A crazy intuition guides him through the streets, right, left, further . . . like hunt-the-thimble where children have to find a hidden object and they are told they are warm if they are near it and cold if they move away. Jeannine never said that correlated photons wanted to get together again. Since they have parted company, they have both changed enormously. Orlanda was expecting it, he welcomed the thought of growing, but it is as if Aline, who was always shrinking, has been liberated. When I consider how she invented a brother, I am stunned. I recall her reserve, she barely dared think. Orlanda leaves her and she thinks uninhibitedly, comes up with a theory for *Orlando* that astonishes Charles and investigates it, ignoring received ideas, whereas before, she had not even been bold enough to develop her comparison between Mme de Guermantes and Mme Verdurin! And worse still, she rinses her hair and then takes a deep breath and immerses herself, knowing he is watching her. She is vaguely perturbed, this morning she looked at his naked body and said: Nothing! almost with pique, now she is fighting a bit – It's me looking at myself! – but this me here is also an attractive young man who is talking to her about her beauty, which, it suddenly occurs to her, she had never even talked to herself about, and she blushes. Conscious she is blushing, she remembers the words that had shocked her: *Yes, you're blushing, and I'm getting a hard-on.* What was going on inside her?

I think I am beginning to understand, and as I had told myself time and time again, it is quite simple: Orlanda contained everything her mother had disapproved of when she was twelve. Today, she is her own judge. On leaving, Orlanda had taken away the terrible *You're such a tomboy!* which had torn her and which he had made his identity. Aline is no longer afraid. She gets out of the bath, laughing, wraps herself in a huge towel and thinks he is right, that she has a lot more charm than she had dared believe. It is one o'clock in the morning, they are sleepy, they will sleep with their heads together, a reconstituted whole that is delighted with itself.

The telephone roused them at ten o'clock. Orlanda automatically stretched out his hand, but Aline rapped his knuckles.

"Not *your* voice," she said.

It was Albert, calling from Hong Kong.

"Were you still asleep?"

"I had dinner with Jacqueline and Olga, and I went to bed very late. How was your journey?"

"As boring as I predicted."

Of course he hadn't had a wink of sleep in the plane. He had been met at the airport by Chinese people in a hurry, they had crossed Hong Kong which was as noisy and crowded as Albert had imagined. Aline could tell Olga there were no more rickshaws.

"It was sheer stupidity to leave on a Saturday! As the bank is closed, and the best time to visit it is when it's busy, but they were so eager to impress us, the cars – three, can you believe it? the Bordiers, Régnier and myself, then our hosts and the interpreters – drove around the masterpiece twice, we had to crane our necks to see just a bit higher than the ground floor, then they took a vast detour to drive over the viaduct which gave us a view of the whole building, we made suitable exclamations of admiration, which were translated immediately. I can tell you how to say 'oh! oh!' and 'ah! ah!' in Chinese."

"Don't be too hard on them!"

"Even better, I'll be generous. We felt we had to comment on the superb way the bank blends in with the urban fabric, the respect for proportions, Bank Street is not dwarfed, etcetera, and you could tell from looking at the façade that all the occupants must enjoy magnificent views over the bay and the port, which I did, because you can't expect the Bordiers to say so, but all I needed to do was look at the plans, I didn't need to risk dislocating my neck or to fly a quarter of the way round the world in a cramped seat designed for someone under five foot five!"

"I adore him!" whispered Orlanda who had edged closer to the receiver.

"You are adorable," said Aline.

"I should hope so, I've been a martyr! Now I'm going to get dressed for dinner: it'll be an intimate affair, just fifteen of us. Cry for me."

"I'll cry my eyes out," promised Aline.

"What a wonderful man!" cried Orlanda when she had hung up. "Although I have no regrets, I do think it's a pity he's only interested in girls."

Aline felt vaguely surprised by this enthusiasm.

The telephone would not leave them in peace. In Ohain, Madame Berger was worried about her daughter alone in town, and, convinced that Aline would be at a loss and need rescuing, called to invite her over for her favourite dish, macaroni cheese.

"But mummy, I was ten years old when that was my favourite!"

"Exactly. It's such a long time since I've cooked it for you!"

Orlanda buried his face in the pillow to stifle his giggles.

"It's very nice of you, but I'm sorry, I'm going over to the Lardinois who had invited us to lunch."

"Without Albert?"

Orlanda groaned.

"I think I can find the way," replied Aline, scarcely able to conceal her annoyance, egged on by the impudent young man.

Marie remained speechless for a moment.

"Yes, of course."

But no invitation was forthcoming and Aline, fearing further phone calls, switched on the answering machine.

"I'll make some coffee."

"No," said Orlanda, "we've got better things to do. Put on a sweater and a pair of trousers. I'm going to take you out for breakfast to one of those big hotels where you find wonderful English breakfasts, with sausages, tomatoes, eggs and bacon. Albert hates going out early in the morning, but we love it."

Aline, surprised and delighted, scrambled into her clothes.

Five minutes later: "Give me your car keys, please. I haven't driven yet since I changed bodies."

When Aline was a little girl, did she dream of dividing herself in half to have a perfect companion? Am I going to be able to recount in detail, as I have done up till now, what goes on between those two – who are in fact one? Suddenly, I sense that the moments dissolve into each other, in a sort of exquisite continuity, everything shines and becomes so powerfully iridescent that I am dazzled, and my eyes fill with tears. I have always been told that you should not gaze at the sun, unless you are wearing very thick-lensed dark glasses. They are running towards the car, borne by the same impulse, they laugh. Are they like lovers at the beginning of an affair or children at the high point of a game? The bond between Aline and Orlanda is so curious! To understand the ties that attach us to each other, we only have a very limited number of models: so me to me? We approve or disapprove of ourselves, we love or hate ourselves, we do not have any more power over ourselves than over others, it is the same struggle that confronts us, victors or vanquished, with our external enemies and our inner contradictions. In the space of a few days, Aline, who struggled violently against Orlanda within her, was won over by his lightheartedness and impudence. She used to be sad, and now she is laughing, oblivious to her mother's agitation at her going out without Albert. Perhaps the explanation is very simple: she had bowed to Madame Berger's wishes without realizing it, and when Orlanda told her, she abandoned an attitude that seemed anachronistic, since it was for her future that her mother feared and that future had become a very enjoyable present. But that is terrible! Are our lives ruled by unspoken laws which surreptitiously restrict us? Suddenly confronted with a part of herself that she did not know, she hesitates briefly, finds it to her liking and joyfully adopts it? Are our principles, our rules, our convictions, everything we believed to be governed by reason, only the product of obsolete docility? If Aline had Orlanda inside her, do I have a whore, a swindler and a murderer inside me? Look at her, a respectable young woman, a professional devoted to her job, who is rushing off to eat pancakes and bacon beside a thief of souls, with whom she slept last night. Who knows what he gets up to in the sleazy districts where his lust takes him? She was touchingly honest, and now she cannot stop lying, and the man summoned by duty to the other side of the world does not know there was someone in his bed last night. All perfectly innocent, some people will say, which I dispute, for I believe that the meeting of souls is more culpable than that of bodies. But Orlanda is Aline, and don't I sleep in the arms of my monsters every night? I'm losing the thread. I must not try to understand but allow myself to be swept along by what they are experiencing.

What is this thing called love that is supposed to be forever? *Ich Tristan, du Isolde*, I am you and you are me. At every moment, you will give me what I need, you speak and it is what I wanted to hear, I joke when you felt like laughing, we are driven by the same desire. You reassure me just as I was about to feel afraid, my hand holds out a glass of cold water and you discover you are thirsty, a perfect harmony is established between us. I have heard musicians say that they do not like playing or singing in unison. I suppose it is because you find yourself on a parallel course without ever meeting, it is not a dialogue. Love can only happen when there is a difference which it then constantly seeks to eliminate. Aline and Orlanda, split but not identical, otherwise they would say the same thing at the same time and would no longer hear each other speak, but each of them knows what the other likes, because it is what they like too. The fear and anger gone, they encounter the joy of the perfect response. Oh! To have no desire that does not find a reverberation in your soul, no longer to fear being unfulfilled, to allow the infinite range of your aspirations to unfold, is to bask in heaven, but to live thus for three days would make coming back down to earth again unbearable! How would it be possible to put up with your own repression once again, the clumsy kind intentions of reality, I am happy at a moment when you are sad, I offer you ambrosia and you wanted soup, *Let me make this clear to you /When I'm asking you for nectar, /Minestrone will not do.* I say it is nice because I know you wanted to please me, we limp from one mistake to the next, I'm sorry, I thought that, but no, darling, it's perfect, and when it goes on for an entire lifetime, without breaking down, we say that it is happiness, pathetic humans that we are, condemned never to see into the soul of another, and, at best, interpreters of an enigmatic smile, alert for revealing looks, keen to please, skilful at hiding disappointment, unfair, infirm, hurtful, loving.

But these two are dancing on air, they wing their way through innocent games. At the Flea Market, where Aline buys a tarnished silver leg of mutton holder, Orlanda's eagle eye spots the hallmark that makes it valuable. At the Marché du Midi which specializes in spices and fabrics that Aline always yearns for, I'll buy some to make some curtains for my new flat, says Orlanda, they look at everything and hang around until the end when the stall-holders knock down the prices. They return to the car with kilos of fruit and vegetables cutting into their shoulders. Aline automatically takes the wheel again and while they are driving up rue Théodore Verhaegen,

Orlanda suddenly swears, leans forward and tries to slide to the floor and hide.

"It's Marie-Jeanne," he gasps, panic-stricken. "She must live around here!"

The street is full of people.

"Where is she? Which one is she?" asks Aline.

"She's blonde. To the right."

Aline looks at the girl walking up the street carrying a small package. We must not forget she now has curly, honey-blonde hair, and is hard to miss. As she has given up saving her money, she is no longer squeezed into the tight imitation leather skirt, but is wearing a long, attractive light beige jersey skirt which Aline rather likes.

"She's not so bad."

"You must be kidding! She wants to go to bed with me."

"You must admit it's rather strange that being a boy, you find girls so repulsive!"

"Can I sit up now?"

"We're way past her. I don't understand how you can be so lacking in curiosity. It must be very different."

"It probably is, but I don't find them attractive. For the time being, I'm making up for your twenty years of repression. You were so demanding and hard to please. When you liked a man, you generally tried your utmost to pretend to be unaware of the fact, and if you didn't manage to delude yourself, you created so many obstacles. Before Albert you just about had three lovers and I had to keep quiet while you turned down Jean, who was charming, Louis, whom I liked a lot, Antoine, Octave, Julien, Jean-Pierre and Jean-Jacques, Edouard and the rest."

Aline interrupted him laughing:

"Stop! I couldn't imagine myself in the arms of a boy who had the same name as my father!"

"Rubbish, daddy's very sexy, it's just that you've never noticed!

He's well-built with grey hair and beautiful gnarled hands!"

"Calm down! We live in a civilization where incest is forbidden."

"More's the pity! But all your repressed desires went into me. You have no idea of the dynamite you made me carry. Unfortunately, it's now too late for some of them. Julien is in Australia, Antoine has grown fat and Jean-Jacques ended up semi-paralysed after his car crash."

"Anyway, I'd like to point out that their interest in me showed that they were straight heterosexuals!"

"There are depths to their souls, my dear Aline, of which you in your innocence have no idea."

*There are more things in heaven and earth, Horatio ...*

They finished the phrase in chorus, amid gales of laughter. They are about to arrive at the apartment and carry up the kilos of provisions. While Aline puts the vegetables away in the fridge, Orlanda will pile the fruit artistically in various bowls and place them on the tables, then he will be hungry and Aline will throw up her arms and say that at this rate he will soon be obese, but he knows he won't, at twenty, you can do anything you like, don't you remember, you used to eat like a horse and you were as thin as a rake, and that makes them laugh too, because everything makes them laugh, they laugh non-stop, they are drunk, they are having fun, they are happy.

On Saturday, Orlanda went off cruising, but on the Sunday and the Monday they stayed together. They had siestas, they went to the cinema, they ate sandwiches wandering around the Grand-Place like Japanese tourists. Orlanda pointed out to the astonished Aline all the men who looked at her and the ones he was missing out on to stay with her. They went to bed late, Aline remembered to switch off the answering machine to pick up Albert's call which dragged them from their sleep at ten o'clock.

"Am I waking you up again?"

"I read till very late."

"Your life goes haywire when I'm not there!"

He told her about the dinner: all their hosts spoke English, but knew that their accent made it impossible for Europeans to understand them and the conversations were systematically translated by an interpreter, which made them exhausting. He was jet-lagged and although he was feeling ill with exhaustion, Albert slept badly. At eight o'clock they had been driven to the Hong Kong Bank where an unimpressive breakfast awaited them.

"It's a strange place, fairly crazy, there are thousands of people carrying out thousands of tasks in front of thousands of computers. In fact, if you walk up an ordinary street, the same thing is happening in all the offices, but you can't see it. Here, the walls and roofs have been removed and everything is visible, only it's an illusion, you don't know any more about what's going on, you're faced with appearances that do not reveal their contents, masses of people sitting at masses of desks and masses of other people come and talk to them. As it's a bank, one imagines that capital is flowing in all directions, according to laws that only the initiated understand, and will accumulate in mysterious places having fed the thousands of industrious ants a few crumbs in the meantime."

"Sounds like hell!"

"The Bordiers adored everything they saw. They think this trip was vital. They now have absolute confidence, we'll be able to do whatever we like, they'll sign the contract without batting an eyelid. In a way, it's not such a bad thing, I think Régnier has come round."

He would not be phoning her the next day as his plane left quite early.

"I'll be home on Wednesday, late morning."

"Then I'll come home as soon as my class is over. We can have lunch together."

"Go back to sleep. And go to bed at a reasonable time tonight."

Faced with Aline on this Easter Monday, I must not think of the sensible woman drinking her mineral water opposite the Gare du Nord, or I too will sink into chaos. Let us be the impartial and puzzled historian, remaining faithful to the facts, the impassive reporter, the witness. Yawning chasms have opened up inside Aline. Her folly is in living for the moment as if there were no future, conscious that Albert will be home in two days. She is happy, but has not taken the time to tell herself so, for she feels somehow, I think, that she might be frightened. The strange identity of the young man who sleeps, laughs and plays beside her does not worry her any more, she is won over by his twelve years, she puts off until tomorrow what she could worry about today. But tomorrow always comes so quickly when you don't want it to! It is impatience that makes time drag, and Albert is already back with Aline.

He had found a way of giving the Bordiers the slip for two hours to buy some lengths of gorgeous pale-coloured silks and some of those fake antique objects made in big cities to delude tourists into believing they have travelled in another century. Aline draped herself in the fabric, Albert joyously threw his arms around her and consummated his homecoming.

Later: "What about this brother of yours? Have you seen your newly-acquired brother?"

Aline who had thought of nothing, thought very fast. She saw that she could not avoid introducing him.

"He's coming to dinner next week."

She had not arranged it with Orlanda, but she was sure she would see him in the meantime.

"Are you still convinced of his innocence?"

"What evil designs could he have?"

"I don't know. I'm not the right man to speculate on evil designs, but I've just spent four days with Régnier who is paranoid about everything and it's contagious. After all, your father, who appears to be his too, is not exactly short of money. Maybe he wants to get his hands on a share of the inheritance?"

"But that's no problem! It goes without saying that, when the time comes, I won't take what he is entitled to. As the son, he has as much right as I do, as the daughter."

Once again, she was so convinced by her story that she was not aware that she was making it up. Actually, she said to herself, if he is part of me, it's true that he is entitled to what I own! Would I leave that excellent half of myself penniless? And can I claim he is not my father's son? His biological body isn't, but his mind is. These ideas made her laugh, she promised to laugh about them with Lucien. He had already spent so much of the savings he had stolen that he would do well to start worrying about his future. He can relax. Guaranteeing her younger brother's future is a sister's duty, I shan't let him down.

Lunch over, the suitcase unpacked and its contents put away, Albert, who could not stop yawning but knew that you don't get over jet lag by sleeping at odd times, suggested a walk as he hoped that the fresh air and exercise would keep him awake. So they set out for the woods. They had barely left place Constantin Meunier when Aline felt a mounting tension which this time she recognized. It was the blind impulse that had made her rush out of the apartment the other Sunday. I miss him, she said to herself. We parted this morning and I'm already missing him! She thought she would probably see him at lunch time the next day, but the evening, the night and the morning felt endless, like stretches of unbroken desert, and her heart sank. But there's no way I can make my life with him!

Paul Renault had come back on Monday evening, thrilled with his young Canadian and convinced he was no longer thinking about Lucien, congratulating himself every ten minutes for putting him out of his mind. He slept well, worked calmly, did not come home for dinner as he was going to a concert, and went to bed well pleased with himself. His heart missed a beat when the bell, which he pretended he was not waiting for, rang on Wednesday at seven o'clock.

"Did you have a good weekend?" he asked calmly.

"Wonderful. I was with my family," replied Orlanda, mentally bowing to Aline.

If he is well brought-up and claims to have no long-term ambitions, the lover of a young man does not question him about his family.

"I went to Paris to see some exhibitions."

He had already realized that a Canadian fling, even with a boy who was as stocky and hairy as a Mediterranean, paled in comparison with the ambiguous charm of the delightful Lucien.

Separated for the first time after four nights lying head to head, Aline and Orlanda slept badly. One immediately understood why, got up and paced up and down, while the other was astonished and wondered whether he had eaten something that had disagreed with him and, at one o'clock in the morning, left his companion's bed. He took his clothes into the living room and got dressed. But where could he go in the middle of the night? Rue Malibran made him shudder, he could not move into his new flat until the following Monday and he did not like the idea of going to a hotel one little bit. He went out all the same, and the minute he was outside, he found himself completely at a loss. Why didn't I stay? He sighed, and felt his feet being drawn towards place Constantin Meunier, but Albert was there, in his place, in his bed! He tried to laugh at himself, and was forced to admit that he felt as wretched as a child lost in a strange city and was horrified. Wasn't he the happiest of fugitives? Was he going to be defeated by . . . by what? The thought had been so fleeting that he had not had time to grasp it; nothing remained but a trail of confusion.

But he could not stay there, standing forlornly on the pavement, he would have to go to a hotel or sleep in the street. He pictured himself stretched out on a bench in the square at Aline's feet, like a transfixed lover, and realized that he was on the move.

Aline drifted from the huge living room to the dining room asking herself where their madness would lead.

Orlanda walked faster and faster, driven by an irrepressible fury.

She stationed herself at the window, her eyes glued to the corner of rue Rodenbach and the square. I suppose I'm waiting for him, she said to herself, and, to her amazement, she saw him arrive at a run. She took a deep breath. How long had she been holding her breath? Orlanda advanced, looking up towards the third floor. Aline opened the window and leaned out. He stopped, saw her, the night was so calm and the area so quiet that the young man's whispers reached her ears without any difficulty: "I don't know where to go!"

"Come in," she said, and ran to the hall on the Molière side, to press the buzzer to let him in.

Orlanda entered the building and climbed noiselessly up the stairs. Aline went down, and they met half-way. Aline checked the impulse that propelled her towards the young man and they stood there facing each other, both equally surprised.

"You can't stay here," she said.

He groaned.

"I know! I didn't even mean to come here."

The light went out. Aline went back up a few steps and groped around for the time switch. They looked at each other in alarm.

"I don't want to go to rue Malibran."

"Then you'll have to go to a hotel."

She kept her hand on the switch, he joined her. They were so agitated, so disconcerted, that neither of them was able to think clearly, so they acted. Aline proffered her forehead, Orlanda bowed his head. As soon as they touched, they became calm and able to think again.

"I'm going to sleep at a hotel, that's obvious," he said. "But I needed . . ."

He stopped in mid-sentence. They did not need to speak, each drew sustenance from the other, quiet descended over them. They remained thus for a time, neither could say how long, allowing the tenderness to fill them, and their identity to reconstitute itself. Then they drew apart and smiled. Aline went back upstairs and Orlanda left, and they both fell into a peaceful sleep.

Aline awoke feeling fresh and in good form. She ate a hearty breakfast, left in excellent spirits and only thought of Orlanda on passing the old, noble residences on avenue Winston Churchill. He had told her about his visit but she did not know precisely where the amazing library was. She was filled with a sensation of sweetness that was so exquisite and so tangible that she smiled. I must have had a nice dream, she said to herself. Then she saw herself on the stairs, her forehead pressed to Orlanda's, she had pushed the time switch several times. It took her a while to realize that it had not been a dream.

In his hotel room, the young man emerged slowly from a delightful sleep. He promised himself he would not go back to rue Malibran until the following Sunday, to pack his bags. For a few days he would live a nomadic existence, then he would settle down. A van would collect his bed with its new mattress, he would scour the junk shops to find a table and a wardrobe, he listed the essentials, electric cooker, saucepans, cutlery and kitchen knives. When Aline had set up house, fifteen years earlier, she had allowed Marie to provide everything a Berger daughter needed, silverware from one grandmother, household linen from another. Orlanda, who had nothing, was going to choose everything. That would really make a dent in Lucien Lefrène's savings! I'm going to have to earn some money, he said to himself, and smiled shamelessly as he thought of the solution that Paul Renault had unwittingly suggested. Putting his body at the service of mathematics seemed to him so exquisitely indecent that he set out to celebrate his new identity once again without delay.

* * *

Poor Lucien's savings make me think of Annie. Madame Lefrène died on Saturday, and with Easter Monday having delayed everything, today was her funeral. Despite Gérard's efforts, they had been unable to find her son, he had not been informed, and Annie would have been alone at the cemetery if Marie-Jeanne had not been sympathetic enough to accompany her. It was drizzling. Annie held herself upright, she did not cry. Orlanda, in taking over Lucien, had stolen the brother from the sister and the lover from Marie-Jeanne. He was unaware that he caused Madame Lefrène's death, and it would not affect him if he knew, he would probably congratulate himself for releasing poor Annie. He would be mistaken. The destiny of daughters burdened with an impossible mother is tragic. When they manage to develop a healthy indifference, people say they are heartless, and when they are devoted, people say they are masochists. Annie, imprisoned in the guilt of loathing a loathsome mother will not be saved by her death, she will dedicate herself to the sick and if we drop by in twenty years' time, we will find her unmarried, selfless and insomniac, living on a meagre income and trembling nervously when she sees a bottle of whisky.

"You should see an analyst!" a friend will say.

"On my salary!"

For women devoted to the good of others never seem to worry about themselves. Their life is ascetic, their generosity boundless, day after day their altruism devours them and sometimes they sink into depression. Then they are found dead holding an empty barbiturate bottle. They have missed out on life, events have passed them by, and one day the boredom that can blot out everything else gets the better of their heroism. It is dangerous to be good.

No such danger threatened Orlanda, that is certain. He had no idea where the danger was to come from.

Aline was going through a difficult time. Apart from the chore of listening to Duchâtel's complaints, the obligations that took up her time had never bothered her as her soul was not in turmoil. Suddenly, she discovered the withdrawal symptoms so familiar to drug addicts and, sober as she was, did not immediately understand what was troubling her. She walked into the lecture theatre where she was teaching and started trembling nervously, she shivered by the radiators and came out in a cold sweat. But she was a brave fighter, which no longer surprises me, and, gritting her teeth, she launched into the attack only groaning inwardly. Orlanda, docile only when it pleased him, was able to alleviate his impatience by going off cruising, but the respectable Aline had only her sense of duty. She thought she was going to pass out several times, people commented on her pallor, everyone fussed over her:

"You look tired."

"I'm looking forward to the holidays."

What would be the use of the holidays?

She was feeling at her lowest ebb, when Orlanda appeared at lunch time with the sandwiches, and she felt fine. For each of them, the other was a drug. They rushed to press their foreheads together, which calmed them and transformed them into Siamese twins, one head and two bodies, and completeness.

On the Thursday, he insisted on hearing every detail of Albert's trip.

"You're not telling it very well, you've forgotten some of it! You should have asked him more about this business of the view. Can you really see the sea from everywhere, or is it one of those lies people tell to impress?"

"Why the hell are you so interested in that?"

"I don't know, I'm curious, that's all."

"It sounds as though you're obsessed with Albert."

"Well I am! Don't forget, when I was still you, I lived with him for more than ten years. I find him attractive, I sometimes wonder whether I don't find him more attractive than you do!"

He became pensive and Aline was embarrassed.

"Going back to the view, I'll ask him if you like," she volunteered, to cover her awkwardness.

Orlanda laughed softly: "What a pity – I know him so well and yet I'm so certain I wouldn't be able to seduce him!"

She felt ill at ease when he spoke of his sexual preferences: "But they are yours, my dear Aline! My attraction to Albert is yours, which you repress as you repress me. I really don't understand why you feel embarrassed about it, you live with him, with him you could at least let yourself follow your nature. Or rather mine, which is no longer in you. Sometimes I get in a muddle! I shock you when I say that daddy is a very desirable man. I suppose it's mummy's modesty that paralyses you, you've never dared admit that she finds him very much to her taste."

"I hate you when you talk to me like that!"

"Of course. But you're not throwing me out. You can smell the odour of truth, you're both scared and intrigued."

"You're so irritating!"

But she could not live without him.

"Of course I irritate you," he replied jauntily, "that's how you made me, in every sense of the word. You created me out of irritation and the things that irritated you!"

That made her laugh.

They quarrelled for a few minutes, and each time Orlanda's sunny nature got the better of Aline's ill humour.

"Why are you so relaxed? Why don't you have any anxieties, if you come from me?"

"You should ask Jacqueline that sort of thing."

"She'd have me locked up."

Aline wondered how much longer the young man's visits would go unnoticed. Sometimes the melancholy Duchâtel would join her at break to tell her every detail of his worries. What would he think of a tousle-headed youth who was not a student?

"Hey! I'm your brother!"

"That's an invention that will only work with Albert. He knows I don't tell lies."

"You don't tell lies to others. I'm the living proof that you have lied a lot to yourself."

He left happy, to go and bury himself in his maths books, and Aline went back to work, calm for a few hours.

On Friday: "When are we going to see your brother?" asked Albert.

She had put the matter out of her mind. She shuddered, and hurriedly tried to regain her composure.

"He phoned me at work yesterday, I forgot to tell you. I suggested next Tuesday."

And that Tuesday immediately began to represent a dangerous boundary that was impossible to cross.

"It won't work," she said to Orlanda. "When he sees us together, he'll sense something."

"Why on earth should he? I'll behave myself. I promise I'll be very formal and polite."

She shook her head.

"You're too naive. We don't act like two people who've only just met."

"Of course not!"

"There's an intimacy that he will be aware of."

"He doesn't get jealous."

"He's never been jealous because he's never seen me behaving intimately with a man. He'll think you're my lover."

"I'll take him aside and confess my vice to him. Maybe that'll give him something to fantasize about."

He explained what kind of fantasy he wanted to provoke, which made Aline rap him on the knuckles.

They had seen each other on the Wednesday, in the middle of the night, and on the Thursday at lunch time, but not in the evening, because Albert, who had at last recovered, felt like eating out, and poor Aline, stretched to the limit, found it terribly difficult to be as pleasant, chatty and smiling as was required of her. It was nearly midnight when, on returning to place Constantin Meunier, she saw Orlanda waiting for her, sitting on the worst-lit bench in the square. She began to tremble with impatience and suddenly developed all the cunning of an artful drug addict. She left her handbag in the car, pretended not to notice until she got upstairs, grabbed the keys from the astonished Albert and dived down the stairs before the gallantry of this well brought-up man could stop her. Orlanda was waiting for her at the door. She flung herself at him and for a few seconds they remained pressed together. It is true, an onlooker would have taken them for lovers, but the close contact of their bodies was not important, only their foreheads sought each other. For a few seconds they tasted their new-found oneness, their breathless craving was satisfied, they smiled, Aline walked to the car, retrieved her handbag and went back upstairs.

It's impossible, she said to herself over and over again as she fell asleep, it's impossible. We can't go on living like this, someone will see us, and who will believe in something that is insane?

"I didn't even check whether the nosy neighbour was out walking his dog!" she told Orlanda, that Friday lunch time.

"OK, so you'll remember next time."

"And what about Duchâtel? Not a week goes by without him bursting into my office!"

She paced up and down between the table and the cupboard, wringing her hands.

"Calm down, you're a pathetic sight."

That evening, she walked in just as Albert was leaving a message on the answering machine. He had to work late to finish a plan and would go straight on to his meeting without coming home first. She telephoned Orlanda's hotel at once, but the young man had just left. Was he coming? Could he sense that Albert wasn't there? She began to tremble.

I must get a grip on myself, she said to herself, I manage it when I'm not on my own. She gritted her teeth, then remembered that it was a good idea to breathe deeply to help you relax, but she was not able to, every breath ended in a sort of nervous sob. A hot bath! I'll run myself a scalding bath! She ran to the bathroom, turned on the taps, sat down at the dressing table to remove her make-up and looked at herself in the mirror: she was ashen-faced, with dark circles under her eyes, she looked drawn and there was a wild look about her.

"A junkie! I look like a junkie!"

She was terrified. I must think. But all she could come up with was to hear Jacqueline saying, one evening when they were chatting, that a drug addict suffering withdrawal did not think but just had to find drugs. She gnashed her teeth: where's my drug? What's he doing? The week before, she had asked him how he had found her at the restaurant: "I don't know," had been the answer. "Something guided me, I turned right, it didn't feel right, I turned left, I felt calm."

*I don't know!* Half the time, when I ask him a question, he answers that he doesn't know!

She pulled out the plug, and slipped into a pair of trousers and a sweater. He doesn't know how he left me, and he probably doesn't know how he could get back either!

How he could get back?

She stood stock still, staring. Get back? He would never want to come back, that's certain, he's free, he's enjoying himself. If he sees me twice a day, he's happy, he's enjoying this life and he doesn't want to change it. Later on, when he's finished having fun, he'll drop by here, he won't be anxious, he'll wait patiently for me to find a way to join him. It won't occur to him that I can't make up a different story every evening, Albert will end up suspecting something, he's no fool. I can hear him already: Well, leave Albert! What a monster. I shouldn't be surprised, he's told me often enough, he's made of all the bits of me I didn't want. So why is it that I can't do without him? If I didn't want what he is, why aren't I delighted to be rid of him and what's stopping me from enjoying a clean conscience in peace? My soul aches in the way amputees feel phantom pains in their missing limbs. In my brain there are nerve endings that are suffering from the loss. Apparently I'm missing him more than he's missing me, but I had his departure inflicted on me, he wanted it, the novelty of his condition gives him infinite pleasure while I have to carry on with my everyday life around a hole which I feel in constant danger of falling into. He won't come back of his own accord, that's for certain.

But here she is, thinking! No! I can hear Jacqueline: she's thinking about her drug.

She had busied herself again and was going out, after leaving a note on the hall table: I couldn't sleep, so I've gone out for a walk, for she was afraid Albert would be back before her.

This is madness, she repeated, as she went down the stairs. At the bottom, she hesitated: right or left? Would the strange intuition that guided the young man direct her? As she felt nothing, she went straight ahead. At the end of the square, she had to choose between avenue Molière and rue Rodenbach. A few steps down avenue Molière and she felt an uneasiness that stopped as soon as she turned towards Rodenbach. She tried valiantly to joke: and I don't even like Rodenbach's novels! and followed the needle of this curious compass which guided her from street to street. She reached the end of rue Berkendael when she realized she was heading for avenue Lepoutre.

So, he was at Paul Renault's place.

Paul had abandoned the attempts at self-deception which no longer convinced him: every evening, he waited for Lucien, and Lucien came. I am mad, he said to himself, and realized with despair that he was happy. The young man's impulses had a passion, a violence, that deeply perturbed poor Paul. It is hard to fight against happiness, and this sunny young man who arrived unannounced sought pleasure with utter simplicity and got carried away speaking of Pythagoras's theorem, swept aside all the prejudices of a man who believed himself to be informed about the world he lived in – and enchanted him. Orlanda was not a hypocrite, I think that if he had realized the misunderstanding he had created, he would have warned Paul, but he had no idea, he still saw him as a seductive forty-year-old who did not want a lasting relationship and, glad to receive a warm welcome, he did not see love blossoming before his eyes.

But he left every night and still would not say where he could be contacted, which was beginning to make Paul unhappy. On the Wednesday, the two lovers had fallen asleep side by side, and at dawn, Paul had been surprised to find himself alone. On the Thursday evening, when he saw the boy rise and get dressed at around eleven o'clock, he wanted to question him, but refrained, as a matter of principle, but on the Friday, it was only ten o'clock when Lucien announced that he was leaving. Paul found it hard to suppress the "Already?" full of regret that came to his lips. He also held back a "Will you be coming tomorrow?" which would have sounded like an entreaty.

As he left the room, Orlanda turned round: "Would you like me to come tomorrow?"

"I'd love you to."

Stated politely, these true words sounded like a lie.

Why on earth doesn't he stay? What is this haste propelling him towards Aline? The week before he spent the night and even a whole day at Paul Renault's, so why are things different? Sadly, the answer is all too simple: morphine, glory or perversion, people become addicted to whatever gives them pleasure. Orlanda could manage without the joining of foreheads while he had not experienced it, but the nights spent in a capital V in Albert's big bed had created a craving and as soon as his puppy-like appetite for sex was satisfied, he ran to Aline. So he was unaware of the grief-stricken look that followed him. Paul bit his tongue to stop himself calling him back, he told himself at length how stupid it was to allow himself to grow fond of someone he knew nothing about and, as his heart was sinking and he saw the hideous spectre of suffering looming, he took a sleeping pill.

Aline had been there for an hour. On arriving at the apartment block, she had remembered Lucien, sitting on the steps in rue de Florence, and sighed. She leaned against the wall, in the shadow of the big entrance door, and began her vigil. The tension was not so powerful, but the young woman sensed that if she were to move a few metres away, the pain would erupt again. I'm in a bind, she said to herself, for she could see with absolute clarity what would happen. Every lunch time he would come to her office and, soon, Duchâtel would walk in suffering a bout of neurosis and eye this unknown visitor with curiosity.

"He's my brother."

"I see. You don't look alike."

She let out a little groan, a mixture of fear and anger. The coming Tuesday would be no better: before a quarter of an hour had elapsed, Albert would be taking her to one side and asking for an explanation. She saw her life falling apart and felt desperate. And yet, she said to herself, last week, when I came back from Paris, I was utterly wretched. I thought that I was always sad and that would never change. I'm not sad any more! I'm perturbed, furious, tense – or happy when he's there. I no longer trail around that feeling of misery that was ruining my life. The truth is that I don't want to go back to what I was before, when, according to what he says, I spent my time repressing and crushing him. But at this rate, I'm heading for disaster! She wanted to be angry at herself for having agreed to speak to him, to see him and to see him again, but, like Paul Renault, was aware of the pointlessness of recriminations when it is too late and sighed again. If he only exists because I made him, how can I unmake him? I'd have to go back to being twelve and begin all over again, I'm stuck in the here and now and I can't live without Lucien.

Lucien! That stolen name was truly irritating. She tried, as I did, to find something else, but didn't because she stopped: it's not a matter of finding a name that I like, but of saving myself, and I don't see how I can do that. It's obvious I am quite incapable of breaking off this dangerous relationship. God! Just look at me at the moment, my hair crammed under a black woollen hat, disguised by a jacket that's too big for me, petrified that someone will recognize me and incapable of going back to the nice apartment I live in and spending a pleasant evening reading on the bed and drinking fruit juice! How long have I got until the whole thing blows up in my face?

She was well aware that these thoughts – if you can call the hiccups of this tormented soul thoughts – were the thin layer of ice between the reckless skater and drowning, and that she was teetering on the edge of an abyss, distracting herself as best she could, the only truth being the wait for Orlanda and the moment when she plunged with him – into him – to swim deliciously in the mysterious waters where they could only go together, intoxicated by the mortal delights of being reunited again.

Twice the door opened: a lady taking her dog for a walk, and a young girl rushing off for a date, but Aline did not need to look to know that it was not him. Nobody noticed her, huddled motionless in the shadows holding her breath.

At last he arrived and walked straight towards her, took her in his arms and they moaned with relief.

Five minutes later, as they walked in the direction of place Constantin Meunier:

"I wasn't very nice to Paul," said Orlanda grumpily.

"Why not?"

"I was impatient, I left him rather suddenly. He was expecting me to stay."

"Go back," she suggested, with the generosity of a sated child unable to imagine that she will soon be hungry again.

"No, he wouldn't understand. I'm very fond of him, but I don't want any ties. You kept me too tightly chained, I want to stay free, and above all, not to become faithful. I've already thought of not going there any more, but I don't want to deprive myself of something I like."

He kicked a loose stone in aggravation.

"There's no way out," said Aline.

"That's right, laugh!"

"You like him, he wants to love you, I don't see the problem."

"In no time at all, I'd find myself like you, stable and depressed."

"I'm not depressed," she retorted, in perfect bad faith.

"You aren't any more, thanks to me. I've added the spice that was missing from your life. For ten years, you haven't made love with Albert because you enjoy it, but because he's there. Your fidelity is worthless, you're only faithful out of habit, emulating your mother, her mother, and her mother's mother."

"You come from those same women!"

"I reject them. I like men. You suppressed your liking for men along with everything else that mummy didn't approve of, which is fine as far as I'm concerned. You could have been what I am, but you didn't want to."

He began to laugh.

"Thanks a million! It's a great improvement on poor old Lucien who had no character but a pretty little face and curly hair!"

"You are outrageously impudent, and you'd do well to remember it. I don't know exactly what you do with your men, and I don't want to know, as you can imagine, because you know me inside out, but if you carry on like this, you'll end up getting AIDS."

"Don't be stupid! I only sleep with very respectable gentlemen."

"Everyone knows that the virus is afraid of a suit and tie!"

She thought it best to part company with Orlanda as soon as they reached rue Rodenbach. She was very relieved to see that Albert was not back yet. She threw away the note and quickly got into bed.

I'm saved this evening. But what about tomorrow?

And what about Sunday?

A shudder ran through her. The drawings would be finished, Albert would not go to the office, on Saturday they would both go to dinner at Jacqueline's to celebrate her husband's return, they would be home late, and in the morning Albert would want to go for a walk and she might have to go to Ohain. When would she see Lucien?

It was impossible to wait until Monday, and it was impossible to escape from a life that was so well ordered that there was no opportunity for a secret rendezvous. And even if she found some pretext this time, what would she do the following week? She could hear Orlanda once again saying: Well, leave Albert! and saw in a flash the life she would have: her friends, shocked at a break-up they would not be able to understand, would turn their backs on her in support of the unfortunate Albert. She would go and live on her own, unless the boy were to decide that they would live together. She would wait for him to return from his debauchery and would grow old and bitter.

She sat up in bed without putting the light on, staring into the darkness while a furious NO! welled up inside her. It would not be like that, she thought, closing her mind to the strange resolutions forming in the depths of her half-soul.

After leaving Aline, Orlanda felt so disgusted at the idea of returning to his cheap hotel that he even considered going back to rue Malibran to sleep. There's no danger of anyone coming to visit me at this hour, he said to reassure himself, but a shudder of revulsion warned him that he was not being realistic. Marie-Jeanne probably did not work on Saturday mornings and Annie would want to give him news of his mother. He imagined them turning up at dawn, the one in love and the other angry, groaned and set off in the direction of avenue Lepoutre.

Paul was not asleep. He was in the sitting room, listening to the Schumann concerto, without noticing that, since the concert where he had met Lucien, he listened to practically nothing else. The doorbell made him jump, and, during the few seconds it took Orlanda to climb the stairs, Paul thought of, considered and rejected ten different greetings, all inappropriate, so that when he opened the door, he just stared at the young man in silence.

"You must think I don't know what I'm doing."

Paul shook his head. "I don't think anything."

And this man, who exercised such rigid self-control, made a huge effort: "I'm glad you're here."

For he had the feeling that, even if he did not understand a thing, this return was something to celebrate.

His usual reaction would have been to try and fathom these strange comings and goings. In his business dealings, he often had to discover his customers' motives, he was skilful at a certain game of subtle questioning, of beating around the bush so discreetly that eventually the bush emerged quite clearly. Certainly a boy of twenty would be completely taken in and would reveal everything. He balked at the prospect – playing this game would be dishonest. We know that he would not have discovered the truth and that he would not have believed it if Orlanda had told him: but that should not stop us from acknowledging the sensitivity of his sacrifice. He was moved by Lucien's naturalness, which allowed the floundering of his soul to show through, he wanted to be worthy of what he perceived as trust and, in this gesture which was no longer that of a libertine, he did not see the collapse of all the barriers that he had so meticulously constructed. This impulsive return convinced Paul of a genuine simplicity: whatever the reason for his leaving, Lucien had come back because he wanted to. He preferred Paul to anything else. He told himself he did not have the right to discover what it was through artfulness, and that Lucien would tell him when he was ready. He thought that, if he had to suffer, it would not be tonight, and that he was not going to mar his happiness.

It was the last time he saw the young man.

That Saturday was a strange torment.

Aline and Orlanda slept badly and woke early, and were immediately assailed by their situation. They were sleeping next to a loving partner whose affection could do nothing for them. Paul and Albert both sensed their tension and wanted to help: "You're tired," said Albert.

And Paul: "Don't move. I'll bring you breakfast."

All they could do was accept with an air of gratitude these attentions which brought no relief. Orlanda understood less well than Aline the dull pain that gripped him, for, until now, whenever he had wanted to see her, he had been able to join her without any difficulty. It was the first time he was aware of the powerful obstacles in their way. There would not be Hong Kong every week, she'll have to leave Albert, he said to himself, without realizing that he was confirming Aline's prophecy. Meanwhile, how would he survive until Monday?

"Stay in bed and go back to sleep for a while," suggested Albert.

She forced a pleasant smile.

"I'm not sleepy any more, I'm restless."

She busied herself as much as she could in the kitchen, but when she had squeezed some oranges, broken some eggs over the frying pan and some bowls on the tiled floor, there was nothing more for her to do.

Orlanda drank the very strong, aromatic coffee that Paul had brought him. Strong coffee has never been known to soothe a troubled mind.

"I've got some errands to do," he said, leaping into his clothes.

Paul tried his best not to show any disappointment. He hesitated: should he tell the young man that he would be home late that night as he was having dinner with friends? That would be to assume that Lucien would want to come, which seemed unwise, and he held his tongue, allowing the madness to walk out of his life without trying to restrain it.

What errands? wondered Orlanda when he was in the street.

Albert asked whether they needed to do the usual weekend shop, as Aline had bought so much food, and suggested the Flea Market instead. They were just on their way out when the phone rang: Madame Berger was inviting them to lunch. Aline, who felt unable to cope with her fretting, turned down the invitation but agreed to go and have dinner with her on Sunday.

So Sunday evening is the end, she said to herself, without really knowing what she meant.

She took the wheel and, without thinking, drove straight to avenue Lepoutre.

"You're taking a strange route," said Albert.

"Sorry, I wasn't thinking!"

Orlanda smiled as she drove past, and jumped into a taxi to go to the Flea Market.

As the weather had turned fine again, the market was crowded. Aline and Orlanda, protected by the throng, found several opportunities to meet for a few seconds, which sustained them until the early afternoon. But then, Albert felt like peace and quiet. He had heard about a farm just outside Gaesbeek where they served fromage frais and radish on bread, may as well have a light lunch and save their appetites for the delicious beef stew that Jacqueline had promised.

Aline gritted her teeth.

Orlanda was waiting for her on a bench in the square, revising his quadratic equations, but she could find no way to join him. So he went cruising and, suffering from withdrawal, he was less careful than usual to restrict himself to suits and ties, thus justifying Aline's concerns.

She mustered all her energy and managed to conceal her agitation. After all, I'm not a weakling, she said to herself. Strange as the separation that took place inside me may be, I was the author of it, he certainly hasn't taken everything with him and I must still have the strength to put on a brave face. So she tucked into her food, pretending she was hungry, and laughed at the right moments. She managed so well that Albert was taken in. At around ten o'clock he told her he was delighted to see that she seemed back on form again, but in fact she was collapsing with exhaustion and could not think straight. This could not go on.

Orlanda, pacing up and down outside Jacqueline's door, was fantasizing about ringing the bell. They would stare at him in amazement.

"I'm Aline's brother," he would declare sounding completely natural.

And then he would rush into the sitting room where Aline would look at him without the least surprise. Olga, amazed, would have the same reaction as Duchâtel: "Really! You don't look alike."

Aline would be furious, but would not be able to say anything. Wasn't this fictitious kinship the answer? He could even stay with her, they would only need to set up a divan in the study. But unfortunately Edouard Berger knew full well that he had never paid a penny to an illegitimate son!

Jacqueline lived on the first floor, Aline and Orlanda were only ten metres apart. This proximity calmed their agitation a little, but when Aline came out with Albert and drove off, the distance increased and was almost unbearable. Orlanda ran to the apartment, and stopped breathless outside the door. Now what? Would Aline find a way of coming down? He heard the buzzer: she knew he was there and was letting him into the hall. He climbed the stairs without putting on the light, he knew every nook and cranny of the staircase by heart, and glued himself to the door on the Molière side. After a few moments, Aline opened the door a fraction, they pressed their foreheads together and tasted, at last, the exquisite silence of being together again. They could hear Albert pattering about, chatting happily.

He spent the night crouched on the stairs. A couple of times he heard people coming home, but nobody ever came up the stairs, and he remained undisturbed. Aline, terrified of being discovered, left the apartment three times to snuggle up to him.

*This can't go on.*

# LAST MORNING

AT DAWN, ORLANDA had to leave: the morning was unbearable. It was two o'clock, Albert and Aline were finishing lunch in the big kitchen when she suddenly exclaimed:

"I know why I was in such a state yesterday! How dreadful, I nearly forgot! I've got to prepare my seminar for tomorrow. I'd put it off until the last minute and then I got distracted by your coming back and I clean forgot about it. I've got to dash over to my office, all my papers are there. I need two or three hours. The best thing will be for us to meet at my parents'."

She grabbed her handbag, keys and coat and was out of the door before Albert could say a word.

She arrived at rue Malibran ten minutes after Orlanda who, standing in the middle of the room, was surveying the few belongings he would be taking with him the next day.

# THE LAST HOUR

ALINE HAD NEVER seen the humble room where Lucien Lefrène had lived. When she moved away from Orlanda she stared about her with the same horror as the young man setting foot inside it for the first time.

"I suppose that's what poverty is."

"Not even," said Orlanda, "don't forget his savings."

"This young man must have been some sort of saint to live like this."

"Or have had an obsessive love of money."

"Love makes people stoic."

"The problem is, I don't even know whether these things are his or whether he rented this cubby-hole furnished."

Lucien Lefrène's funeral oration was over.

"I don't want to take any of these ghastly things with me, but if I leave things behind that I am supposed to take with me, I'll have to come back, which is an extremely unpleasant prospect. And the tenant can hardly phone up the landlord and ask whether this cupboard is yours or mine, can he?"

"Unless it's not you who moves your things, but a friend who isn't too sure?"

"I'll be away on business and you can do it for me!"

"If you like, I'll phone on Monday morning."

"Brilliant! I'll just pack the bedding, my clothes and the Balzac!"

These important practical details dealt with, he began emptying the wardrobe and packed his shirts in the overnight bag. Aline watched him, happy and relaxed as usual.

"Do you think we can carry on living the way we are at the moment?" she asked.

He looked up in amazement: "But it's fine, isn't it?"

"Sitting on the stairs at night and me stealing out in secret to join you?"

"Bah! We'll find something!"

He judged it unwise to suggest she should leave Albert.

"It's a question of organization. At the moment, we're improvising. I agree that last night was a rather poor, stopgap solution. But last weekend was perfect, wasn't it?"

Aline began to feel annoyed.

"It won't be news to you if I tell you that in the ten years Albert and I have lived together, that was the first time we've spent the weekend apart."

He shrugged: "Don't worry. We're here, everything's fine. We'll think about that later."

"You're being childish. You can't see any further than the end of your nose. I told Albert a whopper to get away, he knows me, it's unthinkable that I would forget to prepare a seminar. He believed me, but he won't next time. Supposing he had woken up last night when I was on the stairs?"

For the next ten minutes, they were like two deaf people obstinately repeating two different ideas: we'll find something and no, we won't find anything, after which Orlanda came out with the "Well, leave Albert then!" that Aline had foreseen. She turned very pale: "So you would destroy my life without the slightest scruple."

"Oh! Your life! Your life! I lived that life, and I ran away from it as soon as I could, I don't see why you think it's so special! You were bored with your life, you were sad, I've put some colour back into it. Without me, you'd be as miserable as before."

Irked, he turned his back and took the pile of underpants out of the wardrobe, placing it on top of the shirts. Aline saw the little black revolver. She shuddered.

"Be reasonable," she said in a flat voice. "Try to imagine our future, we will have to stay glued together like Siamese twins. You must have realized that these separations are harder and harder to bear. You'll have to come back."

"Come back?" he echoed, as if he did not understand the meaning of the word. "Come back where?"

"Inside me. You left: you must be able to come back."

"You're dreaming! I'll never come back!"

"We can't remain apart. We will forever be like two cripples, condemned never to leave each other, hanging on to each other, limping through each day, and gradually we will come to hate each other. If you make me leave Albert, I'll hate you, and you have no scruples, you can't live without me, you'll engineer things so that he leaves me and I'm free for you."

"You're not unhappy when you're with me. We have fun together."

So, he was going to be intractable! Everything fell into place, she knew what she was going to do. She felt a great wave of peace, the quiet waters of certainty flowed through her torn soul, the battle was over, no misgivings would restrain her hand, she was completely resolved in the intention that burst out into the light. A powerful conviction rose up and spread, dispersing the darkness, dispelling all doubts. She was the undisputed mistress of her destiny.

She sighed. "What kind of a life will I have? I'll lose all my friends, I'll go to work and I'll come home and wait for you to come back for a few moments' respite between sexual adventures, until you die of AIDS. Then, as I won't be able to bear your death, because it will also be mine, I'll die too. Come back."

Orlanda suddenly realized that she was utterly determined, she really wanted him to give up the delightful life he had been leading for the last two weeks, and would not take no for an answer. He had an outburst of anger.

"Never! I'll never come back to you," he cried furiously. "You'd lock me up in the caverns where you made me live, anaemic and castrated, I thought I'd suffocate to death in your narrow soul, you'd deprive me once again of men, and I would have to walk gracefully instead of running with huge strides. I want to be young and sexy and have fun. You go to work on time, you make love out of habit and you smile out of politeness. You kept me in chains for more than twenty years, I'd rather die than come back under your control!"

"Yes, you are going to die," she said.

And Orlanda saw to his astonishment that she was pointing the revolver at him.

"I don't want to live with only half of myself any more."

"You're crazy!"

"Come back."

"No."

She was ashen, her nostrils pinched. He understood the terrible plan she had in mind.

"You're not going to kill me?" he moaned.

"Not you. All you need to do is escape and come back to me. If you did it once, you can do it again."

She gave an icy smile.

"See you in a minute," she said.

Orlanda thought of jumping and realized that it was too late, the revolver was cocked, she was pulling the trigger, then he let out a great howl of rage and his survival instinct got the better of him, he left Lucien Lefrène. He entered the space where time moves at a different pace – or does not exist at all, since it is bound up with matter which, in the space of the infinitely small, occupies so little space that it takes incredible strength to make atoms bump into each other. The bullet left the barrel and started on the trajectory that would end up at Lucien's forehead, for driven by rage, Aline had aimed with perfect precision. Orlanda in his despair tried to stop it, he flung himself forward, held out imaginary hands to the projectile moving with an absolute slowness through the nothingness, going from nothing to nothing, crossing eternity, but still advancing because it was moving in the real world. But Orlanda had entered the singularity of the quantic world, he was no more than a set of forces among other forces. He had entered the strange realm where Schrödinger's cat exists at the same time as it does not exist. He fully realized that in trying vainly to stop the bullet he was following it, he was returning to Lucien and risked being taken with it into the condemned man's forehead. He imagined the hole, the blood, the brain shot through, and pulled back, terrified.

"I don't want to die," he said, but as he no longer had a body, it was only a thought. Energy among other energies, he wanted to conceive of his voice, his larynx and lips that could move and he turned his unreal gaze to Aline who was standing there, cruel and implacable.

"Bitch!" he cried.

And as this was not taking place within normal dimensions, Aline heard the insult.

"I warned you," she replied.

"But you're a murderer! You're a criminal!"

"Didn't you say that he was barely alive and that perhaps he wanted to die?"

They did not speak, half souls communicate through vibrations.

The bullet had practically reached his forehead, Lucien Lefrène was lost, Orlanda realized that he could not remain in space, that being only a vibration himself, he would not maintain his unity for long in the dimension – the dimensions? – where he now was, that he would soon be dispersed. Pure energy, he would not be able to preserve his identity from being fragmented among the interactions whose power he was experiencing. The slightest jolt – no, the approach of a force would disperse him, a thought scattered among the thought of the gods. The impetus that had propelled him out of Lucien was holding him together still, but he would soon have to come to the end, leave the realm of quanta and return to reality. In despair, he sought a host. Where was Paul Renault? Where were his delightful partners in love? He could not go through walls because he did not have the time to adjust, only Aline was within his reach. He would rather go back to her than die, and he allowed the natural currents to carry him back to his place of origin, but tears ran down his immaterial cheeks, he wept for his life as a man and made his return sobbing.

Still gripping the revolver, Aline jumped twice – at the recoil from the gun and at Orlanda's reincarnation. She staggered under the impact of the memories, all at once, Paul Renault, the man in the train, Amouradora, Lucien's mother, Annie and Marie-Jeanne, the hotel rooms, his nocturnal prowling and the body that had been occupied entered her at the same time as the detonation deafened her. She looked at her victim. The look of fury on Orlanda's face as he abandoned Lucien had vanished, she saw the bullet pierce the forehead, and for a tenth of a second, Lucien reappeared, his gaze was extinguished, his expression softened, his straight shoulders slouched, he was an unremarkable young man pursuing his unambitious plans. The moment before he had been in Paris, bored as he waited for the 13.40 train and thinking of getting out his tape recorder to listen to the interview with Amouradora. Now, the scene had switched to what he recognized as his room and he could see an unknown woman pointing a revolver at him. He felt bewildered, but he barely had the time to realize that he had no idea what was happening to him. He stared wide-eyed, attempted to gesticulate with his raised hand, which he would have stretched out to the stranger, asking her what was going on, the bullet hit him full in the forehead and he died. He fell backwards, his head struck the bed frame and his body was knocked sideways, so he ended up lying on his right side, his face to the floor.

Silence fell in the room. Below, a few cars drove past.

Aline, distraught, staggered with Orlanda's rage. You killed him! he wanted to cry, but the merging was already complete, he felt that he had not been relegated to the dark passages of exile, he joined Aline as he had done when they pressed their foreheads together and trembled with uncertainty. He was losing his identity of a furious child, but he was no longer rejected. He wanted to resist but was unable to because in this soul, he was at home, everything was familiar. He was like the traveller who has visited exotic lands but cannot deny experiencing a certain joy on rediscovering the habitual landscape of his life. He sighed with contentment, consummating the return, then ceased to have an independent existence and Aline, enhanced, took a deep breath. Orlanda's experience became hers, she had run *joyfully* through the Gare du Nord, leaping over the piles of luggage, laughing as she dived into the last compartment. She had been the arrogant youth picking up the man on the train, master of a compliant organ, shamelessly enjoying her freedom. She shrank panic-stricken from Marie-Jeanne's advances, groaned with disgust at Madame Lefrène and trembled with regret on thinking of Paul Renault, now lost. Orlanda's fortnight became her fortnight, she was amazed at the beauty of her back, smiled at her coyness and sensed that the time of sadness was over. She was twenty, with the supple body of youth, she was thirty-five and mature, she became whole in herself, the only mistress of her soul. She ruled, Orlanda's passion ran through her veins, she could feel that part of her body which her mother had never named throbbing, sniggered at the thought of the line of submissive women from whom she came, Marie Berger, daughter of Jeanne Lemonnier, daughter of Léonie Barneret, each contained in the others, fettered and dispossessed. Then she straightened up, looked at herself in Lucien Lefrène's mirror and said: "I am me."

Her words rang out loud and clear in the room with flaking walls.

"Don't start that again," said the reflection.

She thumbed her nose at it: "That depends on you!"

Then she turned to her victim, whose body had fallen at random. His head was at a ridiculous angle, she knelt down, gently turned his face towards her and felt a terrible pang of nostalgia. Christ! What fun she had had living inside this boy! She regretted for a moment that he had not been entitled to a longer life and thought that she owed him an eternal debt of gratitude. Her hand rested on the shoulder that Orlanda's strength had hardened, on the chest which had expanded with his vigorous breathing, slid down towards the forlorn penis and Aline let out a long sigh of regret at the memory of the ease, the challenge and the violence. I had all that, she said to herself, then looked up: I'll have it when I want, if I want it.

She carefully wiped the revolver to remove all her fingerprints as she had seen it done in films, and left without looking back. Albert would still be at home, she was impatient to get back to him and to give him to Orlanda's passion.

# EPILOGUE

"I HAD A PHONE call from my brother: something's cropped up, he can't make it on Tuesday."

Madame Berger was typing a letter which she signed Lucien Lefrène. In it he wrote: "My dear Aline, I have just received an offer I cannot refuse for South Africa. I'll manage fine with my Flemish and my English, which aren't bad, they want a journalist who is well up on cultural life in Europe, the prospects are excellent and I have always wanted to travel. In a couple of years, my English will be perfect, I dream of going to New York."

The two-page letter contained a perfectly plausible mixture of excitement and common sense. Aline thoroughly enjoyed writing it and then found a private courier company to post it from Pretoria.

Albert shook his head: "Well, you were right, this boy is innocent of any dark ulterior motives."

"I've got a feeling I won't be hearing much more of him," she said with a sigh of regret which was not feigned.

Aline went to the Palais des Beaux-Arts just as it was the interval, one evening when they were performing a Schumann concerto. Apparently the pianist had not attracted many people. Among the sparse audience, standing in front of one of the big pillars, she immediately caught sight of Paul Renault who was calmly screwing a cigarette into the long yellowing ivory cigarette holder she remembered. She approached him, with all of Orlanda's guileless impudence, and proffered a light.

"Thank you," he said, somewhat taken aback.

"Are you enjoying the concert?"

"It's nothing special."

" What's in the second half?"

"The Schumann concerto."

"Isn't it a bit repetitive?"

He said nothing, staring into the distance, and Aline saw a cloud pass across his broad, pale forehead.

"Excuse me," he said.

And turned away.

She left, thinking sadly about her escapade: I told you, he only likes boys!

Escapade? But she killed a young man! What about the crime, the remorse, the guilt gnawing away at her?

From time to time, she wonders why Lucien Lefrène owned a revolver. She reminds herself of the little resistance he put up to the invasion: goodness! that boy wanted to die, he was waiting until he found the courage to shoot. I helped him.

# EPITAPH

LUCIEN LEFRÈNE'S MURDERER was never found. It has to be said that the young man did not have any shady connections, that he was neither a drug addict nor a dealer, nor a criminal of any kind and he paid his taxes when they were due. The police did not put themselves out.

I think he deserves a kind thought: he was thrifty, honest and hard-working. He only made one mistake in his life, and that was to cross Aline's path at the wrong time, which earned him an unjust death.

# MORAL

BESIDES, WHO WOULD have gone on trial? Can Aline be judged for a crime of which she is only partly the author, now that she is whole again? That in her which killed is countered by Orlanda who did not want the murder and, anyway, the body had been stolen from the victim by someone who no longer exists. If I were the judge, I would be faced with a dilemma. People will say that I am responsible for the whole thing. But, it is a novel, a made-up story which only takes place in my head. I have no blood on my hands, just a little ink. My killer impulses never go beyond the page, I walk into police stations holding my head high and I give my lawyer very little work.

I have never claimed to write stories that are morally correct.